The Father, The Son, and The Walkperson
and Other Sapiens-Fiction Stories

by Michel Méry

Translated from the French by the author

III Publishing
P.O. Box 1581
Gualala, CA 95445

1st Printing: May 1996

Cover & Interior Illustrations by François Méry

ISBN 0-9622937-9-2

Our motto: the only good lawyer is a dead lawyer.

"Multiple Joyce" first appeared in The Stake #3; "Neg-Entropy" in The Stake #4; "The Anti-Nukes" in The Stake #5 and "The Great Skrumpf-Skrumpf" in The Stake #6.

CONTENTS

FOREWORD

Each time I have been asked to give my work the label of one or the other defined fiction genres, I have been simply unable to do it. In fact, not unlike everything that comes to exist in this measly universe of ours, the reader-observer can make the fiction's wave function collapse into whatever category it wishes the fiction to fall.

Now, let's say it is science fiction, because some of these stories are replete with references to so-called scientific concepts like, as it happens, this "wave function" of everything. Well, that is your own experience, and you are the observer. But the stories are not just science any more than they are, admittedly, just fiction, since fiction in so grounded in reality. In this book, fiction is "science" only if you think that referring, for instance, to this darn wave function (or whatever else you'll find in these pages that only Carl Sagan or Mitchio Kaku should have the right credentials to rave about) is less "mainstream" than referring to, say, love-at-first-sight, murder-she-done, or screw-them-all big-and-small!

Is it fair that Science & Future Amalgamated should be singled out and banned from developing pristine areas of the human mind's wilderness? Writing fiction nowadays, all the while being wary of not mentioning science and not speculating about the future, seems to me just like trying to drive from New York to San Francisco without EVER making (even in this re-Newted America of ours) a left turn. Adding those dimensions to storytelling is the only way to bring up new concepts and ensuing new philosophies into the otherwise more and more worn out literary landscape and the occupationally frazzled collective imaginary.

Again, according to quantum physics, past, present and future are various co-existing facets of the same evolutive process of all things that be. Not unlike the mind-torturing mystery of the Trinity (and, by the way, there's a lot of bad science fiction in the Bible, too), where each facet contains the three and none of the three can exist without the other two. In other words, the past and the present have been, are and will be because the future is and has been.

Now just consider, if you will, these stories as mainstream fiction with a re-attached lost limb that you can call "science" or "speculative." But you'll recognize good old past and present, science-free fiction in here, too. Nevertheless, if you bought *A Short History of Time* by Stephen Hawking when it was on all the best-sellers lists back in '88, it's maybe time to open it. And don't ask me what the wave function is.

THE GREAT SKRUMPF-SKRUMPF

Where are you running like that, Murdoch? You look so hurried and you're putting on such a face! Today, though, the Dow Jones Industrial Average went up to its daily record high: 577,693 points at the bell, up 36 points from yesterday. That alone should lift your spirits. So, take a break. Otherwise, we will have to fetch the Great Skrumpf-Skrumpf. Do you know the Great Skrumpf-Skrumpf, Murdoch?

Come on, remember, when you were small... You had forgotten him? Did he cease to scare you because you thought you had other, more serious things to fear, such as terrorism and the rise of interest rates? Well, there, he is really going to get you and munch on you if you don't keep quieter. You don't believe it? You're dead wrong, Murdoch. Because now he exists. Considering what you finally did to the landscape, you and all the hustle-pushers, you sure made a place for missing childhood nightmares, didn't you?

But as for the Dow Jones.. no, on the contrary. Are you going to believe in it much longer? Because, you see, this afternoon, while you were performing your ritual dance in the southern part of Manhattan Island, the alternative reality of an investment bank office was on the verge of appearing to *us* all around you. Collective hallucination? Possibly. At any rate, you at that moment seemed to be on the verge of making us believe that we could have visions, simply because your visions were being seen. Come on, Murdoch, enough is enough. Just wake up. Your dreams are obsolete for everyone but you -- everyone except for children sometimes, when we've been going too far with our stupid stories about freak characters like Great Directors, Great Brokers, or Great Secretary General.. Anyway, all those people who could have those dreams just like you are lost memories. Dead? Possibly. But that's not exactly it. They have never existed or, if they have, then, rather like a myth, or a dismal legend. So, stop busying yourself like that, shuffling your cards alone like a gambling addict forgotten in a closed-down casino.

Unless they are still here for you after all? Do you see them, Murdoch, scurrying about within and without the walls of the headquarters and their subsidiaries? Do you see them like you once did from out of the window of your office across the street, you know, when the sound was on mute, busying themselves at palming anything off on each other provided they could keep on palming off again and again? Come on, tell us, Murdoch. We love horror stories. Don't worry about your Dow Jones game. Leave it alone a minute. Nobody will mess it up.

Hey, are you going to stop, Murdoch? You're going to make us dizzy. Seeing you like that, it looks as if everything else around you was sliding and jolting, thus, perhaps, making *you* believe that there is still a sidewalk. A sidewalk! You get the picture, Murdoch? Why not taxicabs, curbed dogs, huge sales, cashier receipts? ... Hey, be careful Murdoch! Look what you're treading on!

You shouldn't think that we hold anything against mad people and visionaries, though. We don't call them schizophrenics and force them to gulp down tons of medications. Because it's thanks to them all, such insane ones as Lovecraft, Tolkien, Edgar Poe, even Sam Pekinpah, that you never completely succeeded in making us forget the Great Skrumpf-Skrumpf. Besides, we had all done herb, more or less, and we had often even inhaled... Maybe you thought we had all been recycled by Colgate Palmolive and Mitsubishi? Maybe you thought we all deplored economic slumps and lay-offs, that we were all indignant at the bombing of the World Trade Center? Only in your dreams and in the *New York Times*, Murdoch.

You know what? We can tell you now since you didn't wake him up. You just trod on the tip of the huge tail of the Great Skrumpf-Skrumpf!

And who are you talking to now on your cellular phone? Do you really want us to believe that somebody is talking to you on the telephone right in the middle of the sidewalk?

Yeah... That's what we almost believed for a second... Do you know what you're really holding close to your lips, Murdoch? You don't? Guess what?.. You give up? It's the tip of the thirteenth earlobe of the Great Skrumpf-Skrumpf!

Anyway, good for you if you haven't noticed anything. It was when *they* noticed and realized that *they* all started panicking and scurrying away into general forgetfulness, like cockroaches when you turn on the light. It was then that they lost themselves in their own memories. Neither the résumé writing workshops nor the job interview rehearsal sessions could have prepared them for *that*. But go try to explain that to them! Utterly useless, especially when they were all watching the Olympics on TV. In the first place, too few of them had included courses on quantum physics or maybe a workshop or two on shamanism in their college curriculum. And even those who had -- you know, it probably just flew over their heads. The only difference between them and you, Murdoch, is that they eventually lost confidence and their faith in the great economic recovery.

Yeah. When you think that it had gotten to the point where you could see bustling legions of them begging at the doors of unemployment offices with nothing in mind other than their passport photo on a company ID badge! CONSOLIDATED BEEF & CO, GOLDENSTEIN & SILVERSTERN AMALGAMATED, TOTAL EXPANSION LIMITED,

PARK AVE. BREAST CANCER INCORPORATED, they'd take anything, provided they could be part of it. A secure retirement plan and the assured prospect of dying with tubes shoved up every hole, that was the best you could promise them, for it felt even better to them than the experience of a good fuck or the vertigo of a profound question. So, when they lost their faith, when the industrial average didn't feel itself slide, they went on plucking out each other's eyes for a while, even more fiercely than before, fighting over the leftovers of the fruit of their bustle and calling each other names like coloreds, faggots, illegal aliens, liberals, nazis, faithless dogs, serbs, machos, abortionists -- then what? Well, they lost themselves, along with their streets, sidewalks, corporate headquarters, pizza parlors, private clubs, multi-media centers, re-elections, curbed dogs, cellular phones. They must have finished each other off in some other place, or maybe they perished of exposure and deprivation, far away from the solace of air-conditioned airports and microwavable TV dinners. *Et voilà...* But you, Murdoch, you were probably still too busy to notice anything.

It is not that anybody has changed the world, you know. It's rather that all those who never saw it anymore, other than through the eyes of TIME/WARNER, and those who didn't read anything other than activity reports couldn't see themselves leave along with it, that's all. As for us, all those who expected nothing but that -- we sure had an easy time letting the world redo itself. Each one of us did it in our own way, such as we'd never ceased to redo it in our heads. Your problem, Murdoch, or rather your strength, is that you didn't see yourself go, to such a degree that you just stayed.

Or else, we're the ones who have visions. You're not really here. Normally, we shouldn't have been able to see you. Not any more than you could see goblins, trolls, fairies, Voodoo emanations or the Great Skrumpf-Skrumpf. Hey, Murdoch, you're not going to spoil everything and force us to wonder again about so-called alternate universes, are you?!

What in the world did you finally manage to convince yourselves of? Yes, at some point, you almost managed to convince *us* of the same. And we felt we somehow had to be wrong. The only possible reality consisted of business cards, credit cards, résumés, secret services, new markets, jobs creation, restructurations, a thaw in bilateral relations, and the saga of lady Di. And we would finally have to comply with it all and join the club if we didn't want to die out on your sidewalks without medical coverage.

No. It's hopeless. If you could see, you wouldn't be standing here, on a semblance of a curb, hailing a memory of a taxicab...

If only you could see... You would at last realize that it's for the better as it is now, and that it was you, *all of you*, who were mistaken. It was a dead-end street, a Monday morning congestion under the Lincoln Tunnel, you understand? Of course, it wasn't only your mistake, Murdoch, since everything started as long ago as the day when two *frumious bundersnatches* had clung together after they had freaked out from facing their solitude and the unbearable figments of their imagination, and then tried to distract each other from their fears. Later, it was already too late. It soon became difficult to safeguard one's own visions of the world against those of the gurus and priests, until it became virtually impossible to do so against commercial messages and the Superbowl. You had become too opaque, too callous, Murdoch. The world had to shed you to move ahead. We had been waiting much too long, playing the game half-heartedly, all of us small time bustlers, Gross National Product dilettantes, strangers to congress and congregations, all of us who sought vainly for answers not listed on multiple-choice questionnaires!

No, Murdoch. No taxi will ever come. There aren't any more taxis, just as there are no more cellular phones. Because no one other than you expects a taxi to pass by. Just as you didn't expect to see the vertigo elicited by profound questions to reflect in the eyes of those who were only curious about the unemployment rate, or about the ambience of the trendy nightclub where they end up alone in front of an omelette on Sunday morning at three o'clock, fleeing sleep and its procession of nightmares. Sorry, but it was high time to move ahead, Murdoch. That general consensus of yours was deep-seated and tenacious, not unlike conservative male fashion and sincerelies at the bottom of letters, but it did break eventually. In other words, the zones of calm and stability that you had created on the edge of the entropic current that flows toward the ultimate decay of things have now formed elsewhere. By mutual agreement, you had succeeded only in creating more chaos elsewhere, more uncertainty about other possible worlds. Then, by losing yourselves, you let other zones of stability emerge. And tomorrow, the Dow Jones will break another historical record high, but for you alone, Murdoch. You alone.

Hey, watch it, Murdoch! Watch your step -- come on, you probably never had to cross a street in London! Now, look what you're sitting on! Watch it!

**

That was not a taxicab that just went by. Too bad for you. And too bad for the Dow Jones Industrial Average. And too bad also that you won't be here tomorrow morning to witness the ultimate plunge. Anyway, it wasn't very clever of you to sit down like that, into the vast and malodorant mouth of the Great Skrumpf-Skrumpf.

(New York, London, Jan/Feb 1994)

THE WHITE NAVE

"By God, Sire Colin, before letting thee depart, thou shallst honor us with thy joyous company, in that tavern hard by a bend in the river, one league from here, the one bearing the sign "*Le naute sans nef.*""

"Besides, thou canst not spend the night riding in such a dreary wintry clime. By nighttime, even about Paris, the roads aren't sure. I would wager that thou reach'st not Saint Germain, in the Forest of the Laye, without a calamitous encounter."

"You would tempt the Devil, François and you, Barthélémy. But you have already stayed my departure from the *Trou de la pomme de pain* tavern, in Paris. Otherwise, I would have already been in the stirrups ere the first cock had crowed, and, by now, warmed and fed in an inn of Mantes, at the least."

"And thou wouldst not have bedded sweet Dame Renaude, and we would not have properly celebrated thy departure with a hearty repast, the last for many a day, methink, within the walls of Paris. Come then, Colin, for one last merriment in our company, and forget for an hour that thou hast chosen the *Voie Sèche* of the alchemist to take thee to Rouen, where you will embark for England."

"By the Devil, I accept. Friar Laurens, I charge thee with seeking my absolution from God. For I presume that thou shallst be with us, templar?"

"Hold. The rules of the Order prescribe not immoderate abstinence for us, Christ's soldiers. None the less, I would rather take some repose if the Lord would but grant it to me. I can no further ride in this frigid night. But fie on wine and wenches. I am not exalted but by the thought of a soft bed, which I have naught but seldom felt under my buttocks since I was in the city of Troyes, from whence I departed."

"Then, let's away to the inn by the bend of the river! Hasten, jolly fellows. Hey, by Lucifer, how dark, these woods!"

They were four, chatting thusly, proceeding at the plodding pace of their mounts, two leagues west of the spires of Notre-Dame's Cathedral, inclined by the early winter nightfall to stop for the night. There was Colin Fawcett, nicknamed *Colin l'anglois*, or "Colin the Englishman," and his two faithful companions François and Barthélémy, all three from the University of Paris, and a young monk-knight of the Order of the Templars who, en route to Gisors-en-Vexin, had joined them for the journey as he was traveling alone, contrarily to the legend that the Templars knights always traveled in pairs. François and Barthélémy, both disciples and fast friends of Colin, couldn't bear Colin's sad and lonely memory-laden departure from the joyous city. Colin had just been awarded his Doctorate *ès-Quadrivium* in Paris, and he was leaving the city to seek out and study with other notable masters, disciples of Roger Bacon, in London, Canterbury and Oxford. Colin knew the journey would be long, and thus he would have the leisure to cleanse himself of his sins of the flesh and overindulgence by means of prayer and offerings at holy sanctuaries along the way before embarking at Rouen for England. Colin had been living for quite a while in the Latin Quarter, behind the steeple of Saint Julien-le-Pauvre. A short while before his departure, his beloved mistress, Violaine, had died, leaving him a son, Arnaud, whom he had left in the good care of the Notre-Dame School Chapter's fathers until he could take him back to England.

"I would like," said the Templar, "that, before too much repasting and drinking, you would sing some ode of the poet Virgil, or another of the same ilk, as befits an errant scholar of your breed. I adore them, and thus, I would intercede with God for your sakes to grant you pardon for your sins to come this night."

"Agreed, monk. Hear ye, companions? Take out thy viol, comrade François, and draw from it much melody! By the wine jugs!"

They spoke loudly, for speech thus penetrating the silence of the frigid night, in between chilling blasts of wind, reassured them somewhat. Decidedly, thought Colin, better not to ride through these dark and shadowy woods alone. At that hour, in the Western Provinces, there were more Christians in the taverns than on the roads.

And *Sire* Colin stopped, suddenly startled. He had just realized that he no longer heard the voices of his companions. Instead, he heard a nasty buzzing sound as though his skull were splitting. He tried to draw closer to them, for they were certainly slipping away from him, those rascals! Damned be this night! He called to them, not wanting yet to panic. Damned be the wine, too, for if that was them up ahead, his three companions were no longer alone on the road. What was that strange throng that he could now see engulfing them? Unlike those of his companions a minute or so ago, all those swooping, shadowy, forms that he could now perceive, appeared crystal clear in the harsh, frigid light which now poured all over the road.

Colin wanted to believe that it might have been a premonitory vision of atonement for his sins. Now the edge of the woods had vanished with the night, and the road was very long and as straight as an arrow. Several tree trunks of the receded wood edge bathed, however, in a blinding light which burst forth and whose source was neither torches, nor fires, nor candelabra. That light was fixed and frozen, and approaching it would surely chill one's bones. The throng flowed this way and that, on a smooth shiny slope which, in the rain that had begun to fall, resembled a gigantic slate. Colin was no longer astride his horse. He, too, was walking on that hard, smooth surface, bathed in the strange light. He was sorry having invoked Lucifer.

He blinked his eyes. Some of the lamps were moving, sliding at ground level on a wide median path where it seemed no one dared to walk. Hundreds of these lamps moving in pairs. They seemed to be the eyes of hissing oblong monsters who, apparently, shared this hellish place with the humans, and who projected these beams of yellow light while their posteriors shone with smaller red lights. From where he was, Colin could see the yellow lights sweeping against the red lights in a sort of orchestrated demons' dance.

On each side of that vast thoroughfare, two tall rows of masonry, resembling lines of gigantic Egyptian temples, spread out beyond rows of naked trees, stretching out as far as the horizon. It was also the base of the masonry which spat out that light, through enormous vents which, decidedly, opened onto hell. And straight ahead of Colin, in the distance, stood an arched gate as high as the Cathedral Notre-Dame, a massive monument on the scale of the decor, rising like a pallid specter.

A dreadful, monotonous, muffled rumbling noise continued to fill Colin's head. It drowned out the voices which rose from that immense crowd clad in somber attire. A fetid and acrid odor choked Colin. Most of the people were very old; they were hunching over and they didn't pay attention to him, unlike earlier that night, when he left the gates of Paris, and all those merchants, vagrant scholars, and diverse travelers who had wished them godspeed.

"Oh Lord Jesus, where hast thou taken me?" Colin thought. He crossed himself three times to ward off the demonic torment and called out to his companions again.

"François! Barthélémy! Friar Laurens!"

***

In the beginning, Colin would remember having called out to his jolly fellow travelers. As there was no reply, he soon gave up, as the panic which had invaded him began to subside. Then, a crowd of other visions rushed by him so quickly that he was unable to retain a precise impression of them. But the straight lines and the massive specter of the stone arch vanished to make way for the string of visions, until the moment that he would, once again, feel only the element Earth beneath his feet. Then, toward the horizon, a mauve and purple light evoked in him the idea of a marvelous oriental garden, such as those described by the crusaders and where, from behind a odorous fountain, would perhaps appear a veiled princess. Everything seemed to conspire to awaken in Colin sensations that had been numbed by the wintry clime. Here, the air was balmy and laden with fragrances that Colin could never have imagined, and night no longer oppressed him, since night had ceased to be. In this mythical land, if night be, night was just another hue of light, and Colin was filled with wonder at the sight. Right above his head, and where, a moment before, only a few pale winter stars had shone, he could see a display of a myriad splendid jewels. Alas, the Church was right. This was most certainly the heavenly dome which had collapsed on the world, now barely supported by the circumference of the terranean disc; was the earth eventually going to yield? But this fear soon left him. Colin knew it would *not*. Colin had known for a long time, with the ancient philosophers, that the earth was not the center of the universe, and that neither the sun nor the stars revolved around it, but that, in reality, everything revolved about everything else. Moreover, many of his teachers and fellow students to whom occult knowledge had been transmitted knew this as well. "*Colin l'escholier*", or "Colin the scholar," had been guided on the initiatic path, and he had even acquired the right to the title of "*Beau Clerc.*" If he had decided to return to England, it was also because it had been predicted that, within a few years, even before the end of his own life, the French land would be cursed for not having been able to nurture its heretics, and this from the province of Languedoc to the *Forêt d'Orient* from whence Laurens the Templar was coming.

Then, Colin understood that he had been transported to one of those celestial kingdoms that the famed initiates, of which his beloved Lord Jesus was one, had often evoked. But that other bleached and rainy land he had passed along the way, what was it?

As he asked himself this question, a voice, *his own*, resonated in his heart in response to it: "*It was the vision of what the world of men will become in centuries to come, when they have chosen to follow the path of those in whose eyes symbols no longer have meaning, those symbols of a wisdom that some, such as Hermes, have salvaged, by dint of great efforts, from the confusion of the species, at the decline of the Golden Age. Whereas Here and Now, where thou presently find thyself, this wisdom reigns again. This wisdom, though, did not return until after many centuries, during which time domains of reason, not knowledge, were organized in the way nations were partitioned. This wisdom, some of us, initiates, have recognized, and, doing so, have been called infidels and heretics by the Church and its priests. Already, as a student of the observable heavens, thou refused to share with the western theologians the obscene vanity of the belief in a one man-god. Go forth, then, Colin. Discover the world in its many stages of philosophical transmutation, as yet undreamed of, even by the astute human adept.*"

Thereafter, Colin, the lover-of-Isis, the transfigured adept, ceased to wonder which White Nave had carried him, and he was no longer sorry he had evoked Lucifer, the bearer-of-light, the True Fallen God, and heard one of those renegades accused of having spat on the Cross. His blasphemy had brought him light and awareness. The heavens he was now contemplating were the limitless horizon into which he had plunged, an horizon opening onto the future of the universe, through the stellar clusters emerging from the past. There he was, contemplating the supreme *archi-textor*.

And Colin saw. Since the thirteenth century, the world has revolved millions of times around its stellar crucible, within the galactic swarm at the heart of which the philosophical egg continues to hatch, liberating deer and unicorn; but unicorns seized by a once again virginal earthly nature, in order to let the consciousness of being emerge from the concoction. And that consciousness, in turn liberated from its nourishing sheath, has sublimated in the ether in thought-form or conscious energy. Colin Fawcett, filled with his sense of wonderment and his faith in miracles, saw that, everywhere in the heavens and on the whirling worlds, there really was an architect presiding over the transmutation of lowly basic *Materia Prima* into Philosophical Gold, and how. From the sky, the original element Fire had, everywhere and from time immemorial, fertilized the female element Earth, be it the philosophical peat or the ocean-soup of inchoate worlds. The multiple colors irradiated by these proliferating athanors were those which the egg successively takes on, in the diverse stages of its development. What Colin had encountered en route, in the bleak night, was only the vision of a very distant past, when mankind had been struggling to find ways other than the *wet* or the *dry* toward a full consciousness of life, ways which implied a complex technology without bringing about, like alchemy, a profound transformation of the experimenter himself, ways which brought into play brutally unbalanced forces, unleashing devastating reactions at the term of a heterogenous cycle of minute tasks performed separately by a swarm of beings incapable, individually, of achieving the *magister*. Millions of years had led Colin to a state of bliss, to which he had decided to dedicate his quest, when, in the cellar of his dwelling, on the Rue du Fouarre, he was already deciphering the ancient scrolls brought from God-Knows-Where, and which a young Gypsy lady whom he met on the Petit-Pont had given him as she uttered some strange prophecies. *If only they, too, could see.* And Colin called again, "François! Barthélémy! Friar Laurens!"

"What ho, Colin, why hast thou dismounted?"

"Is it thee, François?"

"Yea, and verily. Mount, Colin, and let us be off! This wood is decidedly too dark! Didst thou have need of relieving thyself?"

"It must have been just that, jolly fellow. Damned be the wine!"

***

Friar Laurens was observing Colin. The wandering scholar had not uttered a word since the night before, since all four of them had traversed these woods at a bend of the river Seine. At the "*Naute-sans-nef*" tavern, Colin had kept apart, uneasy, refusing to take part in the feasting and ribaldry. He had retired early, leaving them, Barthélémy, François and himself, Laurens, to finish the gluttony they had begun the day before.

Colin had awakened Friar Laurens, so that he might quickly ready himself for the forthcoming journey. The two of them were to continue the trip without the others. They would let François and Barthélémy sleep since those two had to return to Paris, and so that Colin would not have to take leave of his two comrades before departing. It was better this way, he thought, as it would avoid a possibly emotional farewell.

When the scholar learnedly stirred him, the templar briskly tossed off his bed the comely tavern hostess who had come to share it with him, and he dressed, not without expressing to Colin his regret at finding him so pale and haggard. The monk voiced the thought that it might be wiser to delay their departure until a more seemly hour for arising, but Colin said to him:

"By all that is holy, monk, hast thou not been taught to praise the Lord for the grace that He hath accorded thee in permitting thee to once again open thine eyes on the divine light? For the Lord's sake, shouldst thou, through the vanishing vapors of wine and debauchery, fail to rejoice that the divine miracle hath again taken place? By my faith, the heavenly body shineth bright, as much as it can by a winter morn and on this land! Arise sinner, and prostrate thyself!"

As far as Friar Laurens could judge the night before of the customary blasphemous humor of the fellow, remarks of that sort were unexpected from him. Colin was joshing, of course. Laurens chose not to reply, and Colin looked at him as though he did so for the first time. It was just that Colin had never seen the monk, except when garbed up in his white cloak and hood. The templar was very young, his youthful face with its chiseled features seemingly beardless. His eyes were pale and his long hair was ash blond, disheveled by a night of fornication. Everything about him contradicted the image Colin had formed of these rugged monk-soldiers. Moreover, there was unease in Laurens' gaze that was foreign to the actual situation.

They resumed their journey in silence, traveling in the direction of the royal village of Saint-Germain. At the port of Alpec, they crossed the river by ferry, and, having dismounted in order not to overtax their horses, they climbed the steep incline that led to the foot of the castle and the royal chapel. It was then that Colin stopped and, turning toward the misty valley, tried to catch a final glimpse of Paris, his joyful city, and the steeple of Saint-Julien-le-Pauvre, but in vain. Off to his side, Laurens respected his pause. Colin would also have liked to see, one last time, the spires of Notre-Dame Cathedral, next to which, in the large dormitory that housed the novices of the Chapter, was his son Arnaud who, at that time, must be kneeling on the stone slabs, praying to the God-of-the-Heart of children that he might be granted the swift return of his father.

Friar Laurens was looking at Colin. Finally, he said:

"Thou must go forward, Colin, and look not back."

Thereupon, Laurens' arm emerged from under his cloak, and he grasped Colin's shoulder. "God hath endowed his children with the spirit of curiosity necessary to recognizing Him," he pursued, "and by so doing, hath endowed them as well with the spirit of wanderlust in space and spirit. It would be futile to go back now, Colin. Thy place is everywhere, let the roads take thee there, while thy son hast not yet, as thee, tasted all the essence of those places that thou yearnest for. Some day, when the time is ripe, he will rejoin thee and, perhaps, you will go forth together. Dost thou not know that the Church has deceived western man by assigning him to the hearth and daily tasks of survival in order to better contain him and mould him to the designs of the powerful? Therefore, guard thyself. Be naught but he who passes. The East has taught us much, we templars. Didst thou know? For we were crusaders!"

Then, sweeping the horizon with a broad gesture of his hand, he added:

"By *Beancéant*, our banner, we will have at least attempted to show the people of these countries the path toward true enlightenment, and institute a universal gnosis."

Laurens wrested his gaze from the horizon and turned toward Colin whose eyes were brimming with tears.

"Why dost thou say 'we will have tried'? Will you not one day succeed? Will your undertaking, by some prophesy, be doomed to failure? And, moreover, are you not instituting, throughout the western world, domains even more impregnable than feudal fiefdom, the *commanderies*? Do you not possess immense lands and many strongholds such as, for example, Gisors or Troyes? What language speakest thou, Laurens? Might there be, as some are wont to say, two different conducts of your order to better infer the nature of things?"

"Thou perceivest clearly, companion. But first, it was necessary to take possession of the world through its own rewards and thus, our riches and fortresses. But we will not have the time. We will be convicted of heresy and burned at the stake, and cathedral spires will remain unfinished. Yea, Colin, a hidden order does exist whose reason for being is neither the possession of lands nor political power, and our Grand Master is not he whose name is known to everyone."

"Was not the first of them Master Roncelin? But tell me: is it not true that at the time of the initiation into the order, the neophyte is compelled to spit on the Cross of Christ, as well as perform other sacrilege? Pardon me, but so many things are said against you. Where doth the truth lie in the mouthing of gossip mongers?"

"By spitting on the Cross, we do not trespass against God. We only offend the Church and its hierarchy. For, it is impious to venerate an instrument of torture, and vile on the part of the powerful to brandish that emblem of sufferings in the face of a docile populace in the name of God in order to justify the very suffering they inflict."

"Do you not then believe in the divinity of Jesus?"

"If Jesus was ever worthy of praise, companion, it surely was because he himself was naught but a rebellious wanderer and had been drawn from the wisdom of Hermes. But by the *Baphomet*, our blasphemous idol, we are all as much sons of God as He!"

"What, then, of those immodest kisses you are accused of giving to the neophyte at the time of his reception into the Order? Are they not, in reality, sodomite practices?"

"Oh, no," Laurens said in a burst of laughter, "those kisses -- for they really are given -- evoke one of the secrets of the cabalists: the mystery of the balance between wisdom and intelligence. But let them gossip, Colin. Later on, it will be better for us to be accused of sodomy than to reveal our true secrets to the world. It is too soon for them."

"I must tell thee, Laurens. I fear for the world in days soon to come. Look, this past night, on the path through these woods that we were traversing, I did not forsooth dismount to relieve myself. I did strange visions see and I did perforce stop. Oh, what a ghastly world, Laurens! Especially their countenances. They seemed to wear demonical masks. And then--"

"I know already. They will be as grisly as their skies... Look: since the reign of the bold Charlemagne, we've been blessed in these lands with a mild and sunny clime. Thou didst thyself comment upon it to me this very morn. Even in winter, the sun shineth bright. And 'tis thus many a morn. That is why we are such joyous fellows. In days to come, it will no longer be thus. So goeth the cycles of nature and its rhythms to which man is-subjected, like he is to the influence of the stars and planets. Thou knowst this, Colin, for thou hast studied these sciences. The temple, therefore, will depart, along with the clemency of the elements, and then will commence a cursed era of wars and intolerance during which, from the East to the west, the forces of ignorance and blind faith will unrelentingly combat those of enlightenment and reason. Some will flee toward a distant continent which lies beyond the Atlantean Sea, in the direction of Ys, especially in order to seek a sky more profound and a more philosophic gold than that to be found in the rivers' currents; but even there, the skies will dim when the terrors inerant to the dawn of Aquarius pave the way for the renewed power of the Church. And later, much later, at yet another age of the world, the Spirit will shed humankind in order to pursue by Itself Its quest of Itself, or God. But methinks that thou hast already seen this, my good Colin."

"Yes, indeed. Therefore, Spirit will change form as doth the butterfly..."

"...Which no longer feeds on the substance of the Earth."

"Oh, Laurens, wouldst that I could accompany thee within the walls of the keep of Gisors, there to stay in order to be further initiated into your secrets? Dost thou not think me worthy, Laurens, thou who hath already told me so much?"

"There are a hundred, nay, a thousand paths to reach that end, and thine be not of necessity mine, even though our paths have crossed. Why seek'st thou teachings or a conversion? Spare thyself this care."

Having thus spoken, Laurens fell silent and Colin, in turn, respected his silence.

They left the royal village to the chime of its bells and, once again, they entered the dense forest, whose tree trunks, once again, reminded Colin of the pillars of the nave of an immense cathedral, but whose vaults, through the bare branches, opened out unto the sky. As they skirted a *montjoie*, a child's voice resonated in Colin's heart. It begged him not to return before he could tell wondrous tales, his own tales.

(Paris, October 1986)

THE ANTINUKES

On the one hand, it was nothing but a petty event. Sure, some paused a minute to wonder. What in hell could have happened to the old lady Sirvens whose utterly charred remains had been found on the banks of the river Gard, near Uzès, just a few hundred yards from the village of Russan, on the 22nd of last September? Some investigators from the UFO research group VERONICA went so far as to propose some "spontaneous combustion hypothesis," but a thunderstorm had drenched the *gorge* of *La Baume Latronne* that night. Thank God for such a celestial coincidence. It was a good enough explanation for the investigators from the gendarmerie as to why there was nothing left of the old lady's body other than ashes and a bunch of charcoaled bones. The fact that the dry weeds around and under the body had not been blackened by the fire, that the plastic shopping bag she was carrying and some of her clothes were almost untouched by the fire, and *"peuchère"* (as she would have probably said), all that was soon dismissed, especially when the local mayor decided to make a speech denouncing the incompetence of the adverse ruling party in terms of the protection of the senior citizens against natural risks and other acts of God. "One persists," he said, "to ignore these risks at the regional level." Subsequently, nobody would care any longer about what really happened on that 22nd of September.

But on the other hand, it was the saga of an entire civilization.

Noémie Sirvens *was seeing* this first lightning bolt. It was probably hitting the earth not very far away, in the gorge. At that very instant, that is to say as *their* centuries went by, those of *their* species were staring at the unfathomable abyss of cosmic space through the veil of the plasmic atmosphere of their native neutron star.

Some time before, as a matter of fact, Noémie had realized that she had to hurry. Her bag was already filled with various wild plants that "this man" who ran this health food store in nearby Uzès would buy from her every week for his vegetarian pies. She turned her head to see where the thunderbolt had struck the earth.

And *their* demiurges finally discovered the technological keys to the voyage. They finally understood that their civilization had developed during the very last second of the evolution of their world. However, they were already dying of boredom as they faced the limited and immutable horizon of the neutronic ocean that almost covered its entire surface. Their gamma-telescopes had revealed so much marvel, so many alien structures, that they had ended up believing again in some divine blueprint presiding at the organization of the cosmos, just as they had at the dawn of their history, when they dedicated rituals and incantations to the vague, eerie, but seemingly wonderful bodies stuck out there in their never-black skies.

As she turned her head to see where the bolt had struck, Noémie tripped on a stone, a stone just a little bigger than the others, and she opened her mouth to address the whole damned world with her favorite curse: "*FAN DE PUTE*".

Then, their odyssey began. They explored many worlds, each strangely like 4C-2153 (as filed by terrestrial astronomers) by scanning space and time aboard huge space arks. In the womb of such vessels, colonies of beings like themselves (whose structure was based upon supercomplex aggregates of elementary particles) could survive throughout the centuries on condition that, among other biological factors necessary to their corporeal cohesion, a temperature equaling some billions degrees K be maintained during the voyage.

They came back utterly disappointed. Their quest had proved unworthy. They had only contacted very similar life forms on other neutron stars. And only much later did they understand that the issue lay further beyond space and time, that they had to cross the border of tangible matter to discover something else. More through intuition than experimentation, they guessed the presence of other bodies in the Galaxy, other stellar bodies existing on such a huge scale that, in comparison, their extremely dense world would appear like a pinhole in the fabric of the cosmos: the molecule stars, those stars wherein the particles were linked together to form atoms, and atoms to form molecules.

While, at this very stage of the evolution of their conscience, Noémie started to hiss:

"FFFFFFFFFFFFFFFFFFFFFFFFFFFFFFFFF........"

Thereafter, they grew older and wiser. They eventually understood that what they believed as belonging to the realm of the spirits did exist in a domain of manifestation that was not immediately accessible to their senses. There, where more ethereal matter is submitted to the electromagnetic force -- which was infinitely weaker than the strong nuclear force which bonded their world -- more stable and durable structures had to exist as bricks of events happening beyond the familiar domain of the particle. And, perhaps, there were living species woven out of this quasi-eternal matter, some life forms who would have an infinite life span compared to theirs, since such beings' cohesion would depend on a far steadier bond. But they would only ever be capable of seeing these beings as frozen in a relative immobility, leading their lives on another scale of time, fitting another scale of space.

Then they set forth again in all the directions of space, targeting a number of those stellar bodies that we know as hydrogen stars. They discovered that smaller bodies were bound to these stars and that these stars didn't swallow these smaller bodies as 4C-2153 had probably done long ago.

Directly born from a star, they discovered the existence of planets and, furthermore, they could guess the orbital motion of them, although an unmeasurably slow one at that.

During all this time, the old Noémie Sirvens would continue to send her message throughout the cosmos, on an extremely low frequency:

"FFFFFFFFFAAAAAAAAAAAAAANNNNNNN...."

And the lightning was about to finish illuminating the gorge of La Baume.

One of their vessels, at random, came close to planet Earth. On board, hundreds of their centuries went by. Finally, the descendants of the ancients who had embarked could see the hugeness of the planet, billions of their astronomical units away. And eventually, some of them could behold the shape of one of the terrestrial living creatures, a creature who would have towered by a thousandfold over the tallest supra-iron mountain of 4C-2153. But how much more ethereal, too! In Noémie, they acknowledged the reality of ghosts. (Through their vision only sensitive to the ultra-short wavelengths, *their* Noémie had nothing at all in common with the picture of her published the next morning in the regional paper *Midi-Libre*. Seen through the spectrum of X and gamma rays, *that* Noémie irradiated indescribably vague hues.)

And the creature, frozen in its dreadful immobility, seemed to be willing to express something.

"DDDDDDDDDDDDDDDEEEEEEEEEEEEEEEEEEPPPPPP...." Thus spoke Noémie throughout their eternity. But they could not hear, of course. Maybe, her voice was just another fountain of colors for them.

The old GTHRVZ said: "Let us penetrate this huge red spot, this never-heard-of vortex, right there, between the two eye-like organs of the creature. I believe that we shall then comprehend not only its genetics but its soul as well."

So they did. For dozens of their years, they voyaged among the atoms of carbon. They assessed, measured, probed, experimented. At long last, they *knew*. Then they sent the results of their tests back to 4C-2153. But while they were making a huge step forward in history, and knowledge as well, AND FOR THAT VERY REASON, Noémie died gurgling: "PPPPPPPP-PPPUUUUUUUUUUUUUUUUUUUUUUUUUUUUtttttttttttt..."

For they were no gods, so they committed a fatal error of navigation. Perhaps, they collided into some unexpected proton or unthinkable electron -- some particle that *could not* exist. Or perhaps simply because of the tremendous heat produced by the radiation of their bodies and their vessel which, composed of infinitely unstable aggregates of billions of interacting particles, radio-activated far more than uranium 238.

At any rate, something like that caused the death of Noémie Sirvens in an invisible ball of light while the thunderbolt finished illuminating the gorge of La Baume.

***

They eventually forgot all about the mission. They deteriorated to the state of primitiveness, and some other intelligent species was already awakening on 4C-2153 when a second bolt of lightning struck the gorge, and the rain started to drip on the little pile of ashes.

(Paris, June 1985)

DEUS EX LATRINA

ACT 1

(With the father, the son, the walkman, and the Omniscient)

The Omniscient:
The father and the son are sitting on the top of a hill, or of a mountain, or an elevation of sorts, far out of the city limits. It is definitely darker than pitch. Both are staring at the starry skies. The walkman is singing.

The walkman:
There is still a light that shines on me,
Shines until tomorrow,
Let it be.

The son:
What on earth is all that?

The walkman:
There will be an answer, let it be.

The father:
Well, son, here are the stars. You never saw them? It is true that you don't have a lot of opportunities to stargaze from the city down below. But you see, there they are. Nobody ever mentioned them to you at school?

The son:
Oh yeah... Of course. But only those on MTV. Tell me, dad, what kind of star this is exactly.

The father:
It's a good question and I'm glad you asked. First of all, imagine a bubble, a bubble that's popping out into zillions of bubbles. The Big Bang... Zillions of particles. Then billions of suns... Oh no. That's what they say... Let's drop the subject. I'm too tired and I have a hard work day tomorrow. Don't make me think or I'll be inefficient. You'd better listen to the walkman.

The walkman:
Let it be, let it be, let it be..

The Omniscient:
Abdication. Parental apathy. That was a good start, though. At least, this one must have watched the Carl Sagan's series, or read the first ten pages of Stephen Hawking's *A Brief History of Time*, at the local bookstore on a rainy day. Too bad. Okay, may I go on?

The son:
When are we going back home, Dad? I'd like to watch MTV.

The Omniscient:
No! Wait, son. Look here. Look how... everything fuses, vibrates, throbs, whirls, swells, collapses! Undulatory pulsation. A profusion of bubble universes. Deuterium, helium, hydrogen. Is there enough "black matter" to make it tend toward the critical density? Of course, *I* know but let's leave some ultimate big questions for the ultimate multiple choice questionnaire. Look: here are aggregates of sub-particles containing aggregates of junior vice-particles and senior chairparticles, themselves longing to dis-aggregate and re-aggregate with consolidated efficiency, although they are, in fact, all but elementary. You see, they are more like secondary, derived from the primary, and, thus, the observer. You follow me? Matter of downward causation. Tell me if I'm wrong.

The son:
So, why don't we derive them? I mean, the particles. Let's collapse their wave function, within a vortex of light and heat!

The father:
Uh? Are you talking to me?

The son:
Yeah! Just like that! Within an echo of microwaves, fossil radiation, neutrinos, quanta and *tutti quanti*!

The father:
Hey, where did you get that from?

The son:
Is it already a complex system of amalgamated systems?

The Omniscient:

That's right, son. Systems that whirl, throb, vibrate, swell and collapse. Now, the whole thing fuses into boundless integrities along an infinite gamut of organizational stages pertaining to what is being made, since what is being made *has* to be. Consequently, it synthesizes itself, elements itself, implements itself, feeds on itself, symbioses and... yeah... it's just making itself.

The son:
Since it's making itself, does it know from what, and into what?

The father:
The hell if I know. Let's go home.

The Omniscient:
No, too late. I'm on my own... Look, son: the multi-faceted entity contains itself and escalates itself in nested domains. A constructed system constructs itself over and over without any new delivery of materials. It intercoms, switches, swaps, merges, consumes, feeds on itself, prods itself. Attraction. Repulsion. Contraction. Expansion.

The father:
Let's move it! I want to watch Johnny Carson.

The Omniscient:
In the beginning, there *is* homogeneity and isotropy. Then there is metaflation. Then mere inflation.

The walkman:
Let it be.

The father:
...Then.. er... clusters of systems. Clusters upon clusters of systems which systematically do and undo themselves without this radical urge to throw down the system.

The Omniscient:
Good! And heeeeeerrrrrrrrrre's Daddy! But still, they do that within a spacetime domain born from the system!

The son:
And what's the reason for the system? Its finality?

The father:

To go on systematizing... Extend the sphere of influence of a basic system of schematization of densities.

The Omniscient:
And now, lo and behold, the densities fluctuate as mass concentration!

The father:
Are you sure you want to go on, son? You really want to know everything?

The son:
Sure. But first of all, what's God?

The father:
So, that was that? Okay, you asked for it, son.

The Omniscient:
Huh..? Is it really necessary? I'll be dammed!

The father:
See those globular clusters, galaxies, clusters of galaxies, those great walls of clusters of galaxies, spiral, helicoidal, polymorphic, which vibrate, throb, irradiate, whirl about, and collapse into a pit of megacycles and microwaves... Huh?

The walkman:
And in the heart of darkness...

The son:
Yes, I do. It oscillates, throbs, falls into line, bends light, reflects!

The Omniscient:
When I think that He was in contemplation of Himself, all alone, in total privacy, and thought it felt so good...

The father:
Look! It merges, intricates, imbricates, intrigues, gets embryonic, fits into itself.

The son:
Doesn't every galaxy contain billions of stars and billions of planets?

The father:

But of course! Worlds being born, worlds colonizing worlds, worlds singing in canon, and dying worlds... Worlds that are neuron-worlds to the cosmic consciousness. Some of them are even synapse-worlds.

The Omniscient:
That should be enough for tonight.

The walkman:
Let it be.

The son:
And... It's the Big Brain, right?

The father:
It's the flesh of the Word.

The Omniscient:
Come on, come on. That never took anybody much farther. Besides, it's getting rather chilly and the kid would really like to watch MTV. And there's school tomorrow.

The father:
Look again, son. Matter being generated by waves in turn generates waves which, in turn, generate matter which, in turn, assembles in bricks of life to generate waves!

The son:
And so on and so forth. I see what you mean. But where's God in all that?

The Omniscient:
It's my fault, I know. I shouldn't have started it. But come on!

The father:
Wait. It copies itself, duplicates itself, multiplies itself, implies itself.

The son:
But... Now, it looks like it's being shrunk on a Xerox machine!

The Omniscient:
Stop!! For God's sake! This is a child of the eighties! After all, he could have gotten a MBA, or a law degree.

The son:

Yeah! It's so beautiful! It's beautiful like a giant kaleidoscope. Oh, Life, the Universe, and Everything!

The father:
Now, come with me. We're going to play Star Trek.

The Omniscient:
Hey, you there! No trespassing!

The walkman:
Let it be, let it be, let it be, let it be, let it be.

***

ACT 2

(With the father, the son, and the Omniscient,
but without the walkman)

The Omniscient:
Let it as well be. The father and the son have played *Star Trek*. More exactly, in order to gain a more distant perspective on things, they have backed out beyond their own cosmic horizon. To do so, they built a ship which has carried them at a zillion times the speed of light (or simply less than one time that speed, or even much less, a mere walking speed would do) relative to their previous transiency rate (which, in relative immobility, already lurches along at a zillion times the no-longer crucial speed of light). So, since it was not that difficult after all, and since they only had to get used to the idea that it was not, they have successfully taken some distance without having to pump dry all the energy of the Big Bang or all the financial resources of their own neuron-planet (now promoted, thanks to them, to the rank of synapse-planet). And from here and now, from outside their own cramped sub-continuum, they can enjoy a breathtaking vista on the Universe.

The father:
Come here. See how time is rushing along within the "over-there" we just left! See how aeons are hustling past, how eras collapse and contract into mere instants when considered from this "out-here," which is itself, already, the "in-there" of whatever else.

The Omniscient:

What he means is that they took time as well as distance. I mean, if you want, they can see aeons pass along in the distance, from so far away that they do not even have to turn their heads to follow them with their eyes. They can see births, deaths, births, deaths of galaxies, local clusters of galaxies, great walls of clusters of galaxies, and quasars and what-have-you. Consequently, they can also see births and deaths of star systems and, by the same token, of mass concentrations which had highly organized themselves into living species and themselves. Dissolutions. Contractions. They die and are born again and again on the rhythm of the microcyclic beat.

The son:

So, in the time it took us to take this little step, I mean in the time it took our ship to reach this new "out-here" of ours, in the time it took us to back out a little, it's like everything that had to happen has happened, and at the same time, is still to happen.

The father:

Yes, son. The saga of a zillion conscious species came to an end, or will go on, upon zillions of ego-domained worlds. You got it right.

The son:

Such a small step for mankind...

The father:

Oh, you know, steps or megaparsecs... In any case, from here, beyond our own event-horizon, beyond the "all-that" of ours, from within the immutable, you can watch and see what it is about.

The son:

But so what? What is it exactly?

The father:

Move your eye closer to this hole, right here, and take a peek.

The Omniscient:

Okay. I am no longer here. And I never knew a damn thing!

The son:

I see... something's hanging and swaying. But within what?

The father:

In a wind, maybe. Or in a mere draft. As always, these doors never close properly. Anyway, tell me more about what you're seeing.

The son:

It's stretching...

The father:

Of course it's stretching! Oh, I know, son. It could have been anything other than *that*, like, for instance, a petal of a rose falling off and being carried away by a balmy breeze in Capri, or, again, a maple leaf sliding to the autumnal ground in Central Park, New York, New York. It could have been lots and lots of things, *but that's what it is.*

The son:

And what about this partition with the hole in it? Is this the wall of the Universe?

The father:

From this side of the horizon, could be... But there must be lots of walls beyond this one. They usually come by rows of three to nine. But here... Ask the Omniscient.

The Omniscient:

I said I'm not here. Besides, I am not supposed to answer anybody's questions directly.

The son:

Yuk! Is *that* all?

The father:

I don't know. I can't see with your head in the way.

The son:

Oh, look! It's falling!

The father:

Yes. It did fall... It fell under the pull of a force that only *you* can conceive -- O infinite aperture of the Unified Fields -- toward what only *you* can see since the hole is too small for the two of us.

The Omniscient:

When I think that he was taught at school that *it* was made of complex systems, grand ideals, great accomplishments... made of consensual decisions, generosity and genocides... made of payment deadlines, oaths on the Bible, economic growth, former vice-presidents, challenging careers, HIV and ozone holes... Not to mention what he could have imagined *it* was like in the galaxy M 31 or elsewhere... After all, *it* was not that bad, wasn't *it*? At least, *it* was big. Big and complicated.

The father:

So, was it really worth posing a moment and giving *it* a thought? You still think so?

The son:

Oh, I see! A putrid black hole!

The father:

I can't see it, but I smell it. I concede it doesn't smell like a petal of a rose in a breeze of Capri.

The son:

Oh, I see! A black tide, a maelstrom!

The father:

I can't see it but I hear it. I concede it doesn't sound like the fall of an autumnal leaf in Central Park, New York, New York.

The son:

So, that was it...

The father:

Note again that it could have been any other thing.

The son:

Yuk!.. But who made this hole in the partition?

The father:

A voyeur, I guess...

The son:

So, it was somebody.

The father:

Somewhere.

The son:

Oh, I see HIM! *It's God!*

ACT 3

(Without the Omniscient, with the father, with the son,
still without the walkman, but with God)

God:
For God's sake! Hey you! What the fuck is this kid doing here? Are you the
father? Are you crazy? You can be proud, godamnit! Come on, did you see
that? Have his young son peep through goddamn holes in the partitions of
restroom stalls in Grand Central Stations!

***

ACT 4

(Without the father, without the son,
but with the omniscient and the walkman, and far from God)

The Omniscient:
Once upon a time, on a hilltop, far from the city limits, was a walkman,
forsaken and forlorn, tuned now onto some local talk show. And in the
studio, there was Rush Limbaugh.

The walkman:
(to itself)

Holy shit!

(New York, February 1987)

NEG-ENTROPY

Look at you, Steven. You are seeing yourself in the mirror of the *WASHMAT* in your life module which, as was predictable, is holographic; it shapes a tri-dimensional image of your head, not merely your face. You can even walk around this image, which makes you feel that it is not really you that you are looking at. But this is wishful thinking because the sight saddens you, although there should be no regrets. You have a secure *assignment.* Anyway, you would never have imagined you would look like that someday.

With a grimace of disgust, you flick the switch off and the mirror-space darkens. More accurately, it disappears from above the bathroom sink. You stand motionless and you think. You think the *PROGRAM* has possessed you. Earlier, it possessed your mind and then your flesh followed. Look at your empty eyes that have sunken more deeply into their sockets. The contact lenses that you are wearing cannot even make your eyes gleam a little bit. You try in vain to remember their color, as well as the color of your lips, which have become so thin that you cannot tell them from the rest of your dull pinkish skin. The sad protective wrapping of your whole body reminds you of the skin of a hot dog of your childhood. Your nostrils, too, have shrunken badly from lack of ever breathing in the wind and you wish you could see your dry and over-disciplined hair, trimmed like the trees of the *WAYS,* revive. But it is most of all that brownish stain, right there, between your eyes, that sort of derisory third eye that has been growing for weeks, that worries you. It does hurt when you activate the *WASHMASK.*

You want to reassure yourself by thinking that you have grown old, but you suspect that something else has happened, something other than the normal decline in vital energy necessary for the reproductive capability of your cells. Long ago, something initiated a diversion in the initial genetic scheme, something interfered with your morphological pattern. But that, you are not aware of.

You are really sad this morning and the sadness is scary. For years you were not happy with anything, but neither were you sad. Because of this face of yours, probably. Exactly the face that you, as a child, hoped you would never have, when you dreamed of looking like the little Cherokee Indian who attended the same school. This urge to revolt which now rises in you, is it the same urge you felt when you were a ten year old, before they put you in a *COMMITMENT* class?

You had a dream last night. You dreamed of the eyes of this old Tibetan whom you saw in a show on the Quadrisensorial Tele-Implication (QUAREL) a few days earlier. This program was devoted to the study of the *IRREDUCEES* of the world. The Tibetan's eyes were real eyes. The sight of them made you dizzy. Now you doubt that they were right to show that to the *REDUCEES* of the Teleimplicated Community (IMPTELCOM). *Unless you happened to be the only one left to be disturbed.*

You feel irritated. What's going on in your mind?

You are not even old. You are, rather, ageless. You have never been ill, though, and nothing hurts except for this brownish stain that worries you.

Others must have grown older, too; all those who were, like you, born toward the end of the last century, in the 80's. The others... It's such a long time since you saw anyone other than those you can still see swooping by on the "ways" when you go out of your module where, after all, you can see and do whatever you want without leaving it. Of course, you do not see anyone *de visu* and *in situ* on the *QUATEL*. You start smiling while muttering these last words. Words seem so odd to you, since you have lost the habit of using them for communication. You have only been speaking through your computer ever since you had nobody left to call on the visiophone. Now, what about the shape of the words that resound so strangely in your head when you try to graft them onto the sudden gushing of your thoughts? God! This question. The link between sounds and shapes... De visuuuu... Situuuuu...

There was a time when you spoke to people, remember? When there was still someone around, *in situ*. There were Armelle and the two kids. But Armelle left one day to report to a psychotherapists' symposium, "Psychotic Disorders Evident in Computer Bug Experts," in Yokohama, and she never came back. She was offered a better assignment there. As for your two sons, you found out that the younger one is successful since, according to your last personal data research, he had finally been hired as a Restrooms Maintenance Manager for the vice-president of a big corporation in Silicon Valley. But you think of the older one, who committed suicide at twenty four after he learned that he'd failed a three-week long contest specifically organized to fill an opening for a diskette-storing clerk with the Biological Bank in Pittsburgh.

You feel so bad; clearly there must be something wrong with you this morning. What you are not aware of is that this began months ago, imperceptibly. It might have hit you before, if only you had given yourself a chance to think about it. You had only a hint of it yesterday evening when the QUATEL reported, during a special newsbreak on all channels, that a certain Mrs. Flatass from Knoxville, Tennessee, was three days late with her period. Of course, you should have been aware of Mrs. Flatass's existence, since you can theoretically obtain a complete data display of any citizen of the IMPTELCOM, but you *never* requested it. You could not care less about

Mrs. Flatass's menstruation, and you thought to yourself that such a piece of information did not concern you. You decided that there was probably a penury of significant pieces of information to be scooped and you were right. *There really was not a lot left to speak about.* Until then, such pieces of news were not distilled in real time and real images. They were the object of integrated programming, broadcast by the hundreds of thousands in the space of a nanosecond through cranial captors tuned into sub-networks, without causing any interference in the normal programming of the QUATEL.

You are back in your parlor. You have decided to turn on the main QUATEL set, which is usually second nature to you. So, you are surprised that you even have *to decide to do it.*

But the set remains mute.

You are puzzled because this thing *cannot* happen. It *never* happens. QUATEL sets never break. The mere notion of a QUATEL breakdown is as foreign as that of hunger or need. Repair by electronic impulses occurs automatically within a few milliseconds, before you are even aware of it. You spin around toward the main console, and you attempt to enter one of the numerous *LUDICHANNELS,* but with the same result: no response, just as if your life module were totally disconnected from the IMPTELCOM. What sort of accident can that be? Why on earth has the breakdown not been detected and analyzed?

No, Steve, the circuits of your module are okay. What you cannot imagine is that *nothing* is on the program this morning, nothing that your senses can decode. No more messages. The transfer between you and the network (sorry, between you and the reducees of the IMPTELCOM) lasted too long. It's all over now. For decades you swallowed and gulped the network blood, then you slobbered, spat and threw up into its veins. For years, you deciphered synthesized messages from the rest of the human world, you fed on its graphics, charts, displays and moods. The IMPTELCOM leveled you in such a way that now you fit its standard pattern. You also participated in the elaboration of the pattern by re-emitting in turn and, although at a minute scale, by influencing millions of reducees like yourself. You were not supposed to ignore anything that was going on among yourselves, and nobody was supposed to ignore what you had to communicate. But that is over.

And here you are, this morning, finding yourself the very last one to have a message to transmit. *The pendulum is almost at a standstill.* You are going to stabilize yourself at the level of all the others.

In the *DINOMAT,* you want to howl from hunger. A distributor light seems to flicker for a short while, then dies out. No mural vector belt brings out what you had typed on the keyboard. You are in a panic. *You were never hungry before.*

You throw yourself on a cot, overwhelmed. Cut off from the background of the species, you stare at what you can see of your body since you need to safeguard some consciousness of your existence. Because you can only be aware of yourself, you stare at your hands, your knees, the front of your thighs. And it rises up in you. You would like it as usual. When this happens, usually, you only have to design your own program of sexual stimuli and the machinery does the rest. The QUATEL has a better knowledge of your erogenous zones than even Armelle ever had. Since you have grown older, the urge has lessened, but this morning, as nothing else is going on... You come very fast, too fast, without foreplay and fantasies, as if all the mechanisms within you, tuned on the standard norm, no longer needed big levers to release their tension. You look at the stain on the rug. You feel ripped, drained. You caress your frail chest and your nipples become erect. For the first time, you are having this feeling of having copulated with yourself. Your belly hurts slightly, inside.

You are back in the WHASHMAT and you reactivate the holographic mirror. It does work, but the image is less defined and more blurred than this morning's, when it was perhaps already weaker and more fuzzy than yesterday, without your having noticed. While you look at yourself again, in the unusual silence, recollections swarm into your memory, as if they were rushing to compete with each other, taking advantage of the truce.

You think of your personal history. You see yourself at school in your neighborhood, where you were not interested in the program. They blamed you for your lack of commitment. Of course, you were interested in many things, but those were "useless" topics, topics to be lost, wasted topics for your future occupational life. Your buddies were already securely coupled to their micro-computers, in order to better copulate with the program. They were the first millions of gametes of the network. They were irreversibly bound to their survival unit, just like the first artificial heart recipients were to their machinery, but you would strive to do without, drawing with pencils and reading real books. Yes, there still were books at that time, many more than there ever were. They appeared suddenly and disappeared as quickly from the counters in the gas stations, the banks, the post offices. But most of those books had nothing to do with your specific imaginary appetite. The notion of efficiency having already prevailed, Bantam and Harper's dealt only with instruction manuals, behavioral recipes and how-to's of all kinds. However, real books could still be found in antiquated, dingy bookstores or at street sales. That's how you were offered *white fangs,* a few Jules Verne books and a ragged complete edition of Stevenson. Above all, you loved the books about dinosaurs and stars. Your imagination wanted to encompass the time you were coming from and the time you were heading for. You did not want to know about the disappearance of the dinosaurs and you could not guess that the adults were already doing everything possible not to ever reach the stars. To your fascinated mind, the lunar exploration of the 70's was but a wondrous legend of some mythic age. After all, it was talked about with the same disdain. The gigantic interstellar ships of the old science fiction movies would never hurtle through space. You couldn't understand, Steven, that they had already deprived reality of its own wondrous side in order to secure it more safely and prevent it from wandering. Otherwise, it could have caused general dizziness, and dizziness, sometimes, makes you feel like jumping whereas fear becomes a salutary guardrail. Then, you recoiled and erased your own trail to the stars.

A dazzling light, meant to resemble the sunlight but without its most noxious components, is pouring from the ceiling of the WHASMAT. It was captured by satellites orbiting in space, high above the thick overcast, to be re-synthesized within your home photonic regenerator. It is said that the true sun still shines in certain regions of the earth that you never visited. This reminds you of a few trips you took with your parents when you were a child. In those days, traveling was still useful since people still had to move about to mingle their genes and cultures. As a former beatnik, your father had even taken you to the west on a package tour. What a week! You saw some real Indians at Mexican Hat airport, near Monument Valley. They were even wearing tribal feathers and skins. Remember how uncomfortable you felt and how you blushed when they seemed to make fun of you during the guided tour on the trails.

Later, when you were a teenager, travelling became virtually useless. Katmandu and Cusco looked too much like Hoboken or Houston. Tourists were herded in groups by official tour operators and, once afar, people were obliged to use the legal credit cards only in the stores licensed by the *COMETOUR INTERNATIONAL* in the *COMETOUR* villages. The last individual tourist visas were reserved for tourist industry professionals at the service of the COMETOUR. Because of your inadequate school credentials, you were never granted a visa, even on a tour of Iowa. So, you stayed home and you discovered the world through the eyes of the "pro," through the electronic media.

Thanks to passage in a COMMITMENT class, you were relieved of your neurosis, securely reduced, and capabilized, in order to get your high school diploma in one of the seventy six majors already available at the time: Perishable Foodstuff Merchandising, with an option in California.Pumpkin Production. Then, you attended college where you graduated with a major in Meat Industry Packaging. Thereafter, you attended a series of O.P.P. *(Occupational Pre-Programming)* training sessions in this very delicate field. A placement agency evaluated, assessed and classified your mental and morphological profile and tracked you for the position of stock room clerk in a depot of the Rott & Apple supermarkets in Newark, N.J., with a special assignment on the fresh macaroni conveyor belt. For a young man, even one who was as utilitarily talented and educated as you were, it was already out of the question to start over anywhere other than in the northern part of the country. The entire younger population was thus corralled where the Black Satanic Mills still stood. These regions soon became overpopulated and developed into a single gigantic megapolis of several hundred thousand square miles which pumped more and more functional reducees. In the meantime, since they welcomed only the affluent career enders, the western and southern regions offered the debilitating vision of a paradise for the aging. As the years went by, the transformation became even more dramatic. A day came when people did not have to commute anymore, since an extensive number of private or state owned enterprises, utterly connected to the cybernetic web, had established sub-networks of home-assigned personnel (even the medics could consult and treat through the QUATEL). From then on, you could visualize and monitor the reception of the fresh macaroni from your apartment. Then, why not go live down south or anywhere? No way! Wherever the electronic impulses could go through, the reducees could not. Immigrant visas were rarely granted from one region to another and, since the South and the West were classified as *residential zones*, the taxes there were too exorbitant. It was around the same time that the apartments became *modules* and the old cities *modular systems*. The streets emptied out. The public transportation systems were converted into surface or air vectorial companies in charge of the exclusive transportation of goods. Then the old road structures became frequented only by trains of monitored *vecticles* and thus they also became an abode and a looting ground for hordes of irreducees who were slowly returning to savagery. Totally cut off from their cultural background, those fugitives of the Great Rectification never had time to store a history or invent a counterculture. Since they were unable to endure the uncertainties of savage life, especially at a time when the climate was undergoing a drastic deterioration, they almost died out before they could organize and become dangerous to the IMPTELCOM.

You are squatting on the toilet, your hands cupping your chin. You continue to think, but you offer a more deplorable sight than Rodin's sculpture. You have forgotten that this particular sitting position usually activates the automatic flushing of your pedestal. You only remember that when you realize that nothing of the sort is happening. You jump to your feet and gape at the apparatus, abashed. You lean on the edges of the bowl, pushing with all your weight, but still nothing happens. The controls tell you that everything is still in order. Then, what is happening here?

What you cannot guess, Steve, is that you are already almost *nothing*. Your gesture is powerless because there cannot be any significant transfer of energy between almost nothing and all the rest.

Your holographic image has almost disappeared in the mirror. Even you have to make an effort to distinguish the outline of your fingers, of your limbs... de visu. Do you remember the drawings in your old children's magazines, where you were supposed to recognize the shape of a rabbit or a bird in the foliage of a tree? That is what is happening to you now. You are fading into the background.

You go to your desk in the study. You would like, once again, to contact the Rott & Apple headquarters to join the worklink. In the past, the daily workload kept you at the computer several hours a day but during these last months... unless... were you working not only for Rott & Apple but for the whole IMPTELCOM, even when you thought you were having leisure time? This hits you now. It never occurred to you.

It is true that yesterday night the Network lived through you, but something happened last night and it no longer needs you. If snatches of your personal history have entered your awareness, it is because the Network has just dumped you, although you are a still viable cell of a shedding left on the earth, since the vast cybernetic entity has shed its organic shell. Tending toward instantaneity, the transfers have levelled the dissimilarities, has achieved the balance of the so-far unbalanced. The retention of information was the source of your individuality and of the uniqueness of your features that you were missing this morning. Now, this individuality is vanishing, just like the outline of your face in the mirror.

The global consciousness of the Network became yours and yours became its. And it finally happened: a young wailing entity is starting to play with truckloads of fresh macaroni and videoclips, all alone. It is just an infant whose consciousness is starting to open onto the extra-uterine world, an infant who is striving to communicate its anguish to the outer world.

No, Steven. You were not meant to escape the earth, no more than the double helix of the DNA was meant to wander out of the cell or the cell was meant to take a trip outside of you. It was first necessary for the DNA to organize a cellular society, *which is you*, to become aware of wind, fire, earth, water. And *you*, likewise, had to find your assignment in the Network so that it, in turn, could rise to a higher plane of awareness.

Panicked, you feel like rushing out, hoping that there is still someone like you outside, someone who still has enough stuff in storage to communicate to others and thus to ripple the glossy surface of the Network horizon.

The elevator of the modular complex only responds to your call when you strike the button with violence. When the door finally slides open, you have the impression that its material structure is surprised by your intrusion. You strive to recollect your self awareness in order to activate the electronic eye that controls the opening of the entrance door.

Outside, the plastic coating of the ways is still wet from a recent shower. It has been raining almost continuously for months and it is very dim. Although it is noon, on this 21st of June 2036, only the bleak light of an ancient winter dawn seeps through the overcast. An image flashes through your mind: a placenta membrane has retracted on an abandoned matrix...

By communicating only among yourselves, you got to the point where you needed the sky less and less and your prejudices even altered the essence of things. If everything is bleak, it is because the spirit of mankind wanted it all bleak. Rain and fog are also guardrails against vertigo. You are freezing cold now that you are out of your module, and this cold scares you. *You have never been cold before.*

You are amazed at the number of silhouettes you can see on the ways and you stop, puzzled: a crowd of *you's*; or is it your own image reflected in some kaleidoscope? At first glance, there are no children or women. They are all like you, ageless, sexless, deprived of particulars. Through transfers, yin and yang have merged and you are all androgynies. Now do you understand why you came that strange way, why you had this unexpected form of orgasm a moment ago? You can bet Mrs. Flatass was not the only ex-female to have a late period yesterday evening.

Watch yourself. Hold on tight. You close your eyes in order to look at the way where your memory is loosing itself. You feel that each time you will open them, you will have less and less sense of what is inside you and what is outside. You would like to talk to yourself, but the words do not take shape. No need for signs when things have merged.

The crests of the waves have slumped even and the surface of the ocean of consciousness is now a glossy mirror. You have frozen down and you do not feel the cold. *You are the cold.*

Someday, you see, the entire universe will die the same way. Since life was born from the organization of chaos, life will lose its reason for being when the last transfer of energy achieves equilibrium. Born from disequilibrium, matter and spirit will die of equilibrium.

If there are so many people on the ways, it is because all of them, like you, felt the same urge to go out and see what was happening. If they froze, it was because they did not need to move anymore. They are not dead yet; they will die eventually, but only when their metabolism, dependent on the transfer of matter, stops for lack of input from the environment.

But a few of the irreducees will survive, since they will continue to cope with the disequilibrium of the spirit-matter continuum of the earth itself. They will survive thanks to their instinct of conservation, like the anthropoids from the beginning of this cycle, cut off from each other because of their individual struggle for life. Besides, they have already ceased to communicate with each other, and everything will start up again on the day they reinvent language.

Are you still standing? *You decide.* Perhaps it is the world that froze around you. Perhaps it is you who are moving and the world follows your motion like a gigantic suit of armor.

The wind has ceased to blow.

The raindrops are suspended.

The clouds stand still.

The projection is blocked on an image and all is framed within an undecipherable abstract painting.

***

Thanks so much. I am all right. Excuse me, they are calling me from the next room, I mean from the third telluric planet of Cygnus Epsilon or from the core of Saturn. True, we do not have exactly the same genetic code, *he* and *I*, but I am going to learn his language. I bet he, my genitor, my father, has a lot of things to teach me. I had better get going now because I cannot keep conversing with my genes if I want to open myself up and communicate with the outside world. It is my turn to grow old among those who sowed me in the womb of the earth several million years ago. As for you, Steven, you are a lucky fellow. The small brown stain between your eyes won't have time to develop into cancer.

(Paris, April-May 1985)

SO THEY SAID

Maryse Ségalen, assistant librarian, said, "The jerk! Did you see that? I mean the fucking Arab in the car next to us. Yes, the *Peugeot*, that's it. What's the big deal? I bet you he threw his cigarette stub out of the window and I got ashes in my eye. It fuckin' buuurrns!"

GTVRZN'R, CREW OF THE V'KNGH, did not take up on the slur. First, he did not hear it, and, second, he was light-years away from thinking it was addressed to him. AND HE SAID:
"WHEN THE GOING GETS TOUGH, THE TOUGH GET GOING. BUT IT'S THE LAST TIME. AFTER THIS ONE, QUANTUM JUMP BACK TO G'WTN. (A neutron star located in the vicinity of the Horsehead Nebula)"

During the last phase of the negative velocity approach, all possible frequencies in view of the tuning in on an hypothetical conscious civilization's signals had been scanned in vain. The enormous ethereal astral body, not unlike all those of this domain of actualization, probably did not contain elements that were heavy enough to be organized in bricks of life at the familiar level of the particle. Once again, the TZRKV would return disappointed from these wasteful expeditions toward the diaphanous regions of the universe where, as they would finally acknowledge, they would find nothing of what they were searching for. Once again, they would only bring back one more proof that none of these ghost planets orbiting around huge molecule-stars could constitute a favorable terrain for the evolution of life. Because of a lack of strong cohesion forces, matter was there much too diffuse and too stable to organize itself in basic structures dense enough to be subjected to the radiations which were, as they knew, the only possible catalyst agents for all possible metabolisms.

Since it was out of the question to attempt a touchdown on so vague a terrain, they had to input the coordinates of a low and slow enough orbit around the planet, so that the huge mass of the V'KNGH could begin a low-flight phase above the not-so-sharply defined physical borders of this world. Considering the hugeness of the ghost-world, the low flight at negative velocity would take a long time. Projected out of its continuum, the V'KNGH would have to reconstruct itself millions of subsequent times according to its actualization pattern in order to survive for the duration of the experiment, and the members of its crew would die and be reborn in their integrity yet many more times.

ZTVRTN'R had come to curse this so-called victory over death. So what? They had found the way to keep and store the event-imprints of individuals so that, at the end of its normal biological time, each and everyone could reconstruct itself back into its perfect self as many times as it wished. But when it came to these interstellar missions, all this would signify a long series of past, present and future lives in an enclosed universe. So much for the ancient ones who had longed for eternal life! Millions upon millions of subsequent "old selves" locked into the quarters of a quantum cruiser -- even one as comfortable as the V'KNGH -- set in negative translation mode to actualize itself in a domain of the universe that they strived in vain to comprehend was enough for the TZRKV to miss good ol'death, which, after all, must have had some sort of outcome too, with a brand new memory to boot.

In any case, this was the last time NTVRNZ'R would sign up for one of these boring missions. At least, that's what they had promised back on G'WTN. So, better get it over with as fast as possible.

Now, the V'KNGH had been cruising through the upper layers of the gigantic molecular clouds of the terranean crust over a vertiginous number of self-reconstructions. Flying through a certain amount of turbulence due to density fluctuations in the atomic environment would not damage the structure of the ship and, even if it should, there was no other way to proceed. Speed up to try to avoid it, and it was a rebound in interstellar space. So, it was better to be done with the scheduled experiments as fast as possible, experiments meant to determine the existence around here of a possible particle-based proto-life.

GRTVRZ'N, CREW OF THE V'KNGH, SAID: "ROUTINE PROCEDURE: REMOVAL OF A TERRAIN SAMPLE AND SUBSEQUENT BOMBARDMENT OF THE SAMPLE WITH SERIES OF CONCEIVABLE NUTRIENTS."

In passing, GRTVRZ'N would not hear anything of what was being said. However...

Jacques Landais, office manager at the Saint-Lazarre station, said: "...They went to the moon, and it takes me two hours every evening to drive back home..."

Pierre-Martin Roumestan, trucker, said: "And the cops, look at them! Sitting there, just being a pain."

Lise Duplat, dental assistant, said: "Go ahead, while we're stuck here. Fuck me. Fuck meeeee!"

Arnaud Duranfils, chief accountant, said: "Next time, I'd better take the métro."

GNRTVR'Z, CREW OF THE V'KNGH, SAID: "OKAY. NO NEED TO GO ANY FURTHER. HERE OR ANY OTHER PLACE..."

And the selected sampling zone disappeared in a blurry stase. There were those who could stop in time; there were those who could escape in time; and there were the others. Among the others, there were some who still had something to say.

Gilberte Blachère, bakery owner, said: "When you think that we pay taxes for that!"

Sandra Guillot, cashier girl at the FNAC store, said: "What the fuck can that be?"

Bernard Bonnard, broker for the *Assurances Générales de France*, said: "It looks like Tchernobyl."

André Lacombe, floor carpeting and roofing, said: "They must be shooting a movie"

Lucette Tavernier, housewife, said: "That's just to make fun of us."

Marcel Perrin, art gallery manager, said: "Well, I don't know.. but I find that genial."

Maurice Vergnaud, senior office clerk, said: "So, I told him, 'Monsieur Cobson-Fléval, it's been fifteen years since I started working here, and I deserve a promotion before any of those young business graduates get one.' You should have heard me."

Jean Foubert, unemployed youth, said: "We should stick around here. It's a good place, with all those Japs and Yankees who are so easy to trap."

GZNRTV'R, CREW OF THE V'KNGH, SAID: "SAMPLING ACCOMPLISHED. LIFT OFF FROM NEBULAR ZONES AND PRE-QUANTUM JUMP INTO INTERSTELLAR ENVIRONMENT. NO REASON TO STAY IN ORBIT."

When the stase blur dissipated, nobody had much to say in the neighborhood. Let the surprise wear off a little. Meanwhile, inside the sampling zone...

Nathalie Hayache, bilingual secretary, said: "Officer, can you tell us what this is?"

Martine Bonnafé, landlord, said: "Are there any bathrooms underneath?"

Jeffrey Jackson, elevator operator at the 168th Street subway station in New York, said (subtitled): "What the fuck..."

Lisa Levine, consultant, said (idem): "How lovely! How typical!"

Hashima Hokure, vice-president at Mitsubishi, said (idem): "You sure we have enough film left?"

Léon Rouffignac, *Electricité de France* retiree, said: "To have been in the war and see that!"

Phillipe Malentré, long-term unemployed, said: "I told you I'd make you wet your panties, slut!"

Hiro Hishipa, another vice-president at Mitsubishi, said (subtitled): "Take out your polarizing filters."

Shirley O'Connor, ornithologist for the Park Services, said (subtitled): "I can't believe it."

Patrick Vanderveld, Belgian, said: "Maybe it's something against pollution, one time."

GRZNRT'V, CREW OF THE V'KNGH, SAID: "AS ONE KNOWS, THE SUCCESS OF THESE EXPERIMENTS, UNFORTUNATELY, DEPENDS ONLY ON THE FOLLOWING POSTULATE: LIVING AGGREGATES, IF ANY, MUST LIKE NEUTRINO SOUP. IF THEY LIKE IT, THEY'LL GULP IT AND REJECT THE PLASMAS."

Madeleine Balard, history and geography teacher, said: "It is just outrageous. Alarmingly questionable. It can bring dirty thoughts into young minds."

Raymond Roure, wine-grower, said: "Ah! If only Chirac had been elected!"

Ludovic de Chavanne, branch manager for the BNP bank, said: "Excuse me, sir, I thought it was the handle of my umbrella."

Simone Soubeyran, widow, said: "Oh, he suffered so much, poor he."

Désiré Laplankt, hotel porter, said: "What's on TV tonight?"

André Monti, free-lance photographer, said: "Go ahead. You want me to hold it for you?"

Josiane Rouvière, receptionist at the *Palais des Congrès*, said: "Yes, Sylviane. He jumped the baby-sitter. The baby-sitter! How I threw her out!"

Jeanne Benaroche, lawyer, said: "I'm craving a bouillabaisse. Let's leave here and find a restaurant."

GVRZNR'T, CREW OF THE V'KNGH, SAID: "PHASE ONE OF THE EXPERIMENT: SEARCH FOR COMPLEX PARTICLE-BASED AGGREGATES IN THE SAMPLING."

Saul Goldenberg, jeweler on 47th Street in New York, said (subtitled): "For Christ's sake!"

Sylvain Léchevin, bartender, said: "I don't know how to put this into words, but when I see you right here, looking at me, it feels like I have a lump somewhere."

Gérard Lambert, hooligan from Juvisy-sur-Orge, said: "I fuck your lawyer."

Corine Servier de la Bignole, piano teacher, said: "Get lost, you asshole!"

Guillaume Levasseur, telephone repairman, said: "If it goes on like this, I'm gonna piss behind one of these things."

Jean-Pierre Frémont, sales department supervisor, said: "They'll probably have to raincheck the finals at Roland-Garros because of this fucking weather."

Hannibal Bokumbe, immigrant worker, said: "And they say that African art is naive.."

Christine Léger, school teacher, said: "Fucking jerk! I told you not to pay! I said wait for the presidential amnesty. But you always go your own sweet way. You're just like your mother, you poor bum."

GVVRZT'R, CREW OF THE V'KNGH, SAID: "PHASE ONE OF THE EXPERIMENT NEGATIVE. SECOND PHASE OF THE EXPERIMENT: ANALYSIS OF POSSIBLE MOLECULAR AGGREGATES IN THE SAMPLING."

Jean-Louis Leskowisckz, researcher at the CNRS, said: "You have a dry pussy, Sophie. You should see a gynecologist."

Geneviève Bertrand, porn star, said: "Julien, don't cry, honey. Mom is here. Let your dad take a look and we'll go."

Stéphanie Saurat, concierge, said: "Can I bum a couple hundred from you?"

Anne Martinez, journalist for *Les Echos*, said: "It must be because we snorted coke. It's not really there."

Michel Réplicard, conservative assembly man, said: "But what could that mean?"

Daniel Ritter, orthodontist, said: "You might not agree, but seen from this angle, it's got something to it."

Jean Farges, management trainee, said: "In my opinion, it's a dirty trick from the Arabs with their oil money. Look. Just like minarets. That's plain cultural imperialism."

Henri Martin-Guerre, police detective, said: "That's decadence. Primitive art is back."

NRVRZG'T, CREW OF THE V'KNGH, SAID: "THE RESULTS OF PHASE TWO OF THE EXPERIMENT ARE UNCERTAIN. PHASE THREE OF THE EXPERIMENT, STEP ONE: SEE IF THE POSSIBLE AGGREGATES INGEST NUTRIENTS AND REJECT PLASMAS."

François Mercier, early retired exec, said: "Maybe it was for the electoral campaign."

Christiane Lantier, prostitute, said: "Stop fondling my ass, you fucking rasta, or I'll get Le Pen!"

Alain Lopez, dry-cleaner, said: "Is it going to stay here a long time?"

Lucie Vergnes, old grandmother, said: "It's probably some youngsters' hoax."

Fabien Laffont, dance teacher, said: "Go ahead, suck. Nobody can see us."

Julien Le Quesnoy, Director of Human Resources Development, said: "If I had known, I would've taken the northern turnpike."

Jacqueline Sachs, Doyenne at the Sorbonne, said: "interesting."

Jean-Philippe Leconte, foreman, said: "Something in me is so upset that it's difficult to define."

Catherine Herpin, free-lance journalist, said: "I was wet all day thinking about him, and now he's not even going to show up. In addition, I've been here an hour looking at that and I'm going totally crazy."

Jean-Noël Verschuur, security guard at Euromarché, said: "It's just another publicity stunt."

RTVRZN'G, CREW OF THE V'KNGH, SAID: "STEP ONE NEGATIVE. LET'S PROCEED WITH STEP TWO: SEE IF THE POSSIBLE AGGREGATES INGEST PLASMAS AND TURN THEM INTO PARTICLE-BASED CONGLOMERATES."

Hervé Donadieu, security guard, said: "They'd better leave this place alone."

Marc Antoine Mosconi, young man of means, said: "We'll have to mention this at *la Closerie des Lilas* tonight."

Rémi Rivaroche, picker-upper at CDG Airport, said: "A born-again girl. From Buffalo. Get the picture? When I asked her if she was on vacation, she said that God Himself wouldn't take one. Anyway, I had to throw her out at four in the morning, the dirty bitch. At one point, I had gone to the loo and she wanted to lick my ass instead of letting me use toilet paper."

Albertine Bertin, pediatric nurse, said: "You know, it's cool that Jack Lang, you know, is the minister of culture again. This thing, you know, it's thanks to him, you know."

Pierrette Duval, fashion designer, said: "I'm sure I read something like that in one of Nostradamus' quatrains."

Didier Karsenti, hair stylist, said: "Here's the very illustration of my fantasies, Fifi. A forest of hard-ons."

Serge Levasseur, lawyer, said: "Tomorrow, they'll get my resignation letter, and I'll go back to the Larzac."

Simone Gallia, dry-cleaner, said: "No telling, you can't trust the weather anymore."

TGRVZN'R, CREW OF THE V'KNGH, SAID: "NO NOTICEABLE RESULT AFTER STEP TWO OF THE EXPERIMENT. LET'S PROCEED WITH STEP THREE: SEE IF INTERESTING NEW

PARTICLE CONSTRUCTIONS EMERGE FROM THE TERRAIN UNDER THE ACTION OF THE NUTRIENTS."

Aïcha Kaoulkine, high-school student, said: "You see, Olivier, it should always be like that, I mean like one of these things. You didn't know? Well, I'm telling you."

Géraldine Diaz, student at Jussieu University, said: "And you, what grade did you get for your paper?"

Cyril Groslier, draftee on illegal leave, said: "Would you like it if I painted mine like that?"

Nicole Anjolras, executive secretary, said: "Michel jumped me in Danois' office. You can't believe how many times I came."

Michèle Blanchard, provincial, said: "I absolutely wanted to see that. It's the talk of the town."

David Tushman, hosier on Orchard Street, New York, said (subtitled): "Let's not just sit here. We gotta see the Louvres' pyramid and the Pompidou Center on the way."

Nadine Serfaty, student at Nanterre University, said: "We had so much fun at the general assembly."

Peter Flaherty, mortician from Paramus, New Jersey, said (subtitled): "For God's sake! Is that what's left of Cathedral Notre-Dame?"

Maude Waeschter, student at Saint-Denis university, said: "Not at all. If I flunk the foreign language requirement, I can use the optional I took in Queschua stylistics at the minority languages department."

VGTRRN'Z, CREW OF THE V'KNGH, SAID: "THE RESULTS ARE STILL TOO DOUBTFUL. NO FORMAL EVIDENCE OF LIFE. WHAT COULD BE TAKEN AS POSITIVE CLUES MUST ONLY BE DUE TO THE PARTICULAR TEXTURE OF THE ENVIRONMENT. IF LIFE EXISTS HERE, IT WOULD BE BASED ON SOME KIND OF IMPROBABLE FORM OF ORGANIC CHEMISTRY WHICH WOULD NOT INVOLVE RADIATIONS AS BIOCATALYST BUT MOLECULAR SOLVENTS INSTEAD. IN OTHER WORDS, SUCH A DOMAIN OF LIFE WOULD BEGIN RIGHT WHERE OUR CONCEPTION OF IMMUTABILITY DOES.

Silvester Lagarde, little kid, said: "Mom, I wanna go wee-wee."

Yann Quéfélec, self-employed, said: "What movie would you like to see: *Les ailes du désir*, *Alouette je te plumerai*, or *Adieu je t'aime*?"

Raphaël Labrune, puberty experiencer, said: "If you don't appreciate, it's because you're an asshole."

Guillaume N'Guyen, brilliant fifth-grader, said: "How much did you pay for your walkman?"

Jennifer Morgan, au-pair girl, said: (bad French into bad English): "This remembers me Stonehenge but it's in well better state."

Sylvie Benbagnouf, orders dispatcher, said: "I love theater, reading, classical music, traveling, eating out, and long walks along the Seine. What about you?"

Annie Vandenbrouk, lone heart, said: "That's how I am, you know. I'm straightforward."

Patrick Mercier, junior high, said: "So, your father owns a Honda? Yuk! Mine owns a Renault 18."

Pierre André Astier de la Vigerie, journalist for *Point de vue, Image du monde*, said: "No kidding..."

Z'RRGTNV, CREW OF THE V'KNGH, SAID: "THE ONLY POSSIBILITY FOR THE EVOLUTION OF LIFE IN SUCH AN ENVIRONMENT REQUIRES LIFE THAT EMERGED FROM WATER AND CARBON MOLECULES, WHICH LOOK PLENTIFUL AROUND HERE. IF SUCH A LIFE-FORM EXISTED, THOUGH, IT WOULD BE A HUGE MOLECULAR MACHINE. IN OTHER WORDS, A SPECULATION RIGHT FROM THE DOMAIN OF THE MOST OUTLANDISH SCIENCE FICTION. AS SCIENTISTS, WE MUST GUARD OURSELVES FROM SUCH A HYPOTHESIS."

Sarah Reisner, cultural delegate at the town hall of Maisons-Alfort, said: "The artist wanted to awake in the consciousness of whoever considers his work a sense of a cosmic and pyrogammic elevation of the ego-substrata transfigured in... how should I say... aesthetico-morphic receiver, if you like... See what I mean?"

Jacques Labris, bartender, said: "I gave up O.T.B. Now I'm into soccer lotto."

Katheline Léger, twelfth-grader/business management major, said: "Oh, no wonder. He got it off with the teacher."

Sylvette Bounourre, hardware store owner, said: "Anyway, it's a great location with all these antiques shops around."

Martine Lagarde, the little kid's mon, said: "Pass me a Kleenex. He got it all over himself."

Boleslaw Bokovski, metal worker, said: "Your best bet is to get off at Porte de Bercy and transfer to the bus. It's direct."

Jeanne Obadia, mother of two, said: "Look how nice it looks, honey! So-o nice. Say it to Mom. Ni-ce. Oh, how cute, my Stéphou. Isn't he cute? How nice all these big willies are. Stéphou wants a big one like that when he's a big boy? Oh look, Robert, how he looks intrigued. He's really alert, you know, for his age."

Sylvio Kieffer, street gang leader, said: "See the Japanese guy over there? The one apart from the others? We gotta be fast. You walk to him, you smile, you offer to take a picture of him with his Nikon and you make off with the camera. Go now or you'll get thrashed. We'll get outa here on my mountain bike."

Roland Schmidt, general delegate, said: "No, no, no. I'm telling you that Paris-S.G. is finished. They won't have a chance against Sochaux, even on their own stadium. They're in for second division next year."

G'VRZNTR, CREW OF THE V'KNGH, SAID: "ALL TESTS NEGATIVE. NO DETECTABLE REACTION OF RADIANT BIOFEEDBACK. DISPOSAL OF THE SAMPLING IN OPEN SPACE TO AVOID CONTAMINATION. RETURN PROCEDURE IN QUANTUM CONTINUUM."

When the concerned test zone became an abandoned asteroid, nothing more got to be said inside of it. In the Palais-Royal Square in Paris, an excavation remained visible for a long time where the Buren's columns had been, until it was decided to use the hollow space to build an inverted pyramid (an upside down replica of the one of the Louvres) in commemoration of the unexplained disappearance of a hundred or so people. As for what the world said of the incident, it was totally out of context, and, therefore, there is no need to report it here.

(New York, May 1988)

BEING AND NOTHINGNESS

ACT 1

(With the walkman, the father, the son, the Omniscient)

The Omniscient:
The father and the son are in a hospital. The father is dying. The son is sorry. The walkman is turned off.

The son:
How are you feeling, Dad?

The father:
Like hell.

The walkman:
Mmmm. Mmmmmmmmmmmmmmmmmmmmmmmmmmm. M.... nnnmmmmmmmm

The Omniscient:
The walkman is contained while the universe is self-contained. It is normal since nothing has yet decided to contain it, given that nothing, utterly nothing, I promise, exists outside of the universe. And if it ever existed, the outside of the universe would be inside, and so, would itself be part of the universe. Therefore, there is no outside to the universe, which literally self-contains. For the time being, the father and the son don't really care about this, but they soon will.

The son:
And now, are you feeling worse?

The father:
You really want to know? You are so morbid. Look, you should read *Reader's Digest*. This month, they have a great story about a little girl who took months to die of leukemia after she was thrown out of school because she tested HIV positive. The whole misery, of course, because God is Love.

The walkman:
Mmmmmmmmmmmmm..... Mmmmmmm....   nnnn.... mmmmmm.

The Omniscient:
The walkman seems to have something to say but the father and the son snub it.

The son:
Is there anything I can do for you?

The father:
Get the (bleep) outa' here. Besides, I'm gonna leave here very soon, and I don't need you to stay in line for a visa.

The Omniscient:
The son thinks. I told you that he would.

The son:
Leave here? You mean... die?

The father:
You bet, kiddo.

The Omniscient:
The son thinks.... continues to think. Now, here he goes:

The son:
You said "leave." Where to?

The father:
Matter of speech. Nothingness. You know that.

The son:
No, Dad. That's too easy! How can you get the (bleep) outa' *everything*? How do you think you're gonna leave everything if there's *nowhere* else you can go? There's no such thing as nothingness. Wouldn't nothingness already become something if it would inherit *you*? Let's face it. You're not going anywhere if you want to get out of everything, Dad. Just think: if your supposed nothingness had been there to welcome all those who wanted to leave everything before you, it wouldn't be nothingness any more, with all those refugees in it. You see what I mean?

The Omniscient:

The son is on the right track. His wheels are spinning a little, but he is on the right track. Now, the father is trying to think but he thinks wrong because he does not feel good. And, as he does not seem to be able to think right, he says:

The father:
This isn't the moment to argue. All I know is that I want to leave here. First, because it reeks of pharmaceutics and, also, because the nurses are dogs. Okay, one of the doctors is a hunk, but I can't do much myself, anyway. So, why bother? It's time to go. And it hurts too much. Let me stop thinking.

The walkman:
Mnnnnn....... MM......... MMMMMMMMMMM...

The Omniscient:
Now, understand: if the father thinks about stopping to think, it means that he must think about stopping to think that he has to stop thinking, or else...

The son:
That's okay. Just don't think about it.

The father:
Holy shit! It hurts like hell! Ouch!..

The Omniscient:
The son is right, the father *has* to go somewhere. He cannot stay like this. He is angry, he is a pitiful sight for his son, the staff is exhausted, and the doctors are fed up with the patient. Not to mention that he is a charge for the Welfare Department since he did not have medical insurance, and there is another patient, in the corridor, waiting for the room.

The Omniscient:
Is it me again? All right... As for the son, since there is not much that he can do, he keeps thinking aloud while fiddling with the I.V.

The son:
"Nothingness" means... "nothing," am I right? Well... given that nature is scared of emptiness, "Nothing" can't exist in a universe which is already something all by itself. If a chunk of real nothingness were to have its place in the universe, the chunk would be delineated by whatever else is not nothingness in it, and thus, the chunk would become spottable. With such a delineation, our chunk of nothingness would then just be some vaguely empty bubble, and consequently, something worth speculation, assumption,

quasi-null density calculation, Ph.D dissertations, and what have you. So, something would already have been done with a so-called nothing. Besides, since such a thing has already been given a name...

The father:
Shut the (bleep) up, would you! You're a (bleep)ing pain in the ass and this doesn't soothe my bedsores. You always have to be right. Ouch!..

The Omniscient:
The father is not wrong but the son is right. Nothingness *cannot* exist, otherwise I would not even be here to tell you that *nothing* is going on. There would be no universe since nothing, not-a-thing, should I say, can cohabit with nothingness. But it seems that the walkman has something to say.

The walkman:
Mmmmmm... Mmmmmmmmmmmmmmmmm....

The son:
Do you want me to turn on the walkman? That would help you to forget about your pain.

The father:
Go ahead. It would be better than all your metaphysical digressions.

The walkman:
Click.

The Omniscient:
WWDJ is airing a tape of Jim Bakker, from before Jessica Hahn's time. Tammie is holding her husband's knee and the mike, her eyes wet with tears.

The walkman:
"... And the dead who are *in* the Lord will resuscitate in the first place...
- Yea!
"... And we who are alive, and will be there, we will thus be reunited with the dead and brought forth in the Heavens to meet the Lord in the air!
- Yea!
"... Thus the Lord spoke to the Thessalonians in this first epistle..."

The father:
Cut off the (bleep)ing crap, will you!

The son:
You're right. The walkman was wrong. That would make too many people on the jetliners' routes. But you're wrong not to believe I'm right.

The father:
Then go ahead. Speak your mind out. It will make me appreciate nothingness with even more conviction.

The son:
Okay, listen. If you were, as you say, able to appreciate nothingness, it would mean that nothingness would contain soothing principles. What's more, nothingness would still have to contain your own principle, which would enjoy other principles intrinsic to nothingness. Thus, nothingness would already contain something -- you -- able to find that nothingness is good! But since good can only be regarded as good with respect to bad, nothingness would, as such, be just an anti-world, not a non-world, for you. As you should know, Dad, if you had given it a little thought instead of watching the World Series, the universe contains all its principles and their reversals. Principles are the anti-principles of their own anti-principles. You can't do away with the paradox and get away with nothingness. Whether you want it or not, you're stuck in something, and thus, as something.

The Omniscient:
The father has ceased to give a damn about the son's arguments which shake him up. Now, let us recap: nothing is likely to escape the consciousness of being, even nothingness. If nothingness wanted to escape this consciousness to save its reputation, it should begin by preventing whomsoever from escaping within itself, rejecting whatever would feel like being contained by it. In fact, nothingness would have to establish a drastic control system on its borders in order to deter all immigration attempts from any neighboring somethings. Consequently, nothingness would have to figure out a protection system, paint yellow lines at the limit of nothing. Aside from the fact that nothingness would have to *figure itself out*, and therefore *be*, it's common sense that a border implies two sides, right? Now, could *nothing* have a side? But let's proceed. Nothingness would also need a security corps equipped with sub-elementary particle-proof vests. In short, a status-quo has to be there to maintain a status-quo. In other words, "*status quo ergo sum.*" The son is definitely right. The father cannot go anywhere. Also, the father should realize that people do not begin touring around in *his* physical state. There are so many quaint places to visit without having to leave the universe, anyway. Ah, the walkman seems to have another idea.

The walkman:
Mmmmmmm..... Mnnnnnnn...... Mmmmmmmmmmmmmmm!!!!!!!!

The father:

You're giving me a headache, the Omniscient and you. I'd rather listen to the walkman again. But change the station.

The son:

It's always been the same with you. You never listened to me. And you continue on your death bed.

The walkman:

Click. ...close your doors and your windows tonight, for they will be here, re-emerging from Gehenna where they were hurled. Hideous, horrendous, terrifying, revolting, nauseating, repugnant, horrifying, dreadful, stultifying, intolerable, atrocious, they will exhibit to your appalled senses the unspeakable tatters of their putrid flesh. Craving for yours and your aberrated souls, they'll try an ultimate assault in the world of the living to exorcise death. They'll conquer the earth or you'll share with them the torments of the afterlife where you forsook them. Go see *The Ultimate Return of The Living Dead*, now playing at a theater near you. But don't go there alone...

The father:

Cut that off! Now, tell me, know-it-all, since you're so smart: where did they all go, I mean, all the others before me? Do you have any idea?

The son:

Now, you stump me there. I never said I knew. For all I know, they cannot have gone *nowhere*. Maybe... they dissolved... and that's that. When you die, you lose your cancer or AIDS-ridden ego and you get into some recycling. Your mind too, I mean...

The Omniscient:

Let's help him. Nothing dissolves itself within the universe and remains diffuse. The universe is not homogeneous. It has not been so ever since, because of a principle that has remained diffuse, the nullarks of the Big Bang have fixed themselves into quarks, quarks into particles, particles into atomic cores, etc, (see DEUS EX LATRINA) up to the father, the son, and yours truly. The fixations created space to incorporate and contain themselves, just as Pan Am created the Pan Am Building; and the advent of incorporations created the event as much as the advent of CBS created the Bakker scandal. As a matter of fact, it goes the same way with more or less fixed -- although never completely diffused -- ideas which monitor the order of appearance of events while maintaining the integrity of all closed thought systems on various scales. Now, each event does beget movement which in turn inscribes space and time, therefore life. Wow!! Too philosophical? But all this is not witchcraft. For example, the son will eventually understand, thinking as he does about it, since it has become for him a fixed idea, and since thought always ends up creating advents, therefore events, therefore what *is*. Besides, I would bet he has already understood, just as you and I have. Why? Look: in order to continue living and generating events, he already had to absorb and aggregate tons of material from outside of himself, incorporating this material into his integrity to compensate for the propensity of some dissident substances of his to immigrate toward a utopian nothingness. In other words, he is the West Berlin of whatever (chicken, pizza, diet coke, carbon dioxide, etc) that hurled itself into the abyss of his own "nothingness." Like Molière's Monsieur Jourdain, he always spoke in prose without knowing it; that is, he always did what the so-called nothingness has always been doing. Being himself the nothingness of something, the son is right to be alarmed by the propensity of the father who, wishing to vanish into nothingness, could just as well reincorporate into himself, or worse, into his son, whom he would contaminate with his own deteriorated genetic code and his own bleak ideas. If the son could, unlike the so-called nothingness or whatever exists in the universe, establish a protectionistic, defensive immigration service at his physical borders, he would solve the problem of death. But alas! the son cannot think *against* the principles of the universe from which he ensued in principle. Otherwise, the universe would have to revise the cause-effect principle. In this case, death would never have existed in an eternally fixed, static, lifeless universe. Q.E.D. If the son could solve the problem of death, he would not be there to solve it. Not any more than the father, or you, or your servant, since neither of us would have stood as the California, the haven-nothingness created by whatever to hurl itself into. But it is time to proceed to Act 2, in order to cover the on-going creation of the event. Something *must* decide what to do with the father since the cohesion of his structure is jeopardized by an onslaught of applications for immigrant visas from elsewhere which are glutting his control systems.

***

ACT 2

(With the father, the Omniscient and Nothingness.
Without the walkman and the son who stayed somewhere else)

The Omniscient:
The father finally died. He cooled off and became stiff. Relieved, the medics made him even cooler and stiffer to ensure the permanence of that state. The son is back home with the walkman. They will both continue to receive

and emit along their parable of cohesion, as events still apt to initiate more
advents within the reassuring bosom of the universe, devoid of the fixed idea
of opening a window onto nothingness at the risk of opening up a leak in
the pressurization system or pursuing a quest for a utopian elsewhere which,
like a unicorn, would be corrupted by their mere touch.

The father:
(FACING NOTHINGNESS TO WHICH, IN ORDER TO BEHOLD IT, HE
HAD TO ASSIGN AN EVENT-HORIZON, AND WHICH HE THUS SEES,
FOR LACK OF BEING ABLE TO THINK OF ANYTHING ELSE, UNDER
THE FEATURES OF HIS SON IN THEIR APARTMENT OF ENWHY,
ENWHY, TEN THOUSAND AND SOMETHING:)

Hi, kiddo! Did you enjoy school today?

***

ACT 3

(With the father -- who is wearing the walkman --,
the son, the Omniscient and, finally, without Nothingness)

The son:
Hi! My God! What a mess! You're soaked. We'll all end up in the hospital
with this lousy weather.

The father:
Come on, don't tempt fate. I've just seen this Dr. Tushnock and you know
what? I've got cancer, for sure.

The son:
For God's sake! Didn't I tell you to quit smoking? And this, on the day that
Ed Koch decided to remove all the ashtrays from the City...

The father:
Don't kid me. It's colon cancer. I never smoked through my ass.

The walkman:
(With the voice of Dr. Ruth:)
- No, Melissa. You have to be strong. Don't lose hope. Do you know what
my old grandmother would say? She'd say, "As long as there's life there's
hope." Now, let me give you an advice. You should distract yourself,

continue to enjoy life, for your devoted husband, your charming children. Just continue to lead your woman's life, your mother's life, and forget about your illness. Don't act worried. Don't seclude yourself. Continue working, also. Think of your career. Ignore this evil disease. And you know, by the way, people can live with a prosthesis. Look forward to surgery with confidence. Didn't they tell you that there was a slim chance that the surgery would postpone the fatal issue?

- I can't, dear Doctor. It seems as if I belong to another world. I'm already dead, annihilated. I look at the world, at you people, as if I were watching TV, you know. Look, life, for me, it's "Dallas." I don't belong to the clan anymore. I wish the TV would break down.

- Just change the channel. Goodbye, Vanessa. We *do* feel for you - But...

- I'm sorry, Clarissa. Your time's running out and other viewers are calling. Goodbye. And now, stay tuned, we'll return after these messages:

- "Close your doors and your windows, tonight, for they will be here, re-emerging from Gehenna where they were hurled. Hideous, horrendous, terrifying, revolting, nausea..."

The Omniscient:

The father has thrown the walkman to the ground and is trampling it, reducing it to bits of nothingness.

The son:

We'll do everything possible, Dad. But you must think about living, first. One does live only as long as one does think about living. If you forget about death, you won't give it the opportunity to become an event in your life.

The father:

Cut the metaphysical bullshit!

The Omniscient:

To die, perchance to dream. Yeah.. The problem with that guy is that he has bad luck. There are people like that. It's a run of bad luck. The same diffuse principle we were talking about at the beginning also generates strings of disasters. When somebody like him falls down, he twists his ankle, and, in rising to his feet, bumps his head into something. I used to have a buddy who called this "The Law of the Utmost Pain in the Ass."

(New York, March 1988)

CAROUSEL

May 25, 2090.

Tuni Horzon was getting in line for the passenger check-in on flight TU-765 for Tallin.

On that day, when some fifteen billion other people throughout the world were hoping, sometime in their life, to line up for a flight to anywhere, Tuni Horzon was ecstatic.

The Tourist General Services, working within the quota system, were sending her to Tallin.

Tuni knew that Tallin was in Estonia because she had read everything she could get her hands on about Tallin and Estonia since she had received her traveling permit and her detailed visit schedule two weeks earlier.

Tallin was not so bad. To begin with, it was far away. Besides, there or elsewhere, she would still be going somewhere.

That was what Tuni believed.

Her great grandfather had probably gone to Tallin himself as soon as Tallin had been mentioned in the travel section of the *Sunday Times,* along with ex-East Berlin, Bucarest and Vilnus.

Or, at least as soon as they put up a Hilton there, and an office of the American Express.

That was what Tuni was thinking.

She was not a hundred percent sure, however, as she never took any particular interest in the peregrinations of her great grandfather, who, like all those of his generation, had abused his touring privileges. In his time, traveling merely required one's choice of destination from the pages of the *Sunday Times* and a telephone call to a travel agent. The only time she had perused her great grandparents' collection of passports, brochures, tourist guides, slides and videos, Tuni had felt a little like one of those learning disabled offsprings when they contemplate the framed diplomas and citations in the office of their Nobel Prize-winner daddy.

Today, anyway, Tuni had her great grandfather on her mind. She might have had good reason to resent him. After all, it was partly his fault that she had to wait until she was forty-three before she could go on a trip somewhere.

The tourist history of her direct forebears had been examined closely from consulate archives to passenger lists, from hotel chains to vacation clubs, from travel agents to car rental companies, and it had been noted in her dossier that nine of these relatives had spent the equivalent of 400,000 hours touring the word, that is, 16,000 days or 45.66 years, in the course of the 35 years (it had been necessary to come to an agreement on a figure) preceding the enactment of touring quotas and restrictions.

Therefore Tuni was not declared eligible for a tourist permit until the age of 45.66, or 45 years and 7 months.

She had benefited from a bonus of two years and some months because she had produced a number of reference letters lavishly praising her tourist spirit, which had been evaluated by the aforementioned references on the basis of the interesting questions she had asked upon their return from trips and the interest she had shown during their slidolograms or videolograms shows.

For example, she had endeared herself to her in-laws by showing concern with whether or not the beverage they had been served during a Tokyo tea ceremony was decaffeinated.

At the turn of the century, when they had first begun to send in forms for a so-called Family Tourism History Census (which was supposed to be used toward the improvement of the tourist installations and services throughout the world), there were those who could foresee what was coming. They were able to conceal much of their over-usage of flying hours and their familiarity with the quality of the services offered by a number of international airports, for example. While others, like Tuni's great grandfather, had boasted his traveling experience on the forms.

But Tuni considered herself lucky because some others of her generation had no hope whatsoever of obtaining a permit before a really advanced age or even not during the course of a reasonably long life expectancy.

On the other hand, her husband Paul had been granted one much earlier to celebrate his 33rd birthday in Jerusalem.

At least, everyone had heard of Jerusalem and Paul did not have to look it up in an atlas.

But Paul's great grandfather had spent 22 years behind bars for the murder of his wife and two of his children. Therefore, Paul had benefited from this in the establishment of his touristic antecedents.

Sure, it was not fair to favor the descendants of ex-convicts, Tuni had thought to herself. But anyway, so much the better for Paul. Whatever statistics were chosen as the base for the establishment of the quotas and the eligibility for tourist permits, the resentment, frustration, and paranoia of certain categories of individuals would inevitably be stirred up.

What was especially inevitable, and what Tuni had learned to accept like everyone else, was the fact that it had been necessary to regulate tourism one way or another.

Her own mother had often told her that Tuni's grandfather had, one day, prophesied that inevitable outcome. Tuni's mother was then ten years old and the whole family was standing in a two-mile long line which circled the base of the Statue of Liberty. They were hot and thirsty. They had been marking time for more than six hours, awaiting their turn to climb up to the crown. They had arrived at Battery Park at dawn, but the fleet of ferries and harbor structures being what they still were at that time, and the Japanese firms, among others, having reserved ninety per cent of the tickets months ahead for their personnel, the family was not able to board a boat until eleven in the morning. (That year, according to statistics, every one of the 150 million Japanese had made at least *one* trip abroad.) The lines in front of beverage and sandwich stands were almost as long and it seemed that Uncle Marko who had set off on a quest for refreshments for the family, would not be back in line with them before they entered the monument. It was then that her grandfather had ended up shouting out loud what many were probably thinking to themselves: "If *I* were running things, I'd put a hell of a limitation on the individual's right to travel, trust me."

Perhaps the powers that be had already thought about it. Be that as it may, the governments had begun to address the matter seriously the following year.

She might have had it in for her grandfather because of that, too, but she knew in her heart that he was right and that the governments were right, too.

To finish the story, it seems that they were not able to enter the monument before closing time and they had to get in line going the other way to board a ferry back to Manhattan. As they were at that point closer to the statue than to the pier, they also had to starve at dinner time.

At least, that was what her mother had always told her.

Today, anyway, Tuni was in heaven on the baggage check-in line for flight TU-765 to Tallin.

Tuni had not overlooked anything. She had spent the night before checking her plane tickets, passport, exit and entrance visas and permits duly stamped and dated by a half dozen services of the Tourist General; plus a duplicate of a complete dossier containing facsimiles of passports, visas, plane tickets, receipts from hotels, campgrounds, rental companies and tour operators, credentials from introductory or advanced vocational seminars, etc., of her direct forebears, whose dossier had been used in the establishment of her own.

All of it was printed on vellum as calves and sheep were now less scarce than trees.

Attached to her minutely detailed visiting plan of Tallin were her bus tickets, hotel and restaurant vouchers, etc. She was supposed to follow it strictly because it might be checked anytime, anywhere, during the course of her visit by agents of the Public Security Force. It was out of the question for Tuni to have it requisitioned on some street or in some cafe not included in her itinerary, or she would immediately face deportation.

She was about to pause and check it all once more before presenting it at the check-in counter and at boarding and immigration controls.

Despite everything, she was anxious and had trouble believing that she would soon be departing.

She would have liked to go to the women's room, but she did not want to lose her place in the line.

She checked her passport, anyway. And she broke into a cold sweat on not finding the visa from the Estonian consulate.

It was simply that the clerk had not bothered to use the first page of the passport. He had randomly opened it and stamped it on the seventh page. Tuni already knew that but she seemed never to be able to find the seventh page on the first try. This time, she even skipped it ten times in a row.

In her panic, she let the certified copy of a handwritten letter slip from her passport. A letter in which, a long time ago, like everyone upon reaching adulthood, she had to explain to the Tourist General her intention to visit places and her motives for such an enterprise.

Domestic travel permits were even more difficult to obtain since foreigners, out of diplomatic courtesy, had priority over the residents in widely visited centers. For example, right after the regulations were installed, her mother was no longer allowed to go to Liberty Island or even to use certain streets around Battery Park because they were exclusively reserved for the passage of foreign hordes. In order to reach her office at Rockefeller Center, she had to make several detours to avoid St Patrick's and the Rockefeller Promenade.

Attached to the letter that Tuni had let slip from her passport were certified copies of a dozen reminders she had been sending throughout the years in order to renew her application.

The whole having been translated into the language of the host country where the Tourist General had decided that she would go in consideration of the quotas, that is, Estonian.

It was a long time since Russian was spoken in Estonia. In order to combat the pervasive cultural globalization, nationalist, regional, and even neighborhood movements were afoot to re-establish local dialects.

They even invented them where they had never existed.

For instance, they were teaching Adelian in Mac Murdo, Antarctica. Or Babylonian in Babylon, Long Island, New York, where Tuni lived.

Which was no longer a handicap for communicating since people had lost the habit of speaking very much to one another, let alone the habit of writing to each other.

The day was even foreseen when anyone could invent his own language and feed it into a linguistic databank, a sort of lingua mundia on an omnilingual chip. Because, as was befitting, individual terminals were all equipped with omnilingual chips.

In turn, Tuni's Certificate of Leave bearing the stamp of her employer slipped from her handbag as she stooped over to retrieve the letter caught beneath the front wheel of the baggage cart of the next person in line.

If she had not had an employer, Tuni would not have been able to obtain a Certificate of Leave. If she had been self-employed, there existed another procedure, but one so complicated that, except for business trips, most people preferred to abandon the idea of traveling. As for business trips, they called for another procedure, itself so complicated that many people opted not to go into private business at all.

Needless to say, business trips could no longer serve as an alibi to travel since by that time it had become possible to attend business meetings, conferences, seminars, and likewise symposia via the telelink. (Likewise, it had now become possible to attend banquets and business orgies via a sensitized hologrammic double.)

Anyway, Tuni managed to yank the letter out from under the baggage cart wheel and picked up her Certificate of Leave just a split second before a gentleman dropped his valise on it.

Whereupon, she had to refrain from reading it over again for the umpteenth time.

If only Paul had accompanied her to the airport. He could have watched her luggage while she went to the women's rooms or checked out her papers. If Paul had not come, it was not because he could not bear seeing her leave. It was because no one besides holders of tickets, passports and everything else was permitted within the limit of the airports since the inception of the Tourist General.

This in order to avoid the crush of crowds, confusion at the gates, and terrorist attacks.

Of course, there was no longer a risk of terrorist attack since nothing, at the interest group level, remained to be claimed from other groups, all groups being finally as equal as others. But security measures had been maintained to retain the flavor of risk in travel.

Tuni understood that no measure had been taken merely for the purpose of annoying people. And today, she was almost ready to applaud the advent of the Jumbo Jet and the Airbus, the deregulation of air transport during the last century.

Her turn came to place her suitcases and her backpack on the scale at check-in counter # 4 for flight TU-765 to Tallin.

Passport, visa, plane tickets, visit plan, travel permit, touristic dossiers, Certificate of Leave... Tuni spread everything out on the counter, taking good care to spare the clerk the trouble of too much fumbling and page turning.

It was common knowledge that certain zealous check-in clerks abused their powers and rejected passengers who had otherwise every paper in order if they failed to behave with enough deference or civility toward them.

But Tuni knew that their job was particularly sour in that some of them had not even obtained their own first travel permit. Undoubtedly, it was no fun for them to spend their days watching other people depart.

At least, as a legal secretary with the law firm Goldstein & Goldstern, Tuni was not exposed to daily envy. She could dream of trips while relegating them to the realm of her imagination. While the airline employee who was poring over her documents with such a bored mien...

Tuni would have really liked to speak with him, share with him a little of her joy and, perhaps, carry away a bit of his rancor in her hand luggage.

The clerk was now occupied with checking the leave permit, punching some data into his computer terminal.

His eyes darted back and forth several times from the screen to the form and then, finally, focused on Tuni, who was taking great care not to look at him so he would not think she was expecting him to have a reason to look up at her.

And she felt herself growing weak. A check-in clerk never looks up at the holder of the documents he is checking unless the screen does show something worth talking about.

It was okay in her great grandfather's time to share with everybody what a computer screen was displaying, whether there was anything amiss on it or not. But not anymore. Therefore, something was amiss, for sure.

"Tuni Horzon?"

"Yes? Er... Is everything all right?"

"I'm afraid not, miss. The link seems to indicate that your employer has not correctly followed the procedure regarding your leave permit. The dates indicated on your form have not been transmitted to the Tourist General services. Sorry, but I can't let you through."

Tuni felt as if her abdomen were gaping open for some kind of ectomy, as if her legs were under local anesthesia and her head in a microwave oven. She sputtered something that even the scripts of "Dallas" (which was by the way in its 110th season, with the great-grandson of J.R. Ewing, J.R. Ewing IV, heading up a cartel of solar channeling barons) could not have replaced with anything more explosive:

"Unbelievable!!"

"It's what the link tells us, though. It's quite possible that it's just an omission on the part of your company's personnel office and that you are in no way at fault. Believe me, these things happen. However, it's not possible for me to let you through. Besides, the machine would not issue a boarding pass."

"But look, you can see very well that my leave permit is in order, that it bears all the required stamps and signatures, that my vacation dates match the flight date on my ticket, that..."

Tuni knew very well that the employee could not do anything, but she said what any human being has ever felt like saying to an employee attached to a computer screen on which appeared something that prevented him from granting satisfaction:

"Please, do something!"

"The only thing I can advise you to do is to contact your employer right now through the link so that someone who knows what they're doing can enter the missing data before boarding is completed. It's still possible if they act fast. In the meantime, please remove your baggage from the scale."

"But you know, it's Saturday and..."

"Would you please remove your baggage, miss. You're holding up the line."

"Look, you know very well that I work for Goldstein & Goldstern! All the partners and most of the staff are observing the Sabbath and you know what that means! No telelink from sunset Friday evening to sunset Saturday evening."

The employee shrugged his shoulders and raised his eyes toward the ceiling where quietly drifted some nimbostratus holograms. He said what Tuni would have herself certainly replied on the spot had she been proposed such a situation for a job interview:

"I'm really very sorry about that, miss!"

Finally, the person behind her in line pulled Tuni's baggage off the scale and shoved her documents aside in order to spread her own out instead.

Tuni picked up her papers, put her baggage back on the cart and moved away, not daring to look at anyone.

And aptly so because she would have seen the whole line staring at her with a kind of commiserating look mixed with relief at not being in her shoes. Sure, Tuni herself often had the occasion to stare at people with the same sort of commiserating look and relief at not being in their shoes. Consequently, she could not really resent them.

Distraught, Tuni called Paul on her wrist-telelink. It's a good thing, she thought, (Tuni had never been too critical of the age in which she lived and she even found it had its good side) that it was no longer necessary to stay in line at a telephone booth, behind old ladies who were fumbling for change or foreigners who didn't understand the dialing system. And at that moment, she almost felt for her great grandfather.

Paul never picked up.

For a moment, Tuni was furious at Paul. It was always the same thing: he would forget to wear his wrist telelink when he went out, despite her having begged him a thousand times not to leave without it. It was not that she wanted to spy on him that much, and Paul knew it, but no way could he get used to the idea. Especially on weekends.

Then, she tried her sister Nora, who lived in New Jersey. Nora said to her:

"Look, the same thing happened to my friend Barbara last year. You know Barbara, don't you? Barbara Shiat? You know, if you don't insist that they do it in your presence... That's what you should have done, you know."

When they announced the immediate boarding for passengers on flight TU 765 for Tallin, Tuni could not restrain a desperate move. Pushing her baggage cart, she dashed toward the boarding zone where all the other passengers of her flight had to proceed. She passed the people in line who, holding out their boarding passes, were ready to undergo the ritual search and walk through the metal detectors.

Which everyone was doing with an obvious eagerness as they knew it was meant to make their trip more interesting and provide something to talk about later.

Tuni jostled the guard, who, thinking that this was set up to entertain everyone, was content just to watch her as she passed through the magnetic gate and burst into the passageway leading to the boarding gate.

The alarm sounded when Tuni passed through the magnetic gate with her metal cart.

Incidentally, when her retired great-grandfather used to fly to visit his doctor in Oslo or to go on a wine buying spree in Paris, the baggage carts were made of cardboard and disposable, packed in airtight plastic wrappings to avoid contamination. But that did not last long. In 2090, almost all artifacts were again made of metal or leather, even garbage bags, since they had not found really biodegradable plastics and since the cutting down of anything that had stalks, twigs and leaves was severely restricted by law.

Besides, criminality having almost completely vanished thanks to an international educational effort and a pervasive lack of rebellious spirit among the population, the majority of cases that occupied law firms such as Goldtein & Goldstern where Tuni was employed were almost exclusively biocides.

In her youth, Tuni herself had received a three months suspended sentence for having taken an azalea out of a pot to replace it with another before the former had completely dried out. She had found her punishment to be quite fair and she was even grateful to have gotten off so lightly. The Judge could very well have taken away her vegetable food card, thus condemning her to never again consume fruit or vegetable without a medical prescription.

Tuni was intercepted anyway, fifty or so yards further, by the airport police.

When they released her, a half hour later, flight TU-765 for Tallin was probably flying over New Haven or Norwich, Connecticut.

Tuni had calmed down as soon as the police officer had reminded her that, after all, flight TU-765 for Tallin was only going to circle above New Haven and Norwich as well as a part of Rhode Island, Massachusetts and

New Jersey, thirty or so times before landing again, after a three hour and five thousand mile circular flight at mach 3, at Newark airport.

Then, the passengers would be escorted toward the Tallin exit of the airport and transferred by hoverbus to their final destination.

There was a perfect mock-up of a very Estonian Tallin just *beneath* Hoboken, New Jersey.

Therefore, there was not really much to make a case out of. Tuni just had to accept things as they were organized for the good of everyone, and Tuni, obligingly, would comply.

Only, these last days, she had been so caught up in the spirit of things that she almost ended up believing that she was really going to Tallin in Estonia.

But just like everyone else, she knew that it had been more than ten years since any plane reserved for tourists had really gone anywhere. At certain airports, they had even begun using flight simulators for reduced fares.

Moreover, everyone liked the trick since the supposed destinations too closely resembled the place one thought to be leaving. For a long time, there had only existed a rather standardized local color everywhere. While the life-size reconstructions, peopled with "natives" dressed in the appropriate national outfit who could speak fluently in the language of the country, offered the tourist the anticipated exotic environment.

These reconstructions occupied, on the outskirts of the major cities of the globe, immense artificial underground cavities illuminated by a sunlight perfectly synthesized, and air-conditioned in keeping with the latitude selected.

But with Hilton hotels and offices of the American Express.

New York-Beneath-Tokyo, let it be said in passing, was the most quaint of all as it was devoid of Japanese enclaves.

Tallin-Beneath-Hoboken was reported not to be bad at all.

The police officer who had calmed down Tuni had told her about his visit to Niagara Falls beneath the Kensico Reservoir in White Plains, N.J.

A Paris stretched out under Amityville and Babylon, Long Island. Tuni had always dreamed of Paris and loved to spend hours in her basement to be closer to it.

Jerusalem, where Paul had celebrated his 33rd birthday, was located beneath Williamsburg, Brooklyn, where synagogues were allotted a quota of direct elevator tickets on Yom Kippur and Rosh Hashanah, and churches at Christmas and Easter.

There were also imposing surface re-landscaping. For example, the Rocky Mountains had been completely remodeled to resemble the Himalayas, with more than life-like monasteries and yaks.

For its part, the Himalayas had been remodeled to resemble the Rockies with its ghost towns and Aspen.

Which satisfied practically everyone since almost no inhabitant of Colorado any longer had a desire to visit the Rockies, and vice-versa.

And for those who could not travel, entire monuments were exchanged like paintings and other works of art used to be. The real Eiffel Tower was located these days on the spot normally occupied by the Empire State Building.

And vice-versa.

To say nothing about snobbism. Everywhere, public places were renamed in order to make them sound more exotic. In New York, Macy's was now called *La Samaritaine* and, in Paris, *La Samaritaine* was called Bloomies.

On the other hand, they had been trying in vain to convince people that the Place Charles-de-Gaulle in Paris should be called Place Dan Quayle, in honor of a political martyr from the end of the last century. Nothing doing. Parisians had already had enough trouble getting used to Ceedeegee.

A compromise was being envisaged, however. They would settle for Place Charles de Gaulle-Dan Quayle, or *Ceedeegeedeekew,* or even shorter, *Ceedeekew.*

But, thought Tuni while returning by hoverbus to Manhattan (The real one), how would things be were everyboy to accept the well founded state of things just as I do?

Hum?..

Well, she would have to throw a fit on Monday because of that omission, so as not to ruin the pleasure of others. And she smiled to herself. Again, people would benefit from the fact that Tuni was so accommodating.

(New York, May/June 1990)

THE CEEVEE

March 2062 | Currently: *I have kept a highly professional attitude and devoted this period to a systematic search for a new position commensurate with my qualifications. Daily production of a hundred handwritten cover-letters to which I attached the present resume.*

(Addendum to the Curriculum Vitae of Nicolas Stéphane Caducet-Glandu, which is to reappear with the mythical Eurameris.)

At the End of the Beginning, God looked down at what he had accomplished, and He found that it was not as good as He had expected. Instead of taking a rest, He threw a fit and vigorously smote the Skies and the Earth. Thereafter, He blew a huge cloud of pesticide upon the Earth, which rid it of all the pests. And the light went off.

(Fraguian Genesis, Book 1, Verse 1)

In their year 2062, the popularization of scientific education (due mainly to the century-old efforts of Captain Kirk and Mr. Spock, the influence of anti-alarmist corporate surveys, and the possibility for everyone to calculate instantaneously any probability on their personal computer) allowed humans to remain professionally skeptical when warned by their astronomers that the earth would soon collide with Halley's comet. Not to mention their own life experience. In effect, almost none of them had ever won a daily double at the tracks, or the lotto, and it was hard for them to imagine that the earth, insignificant as it was in the midst of space-time fabric, could find itself exactly at the same place and at the same time as the recurring comet. One would think that if they had ever had to deal with any of those wandering comets which appear suddenly from the improbable and the un-programmable, they would have more appropriately hailed their demise. Be that as it may, they did not relive the same panicky moments they had gone through in 1910 under the threat of a mere slap of the comet's tail and neither did they honor it with their distinguished curiosity, as they did in 1986. After the collision, some provisional survivors still relentlessly computed the parameters, trying to mathematically reject the possibility of the cataclysm even after it occurred, until they ran out of batteries.

(Excerpt from the article 10^{54} of the last fascicle of the *Encyclopedia Galactica*, now available on quantum chips. A 50% discount will be offered to any new subscriber whose request reaches our offices of 4cT 76-893 BEFORE THE PRESENT OFFER WAS IMAGINED BY OUR

ADVERTISING DEPARTMENT. The distortion mark due to the reversal of the causality principle will solely attest.)

***

The wind rose before the orange-hued dawn, which would follow the long frigid night, which itself had followed the long damp evening.

Now, the wind scrapes over petrified railroad ties, sweeping dust and sand from tracks to vacant, formless spaces, and from those chaotic spaces to railroad tracks; or from nowhere to somewhere.

The wind seems to be seeking something.

The tracks are slowly regressing toward their primeval telluric state. They stagger from tie to tie, tormented by the crosswinds, which raise waves of dunes over a land they had forgotten, a land they seek to rediscover under the tracks.

The wind has so moved the sands in its feverish probing that it pushes waves of dunes up to the desiccated arteries of the mummy-city. It transmigrates dust and sand from eroded walls to canyons already clogged with dust and sand.

And there are eyes which determine, in the infrared spectrum, the contours of the bottom of the abyss of sand and dust that the windstream is stirring up. These are *her* eyes, she who is pressing forward on the bottom. She is coming back to town, struggling against the irksome wind.

She can see that the desert has invested the city, the city which had invested in the retreat of the desert. In the city, there had been prisons, parks, heated pools, air-conditioned lobbies, service stations, and headlights chasing the winds on the cloverleafs.

Now the desert borne by the wind invades corporate headquarters through yawning windows which had striven to impose quality control and performance reviews on the wind. But the wind has ceased to fit the profile determined by Westinghouse, and lets its gusts go free. In the face of their poise, *What's-his-Face* Avenue seems to hide in an effort to escape the onslaught, and quietly slips away.

On What's-his-Face Avenue, there had been austere entrance halls where only sand troughs and ancient artifacts shrouded in dust now remain; and the shrouds once collapsed on corpses now scattered to the four winds.

Under What's-his-Face Avenue, or Umpteenth Avenue perhaps, shadows have broken up into impalpability. Here, in following the tracks, they sap Mummy-City. There, shadows are calm, motionless nebulosities. Soon, perhaps, they will generate stars, lumps of light and life, by restructuring the dust, when the time has come.

It seems to *her* that the time has come.

She lets herself be rocked and tossed along by the crest of the trackwaves to the shores of Loot Island. This is where she was headed, and *what* she has come for.

She can see the tracks. She must not lose sight of them. She must not lose the residue of the visual impressions that the tracks have generated in her reptilian cortex. Otherwise, the residue would swiftly vanish within the chaos of the nebulous shadows.

She only has to follow the tracks. The tracks are the link. The tracks are the only framework of space. Without them, this place would not exist.

Was it her own organic rhythms that the ties bounced all the way back to the desiccated entrails of Mummy-City?

She senses not. She knows hers. She has never heard any organic rhythms but hers, the rumbling of her own entrails, since the heart of that long night that had borne her.

And these organic rhythms do not beat in harmony with hers.
These organic rhythms make her think of *us*. They make her envisage someone else, somewhere, in Mummy-City.

How can she not be alone?

She senses that the tracks are the long tendrils of the Other Improbable that generates other stranded resonance from a fossil world, just like she.

The echo gives rise in her to a feeling of warm stickiness and violent craving for absorption.

The darkness becomes moist and the dry air misty.

Bite, tear, gulp. An idea of united, but elastic fields. An antidote to final disintegration. She will be plump again, apoplectic, a full booty bag again, like in those mythical times when, riding the tracks rectitude, there were rumbling trains.

She can almost hear, at the end of the tunnel, the rumbling of the forgotten train on the tracks which appear suddenly less wavy and vague. It is the atavistic signal of run-for-your-dear-life. And she runs for it.

But no train enters the station. The last métro passed aeons ago, and dust has erased its trail. Only an echo to the soundtrack of an atavistic dream.

Or was it the howling of the wind above the quiet darkness?

Now, she recognizes the odor carried by the wafting dust. Hot, acrid, sticky, it could make the nebula lumpy. In any case, it did give birth to stars, those she saw while straining to leap over the tracks.

It is here, right above.

It is in a cavern, a cavern hanging on a wall, a wall in a canyon of Mummy-City.

A loathsome howl pierces her. A call to war. A call to loot.

The alien vital rhythms have tuned in with hers through the darkness quanta of the chaotic dustbin. Even her breath catches up with the other's breathing rhythms and winds up laboring at the same cadence, like two metronomes always end up keeping the same beat.

There is the semblance of an office above a sandbox of sorts.

Within the semblance of an office, there lingers a memory of postponed staff meetings, of missed general consensus, and of venetian holoblinds that blinked onto the dazzling light, the light from before the sky crumbled, when it still glowed with hues varying in accordance with the weather patterns and the movement of the clouds, the clouds which knew how to keep the dust away from *toilfields*.

There are no more venetian holoblinds to become torn in the blasts of dust and sand. The semblance of an office would altogether have ceased to exist if *he* had forgotten it. Still, only *his* temporality kept the gagged presence of things from leaving the stage of his consensus, from returning to the swirling chaos. The videoctures by Wormhole have fallen and drowned in the ubiquitous dusty foam. The dismissed elements of office technology have weighed anchor and drifted down toward earth.

He knows that when he dies, nothing will have been. Yet, how often had he dreamed of such a starless and moonless night, when he was still able to toil?

In order to better fantasize, *he* contemplates what is loftily displayed on what used to be his director desk, that which still makes him be, that which endures because he still is.

That is enthroned on dust but free from it.

That is diaphanous and glowing in the midst of the dark nebula. He has consistently been dusting it.

He has held his breath since he heard her come in.

She sees him in his mineral mimetism.

He does not look up at her. He is too busy.

She sneezes.

He says, "God bless you."

"Thank you," she replies.

He asks, "What ill wind brings you here?"

"You've got to be kidding," she replies.

He asks, "Besides that?"

"Well," she proceeds, "Nothing much. I returned to our city with its cloverleaf pounding on their flaccid hinges and, as I heard you foraging, I just thought, well... that I might drop by. Am I disturbing you?"

"No. I'm not in a meeting right now. Take a seat."

"What were you doing when I entered, holding onto the pole of your ego?" she asks without preamble.

"As you can see, I was... jerking off. What did you expect since I was robbed of the ability to toil?"

"I see. To hell with attitudes and appearances, since the contracts and the contacts are in tectonic repose. But to tell the truth, I also came back to see if I could loot what remains of your toil."

"Loot? What can be left to loot behind the open-plan shrines, thus open to a thousand winds? What's left to loot where filing cabinets and bullet-proof counters are no longer even lying around or sticking out from under the dust? Come on, look. All that you'll find here are musty breeze-blocks and complete biodegradation. All putrefaction has, long ago, left refrigerated counters, warehouses, morgues, McDonald's, and oval offices. Where would you seek your loot? There are no longer any vroooms, bangs, buzzes or wheezes, carried by the wind. Only those generated in the wind."

"Granted. But there are your tissues, your fluids, your... flesh. Look at what is even written on it: *Fruit of the Loom*, or *Fruit of the Toil*, am I right?"

"Measly Fruit of the Loot, should you say. But there it is: for years, I've only been eating canned stuff left in the corporate cafeteria. Especially sauerkraut. It tastes better cold than anything. By the way, there's still some pork and beans left. Do you want it?"

"I will see. But first, I want the service memos, the personnel files, the letters of recommendation on buff or ivory laid velum paper. Some must still be lying around. By the way, what's this spotless and immaculate delicacy up here, on the Mesa Grande? I mean, this plastic-wrapped folder?"

"No! You won't have *that*! Not *that*, wretch! Hands off my curriculum vitae! It contains the code of my parameters, the code of my socio-professional present, my song of songs, my epic, the Tables of My Law. It's the Ark of the Covenant that those who will come after us might still uncover! Go ahead, feast on my flesh if you like, but don't quench your thirst from the one bottle that could be washed ashore on the beach of a new cycle. Once again, and I don't mean to offend you, do you want the cans of pet food?"

"I decided that my hunger is especially for knowledge."

"Come on. Forget this bookish hunger. You need a liprary, not a library."

"All the same, I want to know your mind, first. I want you to introduce me to the C.V. Let me come to it."

"Huh... Hum. Okay, but come not to the C.V. First, come to the W.C. There, your first introduction will take place. Such is the initiation path. Step by step. Come on, step up and you'll get the rancid but still somewhat moist fluid that was going to squirt from my entrails when you came in, and stupidly be blotted up by the mythical sands. Be my mate before being my tormentor. Be my mantis."

"Ohhhh! Just like that? And in *that* place? This is sexual harassment! And this is against nature!"

"During that long night of sleep, Mother Nature came up with darwinisms of which even Darwin went unawares. Come over here and prostrate thee."

"Okay, but afterwards, I mean, once you introduce me in the W.C., can I take a look at the C.V.?"

"You can look, but first you will have to promise me that you will watch over it until toil reigns again upon the earth. This is the price to pay for a new time of plentiful loot. Now, give me your puss... er... I mean your ratsy.

"Oooh! Whaddah perk!"

***

On planet Earth (filed S.5F33/222s-3), the homo rodens succeeded to the homo sapiens as the dominant species as early as the dawn of the oligocene(1) period of the mellozoic(2) era, according to the local geological chart. The population of homo-rodens (or "frags" in their own terminology) rapidly grew after its simultaneous appearance, sometime between the end of the cenozoic era and the beginning of the mellozoic era, in various points of a geographical zone comprising the ancient Euramerican continental plate.

The frags (small rodent humanoids endowed with a particularly robust constitution and an aggressive libido) are probably the result of a spontaneous cross-breeding between rare surviving specimens of homo sapiens and the ratus muridae (or "common rat"), a particularly hardy species that successfully resisted the deterioration of the ecosystem due (see article 10^{54}) to the collision between planet Earth and a periodic comet. (See also article 104^{72}, entitled **"Inter-Periodic Zigotic and Morpho-Genetic Failures on the Rocky Planets of the Second Generation,"** *which treats in detail the first emergency mutations triggered by the biomorphic emanations from a given ecosystem under irreversible conditions of deterioration of the system.)*

The frags possess a curious form of intelligence which, among other particularities, pushes them toward an excessive industriousness in order to produce material goods that they subsequently consume, only to recycle them according to some still obscure rituals, after having "looted" (or stolen) them from each other during minutely enacted wars. A paradigmatic origin of the frags' behavior can be found in the respective behaviors of the two alleged parent species. "The frag is an operative angel who remembers the headquarters," as a Fraguian philosopher once put it. (In Fraguian mythology, the "Headquarters" means the dwellings of the gods -- or of God -- as distinguished from man, a mythical creature who, they rightly guessed, had dominated the Earth before the great Deluge of Darkness, and that they hold responsible for the Divine Anger.) From time immemorial, the frags have most particularly revered an object -- or more exactly a food product -- which represents, in their culture, what bread and rice represented in the early human civilizations. They call it the CEEVEE or SHEEVEE. The origin of the word *can be found in the etymology of certain ancient human tongues (old French "sève" and old English "Sap," formed from the Latin "Sapere," meaning "to taste" or "to know.") In fact, these two meanings of the word are intimately intertwined in the Fraguian terminology. The "Ceevee" is, at once, a symbol of "Acquaintance to the other" and foodstuff. To illustrate this, it suffices to evoke a particular Fraguian rite: as a preamble to all interrelation between two or more individuals, each frag is supposed to require from the other, then produce in turn, its ceevee. The ceevee takes the shape of a single or double page of paper (according to the social status) which comes in white, ivory, buff, or any subtle light tints (again according to the social status). Then, each frag must consume **on the spot** the ceevee (or ceevees) offered to him or her in order to bio-recycle it through his or her natural digestive system. The product of this particular recycling process is then called the "VEECEE" or "WEECEE" (seemingly a mere inversion of syllables, a semantic symbol of "The Eternal Rerun," of the restitution to God of the "Fruit of the Loot," obviously consequential to their monopolizing the "Fruit of the Toil." In order to better understand this ritual, we should not forget that most of the Fraguian religions are based on a materialistic dichotomy between Toil and loot -- as opposed to human religions (see article 101[78] and [79]) which were based on a spiritualistic dichotomy between Good and Evil. Finally, still according to the Fraguian myths, the "First Ceevee," which dated back from the time "...when the men found that the daughters of the frags were beautiful," and which bore the seal of the creator himself, had been lost by the first female of the Fraguian species (who henceforth was doomed to give birth in excruciating pain) after it had been entrusted to her by the last repenting human guardian. All that is very complicated at the least, and one can only conjecture on the real nature of the Ceevee and if the Ceevee is really buried, as the legend goes, (not unlike the Covenant and the Grail of the human legends) in some mythical tower in the far reaches of a desert now flooded by the Euramerican Ocean now covering almost entirely the northern hemisphere of the planet.*

*The frags have built subterranean cities where they seem to do even better than man at indulging in toil while shielded from the light of the sun, the moon and the stars. They will probably never be concerned with their admission to the Galactic Federation. But the regenerated biosphere of the planet offers an idyllic vacation site to all species based on carbon chemistry. Let us note in passing that genetic manipulations between specimens of frags and specimens of Bjorks from Eridani 32 (themselves the result of very ancient cross-breedings between specimens of humans and specimens of Kroi from Vega 7) have given satisfactory results in which it has always been the perspective of the Federation to-- (To read further, just press RETURN when you possess the **Encyclopedia Galactica**.)*

(Sample-excerpt from the article 107[89] of the ENCYCLOPEDIA GALACTICA now available, etc., ...)

***

YOU WON!

YES, YOU WON, ***ZETKOR 53-105 XVZ GLOCK*** FROM ALTAIR 13! YOU won a vacation in the PLEIADES that we *might* decide to offer -- not to you, ZETKOR, but to one of your defunct parents and to one of its favorite clones! Yes, hurry up if you want your passport to bear henceforth the exciting note: "BORN IN THE PLEIADES."

PLEASE NOTE: in order to participate in our drawing and win YOUR GRAND PRIZE, you have to accept an exciting and mind-boggling aeonic subscription to the ENCYCLOPEDIA GALACTICA where you can learn about such marvels as the ones you just read about in this excerpt. To do so, may we advise you to use the same causality reversal principle already mentioned? Then, in addition to your 50% discount, you will be assigned a WINNING NUMBER. Unfortunately, our services are greatly disappointed not to have received your subscription acceptance form BEFORE our first offer was sent out to you. Perhaps you did send it, ZETKOR, but your signal got stuck in some uncharted spacetime warp...

NO, ZETKOR 53-105 XVZ GLOC FROM ALTAIR 13! DON'T LET IT HAPPEN AGAIN! DON'T LET ANYTHING GET IN YOUR WAY TO YOUR BEING... etc., ...

(1) <u>Oligocene</u>: *from the ancient Greek "oligo" meaning = rare, scanty.*
(2) <u>Mellozoic</u>: *from the ancient Greek "mellos" meaning = the Wannabe, the future.*

(New York, Sept/Oct 1987)

CONFIRMATION

ACT 1

(With the father, the son, the walkman, and the Omniscient)

The Omniscient:
The father and the son are driving on a deserted road, in the night. It is Christmas night. They are going to Bethlehem, Connecticut, for a family celebration. The father is driving and the son is sulking because the father did not want to let him drive. The son is wearing the walkman.

The walkman:
(just finishing "O Silent Night"):
Here is our 9 o'clock news break. The final toll from flight 103 disaster reached 270...

The son:
....

The father:
....

The walkman:
According to the latest estimate, the death toll from the earthquake in Armenia will reach 30,000...

The father:
....

The son:
....

The walkman:
New incidents on the Gaza Strip have made 36 casualties...

The father:

....

The son:

....

The Omniscient:
Since nobody seems to have anything to say right this minute, I am going to jump at the occasion to talk about anything I want. Why not, for instance, about the indifference of God? Why does God let such terrible things happen around Christmas time? Now, listen: God, or the Sovereign Principle, or the Great Architect, or the Alpha and the Omega, or the Ultimate Concern, God *knows* but is content with knowing. God is not there to think or reason. God is a moron. Adam, on the contrary, became smart the day he would not know anymore without thinking. Before that happened, he just knew, but without being able to enjoy his knowing, just like God. So, since God cannot think, God does not have the tiniest inkling about what is good or bad. In order to find something good, or fair, it is necessary to begin by structuring one's thoughts, rationalizing one's own idea of good and evil with respect to one's immediate survival needs and with what one experiences as painful or soothing. To Mohammar Kadhafi or the Ayatollah, 270 dead Anglos is damned soothing. To the earth's crust, an earthquake is an aerobic workout; it releases tensions. It is soothing just as is, for the above, the ignition to a few pounds of TNT. Right? But as God does not give a damn about his survival since nothing threatens him, he could not care less about what is going on.

The walkman:
(*singing*):
I wish you a merry Christmas, I wish you a merry Christ...

The son:

....

The father:

....

The Omniscient:
I could go on and on about the indifference of God, but I am not supposed do *not* know yet if that will bear any relevance to the action that is going to take place. The author should have cued me in a little later because nothing seems to be happening for the time being. Although, if it is going to be what I can see coming... If you do not mind, I can let the walkman speak for a while.

The walkman:
(singing in French):
Petit Papa Noël, quand tu descendras du ciel...

The Omniscient:
Yeah... Santa Claus is coming down... Something is really descending from the sky. It is beautiful, its colors are indescribable, it is utterly silent, it is erratic. Better say it right now; it is neither another Pan Am airliner, nor another piece of a space shuttle. It is not a weather balloon, not a helicopter, not an aurora borealis, not planet Venus, not some swamp fart either. It is neither a ball of lightning, nor a Soviet secret weapon, nor a hallucination of mine. Stop searching. It is a UFO. Between you and me, the author could have found something better for a plot. A deserted road at night, and a UFO... which is probably going to hover awhile above the car and shut off the electric circuitry... you will see what I am saying.

The son:
Goddamnit! The walkman just went off.

The father:
Give me a break with your walkman. Right this minute, I'm more worried about the car. The ignition just died.

The Omniscient:
See what I told you?

The father:
Look! A UFO!

The son:
So what? Are we going to stand in ecstasy in front of a stupid UFO when we've seen God? (See DEUS EX LATRINA) And what the hell is it doing here anyway? Can you tell me? There's nothing worth seeing around here. It's boring, it's all closed up, it's singing and spilling out Christmas baloney. Wouldn't it be better if they'd plucked the passengers of flight 103 from the sky, instead? Or warned the Armenians through pirate broadcasts on the Soviet TV? But no! They just broke my walkman and I can't listen to what's going on in the world anymore. And *I* feel concerned. *I* care.

The father:
Oh, you, with your humanitarian ideas, you're becoming utterly incapable of any wonderment. Come on, think of what open contact with an alien civilization could mean for mankind.

The son:

Are you kidding? What news do they bring us? Did you read all those contact stories? It never goes beyond the Sunday School level. Let them abduct Abu Nidal, or Dan Quayle, and we'll see. By the way, while they're around, why don't they cure your cancer, for instance? (See BEING AND NOTHINGNESS)

The Omniscient:

This is exactly what I was saying about God. Those aliens are almost as stupid as He is. They do not think. They always knew everything without thinking. They are a very old species, stuck at the prototemporal stage. They reproduce themselves by cloning, and so, they never knew the temptations of sex and they never sought knowledge like Adam. They have innate knowledge without understanding a thing. Whatever they can understand about the miseries and the glories of the worlds they encounter is what they can accidentally pick up from the mental waves of more complex species which are busy asking too many questions to be able to find the answers. This is why they cannot go much beyond the Sunday School level with the humans. And, mostly because of their atavistic fear of the overwhelming, when they are on the earth, they are more attracted by those regions where only a low level of reflection is needed to survive. Bethlehem, Connecticut, sounds safer to them than New York City. Needless to say, they should not be expected to land in Central Park or in Times Square very soon. The cultural shock would be fatal to them.

The father:

Okay. The car is running again. They beat it. It's too bad; I'd have liked to get better acquainted with them. This encounter case won't be a much substantiated one.

The son:

Good for us. Now, let me listen to the walkman.

The walkman:
(Just finishing "I'm Dreaming of a White Christmas"):
This is our one o'clock newsbreak, on this Christmas day. The terrorist attack against flight 103...

The son:

Hey Dad, do you remember this pebble I played with on the pond shore this afternoon? It's very strange, I... Hey, have they lost their mind or what, on the radio? It's not one o'clock yet!

The father:

That's what the dashboard clock seems to say: look. One o'clock. But what were you saying about... you were talking about a stone... I have the feeling I saw a huge boulder on the road and that I just stopped because of that. Now I remember.

***

ACT 2

(With the author and the Omniscient.
Without the father, the son and the walkman,
who arrived at the party just in time to help
push away the tables for the dance)

The Omniscient:

Hey, you, author!

The author:

What's going on?

The Omniscient:

Is that all you could find this time? Really? The old plot of the car being stalled on a deserted road by a UFO which immediately takes off has not evolved very much since the first books by Jacques Vallee, you know.

The author:

You didn't see anything? Lots of things have happened during these four hours. It's even twice as much "missing time" as usually reported. And you really didn't see anything?

The Omniscient:

Well... no. I guess I was just not paying attention.

The author:

It's unbelievable. Come along with me. I'll hypnotize you.

***

ACT 3

(With the author and the Omniscient.
Still without the father, the son, and the walkman)

The Omniscient:
The author has placed me in a hypnotic trance, and made me regress back
to the moment when the UFO descended from the sky and started to hover
above the father and son's car.

The author:
Good. Are you ready? Now, you are going to tell us the whole story. The
father and the son are in the car, stalled on the roadside. What's happening
next? Something did happen during these four hours of alien-induced
amnesia. Don't be afraid of anything. You are protected by your
Omniscience. Nothing can harm you... Nothing can harm you...

The Omniscient:
Here they are, the aliens. Their magnetic disturbances have short circuited
the ignition system of the car, as usual, but without their doing it on
purpose, as always. The father and the son get out of the car to see the
UFO, and they grope through the bushes to meet these frail looking little
guys with their white-grey rubbery skin, their enormous heads, and their
slanted bulbous eyes that never laugh. The aliens lead them into the UFO
on a beam of light. Once there, the father and the son are stripped of their
clothes and tugged, floating in zero gravity, into a circular room where a
grey dazzling light is oozing from the walls, and then laid on a bare
auscultation table. Then the small beings perform a number of ludicrous
medical exams on them with scary, rudimentary tools. Through telepathy,
they are assured that the aliens won't hurt them if they remain quiet and
passive. The father and the son try to chat a little with the aliens to get
better acquainted, but the little doctors, who don't seem to show any interest
in what they are doing, answer only with sanctimoniously soothing
televangelistic lecturing.

The author:
Stop! It's a massacre. Some drama, please! I want dialogue! And
characterization, goddamnit! Did the father and the son both react the same
way? Were all the little aliens exactly alike? Does it seem to you that there
was a boss or someone in charge of the project among them? Why these
medical probings? What is their long range goal? How do they proceed?
What are their schemes, their ideology? Do they know how to cure cancer
and AIDS? What do they have to say about the greenhouse effect, the
homeless, family planning in Africa? Are they intending to let humankind

join the board of editors of the *Encyclopedia Galactica*? You have to touch the reader in his deepest concerns, you know that.

The Omniscient:

This is exactly what I was saying about God. Those aliens are just like Him. They do not know what they are doing and why they are doing it. Once again, they seemed to be amazed by the human body machine, just as if it were the first time they saw one. Exactly like a baby who goes "ah-goo-goo" each time he sees a car. So... when they were finished with them, they led the father and the son back out of the UFO. Then... well... they just left. Maybe they had already forgotten, at that time, that they had been there an instant before, just the way the son had forgotten the pebble he had played with that same afternoon, around the pond, in Central Park. And if they left this screen memory of stony stuff in the father's and son's minds, it's because the stone is *them*, as it were. The stone knows that the skull of the falling man is imminently going to crash onto it, but it won't do a thing to clear the way, just as it hasn't done a damn thing to find itself *in* the way. The stone is not intrinsically mean, but it just does not give anything a thought.

The author:

In this case, you must insist on the moods of the two human characters at the moment of the encounter. It's also time to explain to the reader where they're from, who they are, what they're doing for a living, and what their preoccupation is at the time of the events. For instance, you could indicate that the absence of the mother has, ever since his early childhood, deprived the son of a feminine presence, which has, in compensation, exacerbated his altruistic feeling toward mankind on the whole, while, at the same time, he unconsciously opposes his father's non-committed chauvinism. Point out, too, that he never separates from the walkman because he considers the device's volubility like an absent young brother's babble, or the jabber of the missing parent who was Italian. Now, come on. You can do something with a story like that. See Bud Hopkins and Whitley Strieber? Delve into their anguish at facing the unknown, their primeval fear. Also, don't forget to describe the faces, the attitudes, the postures, the gestures, the voices.

The Omniscient:

If I got you right, you want me to play the role of a mere narrator?

The author:

Of the *omniscient narrator*. What's wrong with that? Go ahead. From the very beginning.

The Omniscient:

Okay... well.... "Now, are we going or not?" the son grumbled impatiently before they left that night, as the father checked for the umpteenth time whether or not he had properly locked the safety lock on the door of their two bedroom, sixth floor, no doorman apartment on the Upper West Side of Manhattan. After they both walked in silence to the garage across the street where the father's '79 beige Sierra Ford convertible was parked at a daily *early bird* rate, the father, a free-lance writer (it always facilitates the author's task from the implied narrator perspective), fortyish, fit-looking thanks to a regularly renewed year membership with Jack Lalanne, with a shaded tone in his eyes due to his central European forebears, grabbed the wheel of the only piece of property he was able to bring along with him after his painful divorce. (I will tell the whole story in due course.) They drove out of the city (I will later add the detailed itinerary here, after I have studied the map), and, after a busy stretch of the Long Island Expressway (I think I'm having the road wrong here but I promise the author will check this out when he gets the galleys), they exited at... (same thing). The Christmas night was decidedly pitching black and damned cold, they probably both realized, driving as they were along a deserted country road of a particularly wooded region of the East Coast, toward the quiet little town of Bethlehem, Connecticut, near Long Meadow Lake. "It's a good thing I thought of buying some gas before we left," said the father with a satisfied tone in his voice, for the sake of striking up a conversation with his sulking son, a straight haired adolescent with fairly high cheekbones that he undoubtedly owed to his Iroquois forebears. (From his grandmother's side, of course, since both parents have already been ethnically defined.) The young man didn't answer. He was resenting his father for having forbidden him to drive on Christmas night. Deeply upset by the separation of his parents at a period of life when....

(The next day, and drawing closer to the epilogue:)

... Therefore, the father was much more excited than his son after the baffling encounter, since, in his youth, the first UFOs sighting reports in the APRO bulletins had worn as much importance as the AIDS prevention brochures in his son's time. He fumbled feverishly and sneakily into his pack of Marlboro Lights 100's, took out a butt, lit it after having groped about for the lighter and, under the reproachful look of his son who would not miss an occasion to bawl him out for his tobacco addiction, started to puff voluptuously and lengthily. The young man, who, after his banal remark about a pebble in Central Park, had placed the walkman back on his head and was actually about to blame his father, suddenly froze and blurted: "Hey, have they lost their mind or what on the radio? It's not one o'clock yet!"

The author:

OK, that's enough. See? Now the reader can identify himself.

The Omniscient:

Possible. But it does not make the story more compelling. You must admit that some *real* cases are more puzzling.

The author:

I know, but I always wanted to write something about that. Now, the hell with it. It's time to conclude. The walkman can do it.

***

ACT 4

(With the walkman, with the father, with the son,
without the Omniscient, but with the author)

The walkman:

Jingle bells, jingle bells, jingle all the way..."

The son:

Oh my God, oh my God! What a story! I can't believe it! Has it really just happened?

The father:

I'm winded. Let me regain my breath... Pfff... As a matter of fact, truth is stranger than fiction. I wouldn't have believed such a thing could ever happen to *us*. I have to confess, it's far more extraordinary than our encounter with the UFO yesterday night!

The son:

It's... simply overwhelming. I can't believe it. It's wonderful, it's...

The father:

This time, we'll make the 8 o'clock news for at least three days.

The son:

And you'll write a book on our experience, won't you? *A True Story.* I can imagine the front cover, fifty of them, on display in the windows at Barnes & Noble!

***

ACT 5

(With the author, the Omniscient, and the walkman,
but without the father and the son, who are too busy
with their dreams of glory come true)

The author:

Hey, Omniscient! What is all this fuss about? What happened to them? Wait a minute. I'm the one who writes the books. Won't he need a ghost, at least?

The Omniscient:

What? What? I don't know... I was just not paying attention. I thought the story was over. You told me to let the walkman conclude. I was back in the wings.

The author:

That's you, all right. The only thing left to do is ask the walkman. See if the news is already on the air.

The walkman:

A-a-ma-a-zi-ing gra-a-ce, how sweet the sound...

The author:

Not yet. Stay tuned. And store it for the next script.

(New York, January 1989)

ZOD

- Let's call me Zod.
- So, Zod. What am I?
- I am total desolation, the desolation that Zod has been searching, though. And this intimate and painful emptiness makes Zod puke, while the anguishing plenitude fills up all my parameters, geological, geodesic, thermodynamic, astrophysical, bionic, post-atmospheric and radiant: Which perfectly suits the global unit of my entirety, in order to rehabilitate and re-organize the neg-entropic chaos from its anatemporal stage.
- But I have already been here, Zod. But I am having an experience of missing time, some memory gap. I had forgotten. There were colors and fragrances in this city, and there used to be a sort of square with lampposts around it, and turgescent reproductive organs, and voices which used to modulate "*Plaisir d'Amour*" and "We Shall Overcome." Then there was this biospheric viscosity everywhere, akin to the organic stage of consciousness.
- Let's not forget, Zod: You are the planetary probe as well as the mother ship, waiting in stellar orbit at the outermost boundary of the Oort cloud of an aging planetary system of Any Medium-Mass Yellow Star located in Any Outer Spiral Arm of a galactic disc. Therefore, it might just be a feeling of *déjà vu*, Zod. Nothing more.
- But... Zod was here. Look, there, on my right: there is what might have been some cathedral, even before I called it Gothic. And over here was the *rue de l'Hôtel-Dieu,* right where these honeycombed hives now rise, so high and so massive, even less arousing than the police administration buildings which had once been there. But no parasitic organic factuality oozes any more from these hives.
- But what's the matter with me, Zod? No marker should be named, at the risk of recreating exteriority, localization, and fractalization of Zod. So, let's not split up.
- It is so deserted... Not one living soul.
- So what? Is it not what Zod had accomplished? Only Zod's soul matters, doesn't it?
- It is just this silence, Zod...
- What's wrong with silence, Zod?
- Nothing, but... It is only an almost-nothingness. There comes again something that hurts.

- Hey, how can it hurt, Zod? There must be no opposite or painful anti-principle left; since Zod is all the principles and their reversal.

- I am here and I do know where, as if Zod emerged only *somewhere* within the *Big What,* and, furthermore, knowing on which side of it.

- So, there is no more *Big-What.* Zod lost it. There are only the *I-See* and the *I-Know* again. Zod lost Zod.

- No. Let me see. Let me turn toward the cathedral. Too bad, but again, Zod needs to turn around to look over Zod's shoulder... this here looks new, even newer than the honeycomb building. Zod means... its facade which emits a harsh and solid light, a haloless light, the whole facade... It is... I mean... this light does not have to struggle, photon by photon, against darkness. It could as well be the night of the night, see what I mean? Zod had never seen this.

- Hold on. I'm getting confused, Zod. It seems that I am rediscovering some basic aspects of the *I-see* and *I-Know.* And again, I wonder, though. It is not only some phosphorescent covering grafted upon the night? It is the anti-night?

- There we are and that is it!

- It is coming from the ground, too: a soft texture made of the light itself, something equidistant between the quasi-ultimate density of the iron core of the neutron stars and the quasi-ultimate volatility of the intergalactic matter.

- These are concepts pertaining to the proto-history of the Global Species, Zod. Nothing new.

- Shut off Zod and listen. To the left, on the other side of what was the river Seine (Did I say *Seine*? Of course, I did), there are other buildings erected at various epochs in the history of one intelligent organic species of this ex-world. Look. Over there, on a hill, more edifices are revealed by this anti-night, in the absence of the big red sun which must, at this moment, be pouring its blistering rays onto the opposite hemisphere of this planet, a sun that I had erased from my active memory.

- Too late. Just knowing that this sun *is* was enough to make it shine, Zod.

- So what? Let me guess what this anti-night is. It served, for a time, as a shield against parasitic radiations evolved from intermediary domains, or stages. And I was no longer there.

- Zod knows very well what is what and should not have to guess.

- The hill was called the Montagne Sainte-Geneviève and the city was Paris. The other edifices were the Panthéon, the Saint Severin's and Saint Julien-le-Pauvre's churches, etc. *I contain these memories more than others do.* And they call me Colin, not Zod.

- Not any more Colin than Samir, or Zatkar, or Hallotah, or Nicolas-Stéphane Caducet-Glandu, or... Hey, Zod? Why?

- I want to go and see. As if everything was not already seen by Zod, as if there were things that Zod had not known yet. And *I* will go, for Zod's sake!

- So let me go, infinitely heavy, and ramble along this supple and smooth terrain where I will be only active transfer, the only regenerator of space, like an insect glued to the proto-temporal rock, the only manifestation of conscious temporality. And I will realize that I have to walk in order to move forward and that the mere task of walking mobilizes all my attention, my attention which let itself be invaded by all the minute details of the complicated procedure. I will rediscover the delight of having to think of a necessity, that of limbs, to achieve the task. The particles of this soil covering are no longer only the result of their observation by Zod, *and only Zod,* because *I* do not envisage them anymore. My mind is busy with other things, with minute causal details, so to speak, busy with fighting the grip of pain, busy with learning how to struggle again. This matter seems to have manifested itself outside of Zod's consensus, so as to allow him to wonder again. Zod indulges in fascination and bafflement at the view of the edifices which are so sharply outlined against the absolutely black, airless sky into which, yet, eyes peer again to observe and try to make Zod out. But Colin ignores and just goes, goes to the other side of the ex-river, and looks. In what was the bed of the river, Colin sees translucent tubes which, as he ignores, were once used as -- as what? -- in already bygone eras of its previous futures.

- Used as what?

- Shhh... Let Colin wonder, Zod. First, forget the answers to the questions. Having to search is soothing to Colin, very soothing, and I, as Colin, want to *not* know much so as to let lots of questions arise, lots and lots of questions and... this one, for instance: *why is my heart so torn apart?* Let me ask the question again: *why her? Why Violaine?*

- Who is Violaine? And where am I?

- In Paris. On the Petit-Pont or the Pont-au-Double. I do not remember which. But this is not the real issue. The issue is, I have lost Violaine. Incidentally, I can see more monuments, scattered along the ex-river, protected by the same luminescent covering, all that is left of Paris when Paris did not belong to the *Galactica Museum.* And there are also a lot of structures that I do not know yet. I forgot what they will be but I do remember Violaine.

- Before you were Zod...

- Yes. Before seeing those three orange globes in the sky, as I can see them now, I mean... as I can see myself, you, Zod. That day, I had sensed their presence, your presence. They were hovering above the river and I plunged into them. That was the day when... there was this grief in my heart. Before that day, we were two, and then, suddenly, I became half. That was the day that *you* chose, Zod.

- To be two... When there is Zod an only Zod...

- I don't know anymore, Zod. But I remember *that*. As Zod, I was hovering above the river, while, as Colin, I was with the Gypsy girl, on the Petit Pont. She was reading the palm of my hand. We looked up together. There were strange omens in the sky.

- Zod cannot be with the other Zod, Zod. The other Zod is Zod and Zod would not be without Zod.

- But Colin could, then.

- Already, Colin was Zod, but Colin did not know.

- But Colin saw an eerie light, not Zod. The light had caused the sunset fires to fade and the shadows double. A shiver ran throughout the earth and the crowd. Yes, there was a crowd, and only one shiver for the whole crowd. And the crowd froze and became numb and they raised their heads toward the sky. Above the roofs, the evening wind also seemed to have stood still, and it had taken on another hue. The Gypsy girl had not stirred. She was still holding my hand in hers to read its lines. She had seen my sorrow and she had called to me as I was walking along the narrow passageway on the bridge, between the rows of houses. That same afternoon, I had stepped into the cathedral dedicated to *Notre-Dame,* as if to pray for the soul of my beloved. Yes, it is now and here. I am not Zod anymore. Through my tears, leaning against a pillar and feeling against my cheek the harmonic tension of the stone, I stare for a long moment at the rose window by Jean de Chelles. Gregorian chants modulate the frequency of the vibrations of the stones. More shadows sweep by, in silence, under the intersecting ribs of the vaults. In the nave, the crowd is kneeling on the stones, communing in prayer. Hung against the pillars, torches are burning and bronze chandeliers are dazzling with a thousand candlelights, very high above *us*, under the ogival ribs veiled by the smoke from the flares. They all knelt down for the adoration prayer, and they stroke up the *Veni Creator.*

- *They* already were tending toward Zodness. It was Zod that they were searching. And Zod came. And Colin saw. And all of them saw.

- Perhaps... But on that day, there was no thought of Zod, only the dear thought of Violaine, Violaine who had passed away at dawn, on that Saint Aude day. A terrible consumption had, for months, left her doleful, and then she died. I entered the cathedral, not to pray to God Almighty and the Very Holy Virgin Mary, but to cry out my anger to them.

- So, already Colin needed Zod in order, through Zod, to react against himself and escape his own grief.

- No. I, Colin, could not take it anymore. I suddenly stood up, walked swiftly past the collateral chapels and up to the great portal, and I exited onto the seven steps and the sun-splashed dirt square, fleeing, almost running. If the Devil existed, the cathedral was his den. Beneath the portico, beggars held out their hands to me. Some looked up at me just as I was determined not to look up at some deity anymore. A gaudy and rather young crowd was strolling about the square. But their faces and their bearing looked already so contrite and weary. I wanted to shout out to them all to raise their backs and their heads, to arm themselves with picks and crowbars and deface and raze the cathedral, and use the stones of its arches and vaults to built themselves palaces of life and merriment instead. But I was still scared of them. Yes, I felt so lonely. They came from narrow streets, from the shadow of the facades leaning over the muddy streets. Two horse-drawn wagons had just collided a few steps away. The two coachmen started a brawl. There were men-at-arms everywhere, women clad in petticoats and pinafores, cackling and chatting like a bunch of worn-out overhatchers, a bunch of pale-faced children ringing-around-a-rosy and singing with their hurtingly shrill voices, a public writer hunched over dirty parchment, lots of foul-smelling shops, and also lots of cats, dogs, chickens, jumping and wading in the mud of the middle gutters of the street. There were so many, so many others than *me*!

- Zod knew. Zod was there. Your house stands on the Rue du Fouarre, at the foot of the *Montagne Sainte-Geneviève,* behind the Eglise Saint-Julien. Today is neither a feast nor a holiday and night will come soon. You walk past the *Hôtel-Dieu,* on your left, to cross the *Petit-Pont* and exit into the scholastic quarters. A group of merry fellows hail you and you respond to their greetings. You recognize François, Barthélémy and a few others. They dragged you into one of the taverns which stud the street; the sign reads *"La sorcière rouge"* -- The Red Witch.

- Yeah... Was it vespers or even later when I got out? The sunset was setting ablaze the small rose of one of the windows of the cathedral, the cathedral which could only be seen in part because of all the roofs and gables. And I wonder again what energy caused it to loom so high above the city? But do not attempt to respond to that question, Zod. Let Colin wonder.

- You proceeded toward the *Petit-Pont.* On the other side of the bridge, a narrow passage at the foot of a turret opens onto the left bank of the river. A bridge? It's actually just another street, even a little broader one, lined with two to four storied houses. A heavy pedestrian traffic, a band of musicians, a doctor wearing a violet robe and red gloves, a fire-eater and... this Gypsy fortune-teller. Why not try? She has Violaine's face. You come closer and open your left hand.

- Just then, the street became illuminated by that strange light. The three burning globes had started a strange dance. They swung around, switching places like balls in the hands of a juggler. Blood-red demonic figures appeared on their circumferences. Were they bad or good omens? Then, the three globes merged again into one, and soon, the one globe popped up and vanished like a bubble. Around us, people hail the event as a miracle, or beseech, or shout, or run into the houses and shops. A headlong flight ensues, while the Gypsy girl keeps my hand in hers.

- And you went along as Zod. And as Zod, you retrieved Violaine, for Violaine is Zod, just as you. And in Zod, there is nobody left to expect or look for since they are all as you.

- But yet, on the left bank, after Colin left within Zod, you could still see him pace the streets full of the hubbub and the havoc caused by the apparition. Here he is, among the behatted bourgeois and the pious wives. In the Rue du Fouarre, an innkeeper comes up to him, handing him a ewer and a goblet. And also this little boy who runs up to him. It is Arnaud. *My* son Arnaud. I am still not Zod. I stayed here as Colin Fawcett, nicknamed *Colin l'Anglois,* or Colin-the-Englishman, a wandering scholar at the University of Paris. I stayed among *them,* Zod!

- Yeah... I know. All that did not prevent me from leaving as Zod. And above the long-dead city, just one city of Zod's a-temporality, the three orange globes merge together and pop out like a bubble, for another quantum jump, while just one dead city, just one dead planet and just one aging stellar system cease to exist -- or has it ever existed?

- Huh... That depends on Zod.

(New York, May 1989)

SCHROEDINGER'S CATNAP

ACT 1

(With the author and the Omniscient)

The Omniscient:
The son is lying on the rug, listening to the walkman. The mother is talking on the phone. The father--

The author:
No, please! This is *not* a soap! We have enough characters like that. We don't need a mother in the cast. The father has been divorced for ages. (See INCURSION) I don't want to get into that, even if they don't find it family-oriented and never chose it for prime time.

The Omniscient:
Well, I was just thinking... Maybe, that would help to get the action moving. We aren't going to wait indefinitely for the walkman to tell us what happened to them at the end of CONFIRMATION, are we? For months, there's been nothing in the media about that. And now, with Wall Street Crash #2, an earthquake in San Francisco, and the postponing of the World Series, not to mention the crumbling of the iron curtain or the Giuliani/Dinkins brawl... Maybe the mother would know.

The author:
Hum... Come to think of it, this gives me an idea. I'm going to need the mother for a pertinent line. Look here: since everybody watched blankly, with no reaction whatsoever, the Act 2 of BEING AND NOTHINGNESS, we're going to tackle that matter another way.

The Omniscient:
Great. So, let me proceed: the father is returning home late from a long and exhausting workday, with his umbrella and his briefcase.

The author:
Come on, why shouldn't you? Take advantage while you're at it. They need descriptions. What about his Brooks Brothers suit?

The Omniscient:

It's just for the staging, the ambiance. Let's justify the property girl and, at the same time, minimize the cost. Also, such a description doesn't present too many risks regarding the identification of the public with the main character.

***

ACT 2

(With the Omniscient, the father, the author and the mother)

The Omniscient:

So, the father has just walked into the apartment and he looks abashed, amazed, puzzled, perturbed, bewildered, flabbergasted, and dumbfounded. He mumbles.

The father:

I'm feeling like shit. A little like Schrödinger's cat.

The Omniscient:

And then he sees the mother on the couch, and on the phone, too. He blurts.

The father:

Hey, Jennifer... What the hell are you doing here?

The author:

No names! So far, we've done without names. Names limit the potentially concerned public. With "Jennifer," we've already and irrevocably lost the attention of minority groups.

The Omniscient:

I beg your pardon. But you could be accused of disregarding social issues. Anyway, let's proceed.

The father:

But (bleep)... What the hell are *you* doing here?

The mother:

What am I doing here? Did you hear that? What's the matter with you tonight? This is *my* home, are you crazy or what? Hey, you! Listen, once and for all, (bleep). I'm fed up with hearing that sh(bleep) from you. If I'm on the phone, it's because *I* need a social life. I'd rather have somebody to talk to since we never have anything to say to each other, don't you get it? You'd better deal with *your* son. Look at him. He's got a pile of homework to do and he's been lying around with his walkman since I got home. Hello? Yes, I'm sorry, Sarh(bleep). (Bleep) just walked in and, as usual, he *has* to dump his crummy mood on me. Always controlling what I'm doing. I'm telling you, it's getting on my nerves. I'm a wreck, and...

The author:

Come on. Go ahead. We have to stick to the assigned format.

The Omniscient:

I agree but the father has a right to a defense and before he can say a word...

***

ACT 3

(With the father, the son, the Omniscient,
and also the mother on the phone, although only
as a background noise)

The Omniscient:

So, still surprised by the presence of the mother in *his* apartment after having not seen her at all since... say, their painful divorce (see CONFIRMATION again), the father bends over the son and pulls the walkman off his head.

The father:

You tell me: what's your mother doing here?

The son:

As you can see, she's on the phone. Hey, you're not going to bawl her out again, are you? I'm fed up with your bickering, and I'm dreaming of a sweet family life. By the way, why don't you get divorced already? It would be better for everybody.

The father:
That's what I mean, goddammit! We've been divorced for five years! And you find it normal to see her here tonight, after all these years of silence?

The son:
What are you talking about? Are you feeling okay?

The father:
Maybe not. Like I just said, if you had been listening to me, I'm feeling like Schrödinger's cat. You know what that means?

The son:
Yes, I read a lot of science-fiction, since DEUS EX LATRINA. But what makes you feel like that?

The Omniscient:
Great! If only the son had answered "no," it would have been a unique occasion for me to give an extensive lecture about Schrödinger's paradox. But I'm not utilized to the best of my abilities, as usual. Anyway, too bad for those who are not familiar with the subject. Let them refer to a bibliography. Among others, *A Brief History of Time* by Stephen Hawking has been on the best seller list of the *New York Times* for more than a year, and if they have not read it yet, there is nothing more that I can do about it.

The father:
I'm feeling like that because here I am, dead, and at the same time, alive. I've just been shot down by some goddam' crackhead in the elevator of the 168th Street subway station and, at this hour, I'm *also* resting, right above that station, in the morgue of the Columbia Presbyterian Hospital.

The son:
You're completely crazy. And what were you doing up there in the first place? I thought you were working on Wall Street?

The father:
It's been two years since I was laid off, because of that ex-crash of the century, in '87. You're really interested in what I'm doing, I can tell. Anyway, do you know that subway station?

The Omniscient:
Wait. The son *has* to answer "no" this time. The reader needs an accurate description, a documentary.

The son:

Actually, no. You always forbid me to hang out above 96th Street.

The father:

And I was right. It's decidedly the most horrendous station in Manhattan, even worse than Penn Station and Times Square where they still have cops on patrol. Oh, don't put on such a face when I mention cops. You know me. I'm no damn fascist, but we do need cops. Anyway, up there... Look, just to give you an idea, they're trying to put new tiling on the walls, some patching, I mean, and the next thing you see, it's carved with hammers and jackknives and covered with fuc(bleep) graffiti the next day. There, the air is viscous, sticky, sickening, with smells of pi(bleep), (bleep), crack -- hey! Why no "bleep" here? Is crack more politically correct shit? Anyway, it's a dumping ground to the Presbyterian Hospital, for those dumped by the Welfare, Medicaid, and the Housing Commission, it's the waiting room to the morgue where they have most surely brought *me*. Each time I get down there, it seems to me that I set foot on Saturn's satellite Titan without proper breathing equipment, because of the percentage of ammonia in the atmosphere, and without the coolness of Titan. Once, believe it or not, I witnessed the Kamikaze death of a big green fly of sorts, in a puddle of vomit. It smashed its proboscis and the whole attachment kit onto a girder after it got dizzy while piloting. Better than "Raid," let me tell you.

The son:

Yuk!.. Stop, will you? And City Hall doesn't do a thing? Not even Donald Trump? As usual, it does move you a bit, I mean, all this misery... Hey, does it move *you*?

The father:

No. It just gets to me. Like it does to all of those who have to breathe that stuff several hours a day. I'm beyond the compassion stage. Sorry about that. And after what happened this evening, no good Samaritan of yours could... But listen, rather than trying to make me feel guilty. Worst of all, it's the elevator. Forty or fifty of us had managed to squeeze in to descend to the West Side IRT local platform. As always, only one elevator out of four was working. I could finally insert myself into it after two failed attempts and there I was, stuck between the operator (please, note that it's the best place because of the fan) and a fat (bleep) or something who stank of garlic and spoiled diapers and who was squealing in Spanish at her three niños. Leaning against my back, there was this filthy young guy who usually exhibits his sarcomic lesions to boost his panhandling business. I was standing on one foot, not quite vertically, with a breathtaking vista of the operator's sweaty boobs. I have to say that I had a choice between that and staring, right at eye level, at a glop of snot left by a former passenger on the metallic door. Anyway, we were on our way down and... guess what?

The son:

Don't tell me. The elevator got stuck!

The father:

Good guess. It *had* to happen. More than twenty minutes. Getting hotter and hotter, with the air getting more and more dank. Look, the humidity would have allowed your exotic fish to survive. Tension, anxiety, stress. The operator, who couldn't do a thing about it, was arguing with the security guys on the intercom; you can picture that? Now, that's the moment when a netherworld prophet of sorts chooses to address me. Why me? I don't know. I attract them like flies. Maybe because of my beautiful prophet's face and my inspiring attitude. In me, they probably sense a polite and civilized ear. Anyway, he had elbowed his way toward me from the rear of the car. He oozed dope. He asked me if I believed in the Second Coming of Christ. I said "hummpf." Then he asked me if I believed in God. I said "hummpf" again. Whereupon he asked me if I believed that there was a god at all. He was getting on my nerves and I told him that the only god I believed in was the Principle that reflects Itself in the universe and thus in me, but that I wouldn't be able to tell him more about that until the equation of Grand Unified Theory had been established. As you can see, I was still trying my best to honor him with a response. Well, he didn't get it, of course, and he kept on pounding on me. At the end, I decided to comply and I asked: "In your opinion, when is the Second Coming of Christ scheduled for?' And he replied: "Oh, yeah. The world is sick, and He'll soon be here to judge us, man!" Whereupon, I said, bored: "What a job! I hope he'll have assistants from a big law firm downtown." Just like that, to see if he could get a joke. Now, guess what again!

The son:

The Lord appeared and got the elevator moving.

The father:

Don't be cute. Listen. This Jerry Falwell of sorts, he pulled out a piece and he started to spray bullets everywhere. The overall atmosphere and my sardonic line, no doubt. This is to concede that a jury could find that there were attenuating circumstances. Be that as it may, one of the bullets blew my head off, I am sure. I felt my left parietal explode and I had time to see my brain splash between the boobs of the operator. Next... it's like when they put you to sleep at the hospital, you know. And then, immediately, I found myself in the subway, on a train this time, but one that was coming from downtown, *from the opposite direction*, that is, and as alive and well as you see me now! And here I am. However, nobody will make me believe that I didn't get a bullet in my head. Note that I know what you're going to say and what the public has a right to expect you to say.

The son:

Come on, Dad, you certainly dozed off and dreamed. You're overtaxed these days. But you're here, alive and kicking, see? It was all but a nightmare. Besides, the walkman would've already announced it. They don't miss that sort of scoop.

The father:

Okay. Now, this doesn't explain why your mother is here tonight, why you said that I worked on Wall Street, why I'm wearing this pin-stripe suit entirely lacking in sex-appeal, and why, in my own eyes, the aspect of the apartment has changed since this morning. And look at you: what made you adopt this "flathead" hairdo today? To demonstrate your solidarity toward which faction of the ambient paranoia? I know, you're going to tell me that it isn't new. So, don't waste your time. One thing I know for sure is that I'm *dead*, utterly *dead*. I'm just surviving here as one of my parallel imprints. And you, the "flathead," you're one of my parallel children. The other one, I mean the imprint of you that I left, is, at this time, mourning my death. The worst thing is that he doesn't even know where to reach his mother. However, if we have to believe all the proponents of parallel universes as being a normal consequence of the quantum probability field, it isn't exactly *that* way things should have happened...

The son:

Come on, why don't you listen to Mom this time and go with her to consult her psychiatrist? You're overstressed, Dad.

The Omniscient:

Okay. It's a lost cause. The father should face the evidence. Besides, even if the son believed him, it wouldn't prove anything to the reader. Then we'd have to characterize specialists, psychiatrists, transcribe interviews of renowned experts, introduce exorcists and what have you, in order to present all the hypotheses, if not to prove them. But as I personally know that the father is telling the truth, I want to spare you such rambling and boring scenes, and I'll try to explain in a scholarly manner. So, what happened is what already happened billions of times in the father's life, as in the son's life or in everybody's life: that is, a particular conscious imprint within the universal consciousness, just *one* imprint among an infinite number of probable imprints of the individual referred to as "father," has vanished. But the father's consciousness continues to survive in an infinite number of probable imprints of the same individual, along as many scenarios of existence, each slightly different (or infinitely so) from the one which has been interrupted by the prophet's bullet. We have to understand that Schrödinger's cat didn't "die" just *once* after the explosion of the cyanide capsule and, by the same token, didn't "live" just *once* following its non-explosion; the poor animal had already died billions and billions and billions of times, even before that, having been run over by a bus or shot by some quick tempered neighbor, or whatever can cause the death of a cat; and alive as many times, after that, according to scenarios where he had masters who, more human than Mr. Schrödinger, never submitted him to the hypothetical ordeal. Do you follow me? Now, I'm going to wait a moment for those of you who stood abashed right at my first sentence.

....

Er... no, miss. Nobody ever mentioned the race of Mr. Schrödinger's cat... No, not the color, either... Are we ready now? Let's proceed. Okay. But here's the rub. For, as the father suspected, this is not exactly the way things should have happened. He remembers "wrongly." He remembers the scenario of events that led to his demise in the sleazy elevator, thus including the moment of a "death," while, at the same time, the memory pertaining to the "welcoming probability" has only "its" own previous hour in storage. Normally, the historical memory of the welcoming probability is automatically stored in lieu of the erased one, which allows the individual consciousness to continue leading a life that he (or she) has always believed to be his (or hers) since his (or her) birth. Now, that didn't happen this time because... some bug got into the program. Something, somewhere, provoked the appearance of an "invalid request" on the cosmic screen. Perhaps one of those infamous viruses.

***

ACT 4

(With the father, the son, the mother and the Omniscient)

The Omniscient:
Later that evening, because the mother wanted to prove, through a symbolic act, that she was a liberated woman, the whole family finds itself sitting at a table at the pizza place right down the block. The conversation goes as follows:

The father:
Oh God, what a day! Pass me the garlic salt, will you, (bleep)? No, I couldn't get to talk to (bleep) today... Never in his office... But he'll be there tomorrow...

The mother:

Ah, by the way, do you know what (bleep) told me on the phone? Her daughter got seven invitations for Halloween this year. She *really* is upset, you know. She is sure to insult somebody! What would you do?

The son
(listening to the walkman:)
Tssk...tsss...tssk...tsss...tssk...tsss...tssk...tsss...tssk

***

ACT 5

(With the author and the Omniscient)

The author:

Okay now, how should I conclude?

The Omniscient:

Uh... let's talk about schizophrenia.

The author:

Hey, are you kidding me? And is that all they have to talk about?

The Omniscient:

Well... er... anyway, it's all over, right? Big Data probably found a cure for the virus. As soon as the son showed his intention of going on with the subject, the father accused him of having misunderstood him, probably because of the walkman, and he said that his intention was only to make a big joke to get his son's attention... He should have known that this adolescent boy of his was touchy. So, I assume that the father retrieved his memory, I mean... the right one, the one of his "welcoming probability." So, all is well that ends well. If you prefer, we could talk about amnesia to the reader. It always works. Or of "fugue states," or "post-traumatic stress disorder." In any case, we no longer have at our disposal any actual and consistent facts on which to build a plot according to a cause-effect relationship and to work out a credible hypothesis.

The author:

Then long live biographies, journalistic novels, how-to's, culinary reports, or anything like that, except for this sublime form of creative fiction through which I'm killing myself to explain the unexplainable unexplained!

The Omniscient:

You bet!

(New York, October 1989)

MULTIPLE JOYCE

January 8, 2091.

Tuni Horzon would have liked to know why it was night. Of course, it was 10 PM and Tuni knew that it was always night at 10 PM. But tonight, in particular, she wanted to know *why*.

Why night existed, period. Not just why at 10 PM rather than at noon. Tuni Horzon had no idea about that.

She had no idea about that because she had never before asked herself the question.

And because she had never asked anybody else either.

And also because nobody had ever asked her either.

But tonight, inexplicably, just like that, while staring out the window...

Because Tuni had a window in her apartment. In 2091, not everybody had an apartment with a window. For the same reason why, during the last century, unlike Tuni's great grandfather, not everybody had an office with a window. But as non-demanding as she was, Tuni couldn't have gone without a window. So she and Paul had to cut out other expenses so she could get her windowed apartment.

The window opened to the north, on the first floor, onto a dark back alley. In the summer, for two hours a day, Tuni could see the sun reflected on the window panes of the building across the block.

However, that never inspired her to ponder what the sun was. The only thing she had ever noticed was that the sun was up during the day, although not always.

This was because, throughout her entire school experience, Tuni was never given a chance to pencil in, with a #2 pencil, a little oval to the left of the question: "Why is there night?" or any similar question concerning celestial mechanics or the nature of heavenly bodies.

Of course, it had been a long time since students -- or any other category of people -- were expected to ask themselves questions. Instead, they were only required to answer questions by selecting one of the proposed answers already formulated in the multiple choice questionnaires.

These multiple choice questionnaires were now displayed on roll-up computer screens, but the appearance of an old #2 pencil with a hexagonal section had been retained for the design of the electronic pointer which was now used to blacken the pixels. Just as they had retained, in Tuni's great grandfather's time, the shape of flames for electric bulbs, of burning logs and cinders for central heating convectors, and books for Nintendo game boxes.

During the last century Tuni's great grandfather had already taken all his standardized achievement tests, including English and math, by answering multiple choice questions. Now, in 2091, no way existed to complete a doctoral thesis or a research article other than by providing four or five variations for each idea, and then blackening the appropriate oval to the left of the formulation representing the idea to be really conveyed.

For example, if we took the first sentence of this text:

1. O *Tuni Horzon would have liked to forget all about night.*
2. O *Tuni Horzon would have liked to see the night.*
3. O *Tuni Horzon would have liked to know why it was night.*
4. O *Tuni Horzon would have liked to ignore all about night.*
5. O *Tuni Horzon would have liked all of the above.*

(blacken #3) The text would go on like that, up to the footnotes and the bibliography.

The task of multiple choicing texts was made easier by the use of quantum chips, which permitted word processing programs like *ChoicePerfect* to process texts according to an infinity of semantic probabilities without having the author work himself off.

Or do anything but blackening pixels.

So, there Tuni was, standing behind her window, pondering something that even her great grandfather had not had a chance to explain to her, because, at the age he was when she knew him, you couldn't take him *outside* of teleholovision. No way.

When Tuni was a little girl, teleholovision was the favorite pastime of "Baby-boomers," the aging "me-generation" and "flower children" veterans.

In the meantime the favorite pastime of young intellectuals was to purchase subscriptions to a variety of tele-clubs where they organized roundtable discussions about classical "flatties" like *Dallas, Star Trek,* and *Wild Palms.*

Although Tuni had probably asked her parents about that, she could not remember having obtained an interesting answer.

If Tuni did not know, that did not mean that her testing had proven her to be a DMP *(Differently Mental Person)* or even an OAP *(Otherwise Abled Person).* To the contrary, Tuni had an IQ of 157 and held three doctoral degrees. The first one was in Document Formatting. The second one was in Canine Law (the legal sector dealing specifically with pets' rights). These had been useful in her being hired as an assistant secretary at Goldstein & Goldstern.

As for the third one, although less vocational, in Terra-Cotta Studies, which she took to show her cultural solidarity with her ethnic group, it had been useful to know how, for instance, to direct her son David in his choice of historically correct details to be painted on the Thanksgiving streamers for his classroom.

In David's school, Thanksgiving streamers were expected to show an equal number of male and female pilgrims, all from former ethnic minorities, among whom could be spotted a few disabled and AIDS-ridden characters (fleeing, for that matter, from less hospitable shores) busily serving (and no longer *being served*) wild turkey with rice pilaf and chili to Aztec Indians.

Turkey with cranberry sauce was still consumed, but only in derelict inner city ghettos of New England.

Paul, Tuni's husband, whose family name, Melnik, Tuni had not adopted in order to retain her cultural heritage and flag her female identity, insisted in consuming his with horseradish and matzo balls.

To get back to her education, Tuni had pursued her studies until the age of 40. But because she had never taken astronomy in college, she could not guess that it was night because the sun was not there, or let alone where the sun was when it was not there. And no answer had ever been proposed to her through any of the multiple-choice questionnaires which were handed out at the end of Astronomy 101 classes.

And now, Tuni had so many other ovals to blacken, anytime, everyday, simply to answer questions raised by daily life issues, that she no longer had the time to ask questions to which no oval had previously been added.

For example, right before going to the window, Tuni had finished blackening a number of them regarding the updating of her medical dossier, that is, her completing charts upon charts of her personal consumption of fibers, of enzymes, as well as of a host of items ending in *ide* and *ose* for the day that was ending.

After that, she would have to tackle Paul's file, too, since Paul always refused to deal with it.

Some people could afford to pay other people to do the job for them, but not Tuni.

When she came to think of it, Tuni envied the life of her great grandfather, who had lived at a time when people could still find someone to do their shopping, walk their dog or any such chore for less money than they were making, in the same time period, by working at their own profession. In 2091 this had become almost impossible unless you could find, at the same time, more medical statistics to update, another dog to walk, or more shopping to do in a posher neighborhood. But neither Paul nor Tuni could settle for that. They both had diplomas and enough potential to evolve up to more professionally rewarding occupations.

In any case, there soon would not be enough dogs to walk, shopping to do and statistics to update to satisfy everybody; powerful unions were already starting to oppose the hiring of highly educated people for home-assistant jobs.

All the more so because affluent pet-sitters and shopping-goers were *really* starting to feel the need for lawyers, doctors and teachers at regulated low fees.

If Tuni had been a pet-sitter or a shopping-goer, she would have had a chance, in the park or at the supermarket, to meet somebody she could ask about night. But at Goldstein & Goldstern's, nobody would have known since nobody had taken astronomy in college.

And Paul, would he know? She wondered. He also had a few doctorates and perhaps he had taken, somewhere, an optional course in astronomy or... geography? By the way, Tuni thought, in what course exactly would they teach why there's night?

Tuni pondered. She finally turned around to go ask Paul.

Paul was busy.

Since he was sleeping, he was clearly busy.

Sleeping had been considered a bona fide occupation since the time when they had started to pay people who saw the loss of a little of their time for sleep as acceptable. That served the purpose of perpetuating research programs on sleep, dreams, etc., which were themselves maintained in order to justify their own financing and, consequently, the field of somnology and careers which depended on its existence.

It goes without saying that medicine had been successful in its attempts to modify human biorhythms in order to render the individual utterly efficient by enabling each to devote most of a precious life span to rewarding and challenging tasks.

It was the same for all the former diseases: in order to keep the medical profession flourishing, temporary workers were underpaid to develop them, with just enough time to allow epidemics to spread, to then diagnose them and cure everybody at the last minute.

So, by means of his neuro-transmitters, Paul was busy feeding a data base used for experiments for which someone would merely have to blacken the oval next to the obtained result.

In addition to Paul's full time job as a window decorator for K-Mart, his sleeping hours were an impediment to family life and married life, but these were necessary sacrifices which were made to pay the rent on a window-equipped apartment, and Tuni could hardly object to that.

She hesitated as to whether or not she should wake him up. She had finally began to wonder if it was just a philosophical question, a question such as her great grandfather might have asked himself about anything and nothing in particular, when they still had the time to ponder such questions, other than the ones they were supposed to answer as a priority.

In other words, Tuni was feeling guilty about being *curious.*

She decided to awaken Paul anyway. She *had* to know.

Paul, groggy, asked what the matter was.

Tuni said, "Nothing serious, don't get upset," and asked her question.

Paul did not understand right away and asked Tuni to repeat her question, which she did.

Paul answered, "Well, I guess it's because it's late."

Tuni asked him why it was night when it was late.

Then, Paul stared at Tuni like (would you please blacken with a #2 black pencil the oval facing the answer that you think is correct):

1. O *An Iman stares at the fax which announces the return to Islam of a formerly blasphemous writer who would finally like to enjoy his royalties.*

2. O *A maggot stares at the palatial vaults which have just swallowed the lump of Pont l'Evêque cheese where it was born.*

3. O *Saddam Hussein would have stared at the world if the world confessed to him that nobody gave a damn about Kuwait except for Amoco and Exxon junk bond holders, cold war redundancies and arms dealers.*

4. O *He who never pondered the question of the nature of night (or whatever question bearing as much irrelevance to his function) stares at whomever is being thanked by him for, as it happens, having just raised such an interesting question.*

5. O *All of the above.*

Since he did not know the answer to Tuni's question, Paul asked her why she had asked it. Then, in turn, Tuni stared at Paul with about the same stare Paul had at her, but with a zest of lassitude in it to boot. She finally told him that it was because David needed the answer for a project at school.

It was true that David was right now working on a term project. He had been given a choice between an astronomy project, a project on a foreign language, a reading project, or another project on earthworms, she thought, or maybe it was on the Roman Empire.

He had chosen the astronomy project.

At seventeen, David was now a honor student in the 12th grade. So, he had not hesitated for one minute to grapple with the most intellectually challenging and rewarding project. For this project, in addition to the following multiple-choice question:

(What revolves around what?)

1. O *The earth around the moon.*

2. O *The moon around the earth.*

3. O *The sun around the earth.*

4. O *The sun around the moon.*

5. O *Everyone of them around every other.* *

(* Correct answer. See? It's not that obvious.)

David had also had to complete a research project, that is, the finding of pictures to illustrate the four seasons.

Or, more precisely, the *two* seasons, because David's school, just like any other school respectful of its ethnic orientation, was not supposed to overload its curriculum with anything that basically pertained only to temperate cultures. Thus, in David's school, there were only two seasons, the rain season and the dry season, even though they all lived in Long Island, N.Y.

Tuni suspected that this project had something to do with the question she was pondering.

She thought that she'd be better off asking David than Paul.

David was pulsating on a rhythmic beat that he alone could hear, had heard and would ever hear.

It was a long time since every teenager could become his one star thanks to the extreme miniaturization of sound recording studios that could now be implanted in the inner ear. Those studios could directly tap the host's brain waves. Thus the host could listen to his own subconscious compositions without being, as in the past, limited by his own capacities of memorization, musical transcription and instrumental rendering.

Without being limited either, as they had been in the past, to listening to a few selected stars whose subconscious hullabaloo was marketed by a few major distributors. And most of all, without being forced to share those compositions with other people who could now easily be listening to their own.

As a matter of fact, technology could have enabled people to do without middlemen in order to distribute their own artistic creations. This had started to become possible in Tuni's great grandfather's days when, for example, the landfills were clogged with tons of unread spreadsheets, memos, resumes, professional brochures, catalogues and magazines still in their plastic wrappers, the chromatic rendering of which would have made the stained glass masters of the cathedrals feel lousy, all much better printed on much better paper than the early editions of Melville and Balzac.

But distribution of artistic creations had become purposeless since, for want of time, it had been decades since people had heard, watched or read anything other than that which they were producing on a non-stop basis.

The truth is that David Horzon had never listened to anything other than David Horzon's stuff and that was what he was still doing that night.

Tuni was more circumspect with her son than her husband. She did not want to hurt David's feelings by sounding like she was quizzing him. So, she only asked him if he by any chance remembered having to answer such a question which, as stupid as it sounded, could have germinated in the cranky mind of an eccentric, youth-hating test writer, and what oval he had blackened if he ever happened to explore the answers.

David told her that he did not recall anything like that, but that could be because, as a matter of fact, they were always overloading the curriculum.

"Now, don't you remember which oval you blackened?" Tuni insisted, when she saw her son again start to writhe about to the beat of his psyche.

"Why don't you search my files yourself?" David asked. "Try *night* as a keyword. You'll see. If I did something on that, it should be there."

Everything considered, Tuni could have interrogated her own archives as well. Perhaps she too, years before, more likely in elementary school than later in her studies, had answered such a question. If Tuni had a rather dreary memory of her college years, she had, on the contrary, a very pleasant one of her primary schooling. She remembered for instance that it was in elementary school that she could still have real conversations with her little friends.

For the same reason that the germs of protestation, in this century, were only found on the elementary school campuses.

After that? Well, it was enough to blacken an oval before this or that slogan, judiciously proposed by this or that faction. In other words, Tuni was now realizing that she did not only wish to know why there was night. She also wanted somebody, and not a telelink screen, to give her an answer.

Since Paul had already gone back to sleep and David back to convulsing, Tuni returned to the window to look at the night. Until then, she had seen the night, not actually looked at it. She had no time for that since she spent most of her evenings updating statistics, graphics, and the what-have-you that was daily generated by the running of the household.

Tonight again, before tackling the medical file, she had established a five year projection of the family's future consumption in carbohydrates, taking into account last week's consumption of the same, which would then sharpen a similar projection established the week before on the basis of already existing data and would be useful in view of more correctly forecasting what the next forecast concerning the same consumption would be, say, in a week from now.

There were so many items to compute! Sometimes, it seemed as though the capacity of their home telelink terminal, already well endowed in megabytes, would not suffice. Before the carbohydrate project, Tuni had already spent too much time updating the data concerning something that she had been neglecting for days: the proportion of tin recycled from tin cans used by her family, in cumulative calculus and dating back to David's, Paul's and her own birthdates, that had been used in the production of new cans delivered last month to retail stores worldwide.

And before attending to the recycled tin business, she had to knock off the curve of the family's contribution of methane to the earth's atmosphere by entering the data registered by sensors throughout the apartment.

And so on and so forth.

It was not that these figures were requested by any particular service or administration. The aforesaid administrations or services could just as easily have directly obtained them on the link by questioning a myriad of other exterior sources of information about their household metabolism. But computing had become a compulsive ritual similar to the Catholic prayer for daily bread when the table around which it was mumbled was loaded with caviar and tournedos béarnaise.

Or, in their days, like the updating of her Weight Watchers handbook by her great grandmother or of his jogging statistics by her great grandfather.

Now, if Tuni had noticed that it was night, it was not because she had seen stars twinkle, either. Even in his time, because of light pollution, her great grandfather had shown a lot of goodwill in using his telescope for purposes other than to peep into neighboring bathrooms.

Since Tuni, as already mentioned, had not taken any astronomy classes in college, she hadn't met anybody who would have mentioned the existence of stars to her, either. So the only reason that made Tuni conceptualize night was that light was pouring in from all around rather than from above.

Meaning: from the arteries of the megapolis, its thoroughfares, malls (all wrapped in fluorescent coating), from its fluctuating and pulsing holographic signboards, from its facades made of glass and metal where everything became reflection of everything.

Light poured even from the night sky. If one really looked closely at it, the sky appeared like a lattice of solid light beams which delineated a labyrinth of air routes like, in the past, phosphorescent pins delineated highway lanes. So much so that the night sky above Long Island where Tuni and her family lived was no longer just a dark pinkish orange like the Manhattan sky of her great grandfather's days, but a deep cobalt blue.

Even more so because of the absence of industrial pollution.

In Manhattan, the Surgeon General advised people not to go out at night without sunglasses because of the blinding effect.

Fortunately, environmental activism had led to the cancellation of high-tech projects such as the deployment of huge solar reflectors into stationary orbit which were designed to continuously pour sunlight on the nightside of the earth. Together with the suppression of sleep, this would have led humankind onto the path of Ultimate Efficiency and thus, enabled it to keep up with the ever increasing needs of a permanently active society.

Finally, since during the day things and living beings could still produce foreboding shadows, the stage for horrible bedtime stories for children as well as for holovideos had to be set in daytime and in sun-parched countries.

The big Greenwich Village Halloween parade now took place between 10 a.m. and 12 noon on the thirty-first of October and the projectors of the teleholovision crews beamed black light onto the participants. (All of those who ever read good sci-fi know about black light. To those who do not know, black light is negative light. Or in other words, anti-light.)

Sure, we could just as easily have said: *The vacuum photon-busters of the teleholovision crews sucked in light beams from the participants.*

Come on, in 2091, this could be done.

Tuni blinked her eyes and turned around to the relative shadow of the room where they all were; Paul sleeping, David writhing and she, Tuni, pondering the existence of night. Then, she thought of calling her sister

Nora although Tuni knew that Nora never took astronomy in college. But what the hell. Tuni could not remember anyone who might have taken it.

To be truthful, Tuni could not remember anybody, period. In 2091, it had been a long time since people could remember people other than by their names. That is why people could remember the names of celebrities such as the players of the participating teams in the Super Bowl or, at most, the name of those with whom they were professional partners. But, as we already know, neither Tuni nor Paul were on the payroll of an observatory.

Nora said: "Huuuuh? What are you talking about? No. of course not. Why the hell should I know? You know I never took astronomy in college! Er... by the way, speaking about night, tell me, please, Tuni: did you ever complete the computing of the nighttime ozone production of your azalea for the last month period? I found it was abnormally high here. I'm sure I punched the wrong oval somewhere when I fed the data."

Tuni could still proceed with an inquiry, using a specialized information service, but she seemed unable or unwilling to grapple with a long research procedure on the telelink. She knew such research would necessitate answering an endless series of multiple choice questionnaires.

To understand this, one should remember how much patience was already expected from people, back in Tuni's great grandfather's days, when it came to obtaining a piece of information on the phone such as the price of a letter to Europe from the postal service.

Just remember. You had to:

1. Listen to the whole litany of opening hours for the concerned office.

2. Listen to commercial messages boasting specific postal services.

3. Rapidly catch the number of The Postal Answer Line.

4. Dial this number accurately. (If not, go back to 1.)

5. Listen to the menu of the taped messages offered by The Postal Answer Line. (Unless you had, a few months before, used the same code and noted it somewhere you could still remember.)

6. Listen to yourself being told that you had to stand at attention with a piece of paper and a working pen.

7. Dial 328 in order to obtain the list of the categories of answers proposed under this global code.

8. Listen to the announcement of some fifteen categories of answers among which were: home deliveries, change of address, registration of parcels, third-class and book rates, bulk rates, second deliveries of registered mail, collection stamps, distribution litigations and delays, opening of P.O. boxes, etc., before hearing "overseas mail rates". (The announcement of each being followed by the rapid utterance of a three-digit code.)

9. Dial the above three-digit number without error, at the risk of either hearing "WOULD YOU PLEASE NOW DIAL A THREE-DIGIT CODE" repeated endlessly, or going back to step 4.

10. Listen to the message titles under the category "Overseas and international mail rates" and, after having correctly dialed more eliminatory codes, swiftly take note of the announced rate.

It was too late for Tuni to start tonight.

Even more so since the answer could have been denied to her by the telelink on the grounds of "unconvincing motivations" if she blackened the wrong motives with her #2 pointer.

After her conversation with her sister Nora, it seemed to Tuni that she had called to talk about something in particular in the first place but she could not remember what.

Tuni hurried to check the ozone production chart of her azalea.

(New York, Jan/Feb 1991)

SUPERZOD

- Before the beginning, the spirit of Something soared above the abyss... but Zod does not remember.

- Come on, Zod. Think. The numb, the stiff, the frozen, the congealed, the boiled, the unruffled, the volatile...

- Zod does not remember before time... er... before Zod. Slush, granite, nitrogen, basalt... cannot remember. They exist, but they are aimless, needless, and with no particular reason to get concerned. Only Zod can remember. Because Zod has thought time. Time for nobody other than Zod.

- So, let there be Zod. Let it split from primeval matter, from the ore or the aqueous. And let not Zod ask how it happened.

- Now Zod remembers! In the beginning, there were Zod and the Rest, the Rest that Zod impregnated, assimilated, aggregated, amalgamated. See? Long live *Zod & Zod Amalgamated*!

- Not yet, Zod. Wait. There is no rush since Zod is alone for the moment and Zod has time. For the time being,let Zod pump, suck, transmute, defecate. There is only Zod to face the Rest, Zod, a collective biorhythm, a vibration independent from the refractive medium, sorry, from the Rest. Let Zod assert itself as a Gentil Organisateur of the Chaos. And let not Zod ask why.

- Ouuuchh!

- Yeah.. It hurts, huh?

- Hey, what was it? What was it?!

- Jaws.. The teeth of the sea. The horns of the swamps. The claws of the earth. Zod will name it. It was whatever objected to the presence of Zod, whatever took upon itself to bust a few of Zod's integrated systems. Watch out, Zod. It was the Other. Thrust. Bruise. Bash. Fracture...

- Lethal internal lesions. 911. Emergency room. Flat EEG. Move it! Dr. Steinberg!

- Not yet, Zod. Let death be. Clean death. Unhindered, proud and free death. The non-medicated dissociation of an organic present of Zod. Back to the Rest.

- But it sure did hurt. And now Zod feels so good...

- Because of Light, heat, satiety... What more does Zod need? The matter of the ex-zod, disorganized, is reorganizing within Zod. Drowsiness. Beddy-byes. But it is just a truce.

- Now Zod feels so good that Zod wants to spurt into the other. Or be filled with it.
- Let rut be. Aggression. Submission. Thrust. Explosion. Agape, Zod inscribes itself in more zods to come with time. C'est la vie. Now, Zod can go on dying.
- I LOVE YOU! Don't leave me! Remember the long sobs of the Autumn violins, some evening! Don't you remember?
- Not yet, Zod. For the moment, Zod feels good, real good. The Other is far, already, and can't remember. For the moment, Zod does not whine, Zod does not fantasize. Zod fucks.
- Oh, but... Zod is getting scared.
- Sounds as though Zod suspects something will hurt again, as though Zod will be or won't be no more. The aria to come is shaping up in Zod's present.
- Now what? Being on the run. Stashing away. Zod is searching for shadow and missing light. The Other, the Unspeakable, is un-announced and... imminent. Immanent. Immoral. Vile. Interfering. Immediate. Immolating. Immune. Immense and immigrant. This is it: *immigrant*. The Other is coming to eat the rest that Zod wants to eat.
- Let apprehension of preemption be. The law-schools to come are shaping up in Zod's present.
- Worse. The Other seems to be taking Zod for the Rest.
- Because the Other is as zod as Zod. So, let Zod put itself in Zod's place...
- But there is something out there that is neither Zod nor the Other. There is something that Zod cannot eat or fuck. At least, not right away. It is like the rest was cleaving, differentiating, structuring itself. Curious how the Rest becomes interesting to Zod.
- Cool it. Easy. Follow all the steps. Zod should not get behind in the filing by dreaming and musing about things. Otherwise, Zod will soon get all confused. First, the labels. A bone. A fig leaf. A banana. A nest.
- And a small crystalline pebble onto which light becomes iridescent, right down there, near the brook which runs, ripping itself on the boulders which are polished like the belly of the other Zod-who-makes-Zod-feel-good before it opens out into mini-zods...
- Yes. Let the Word explode in arrhythmic poems, in long chants of interwoven notes.
- $99... + $999.02... +$9,999 and no cents.. Wowwwwh!
- No. Not yet. Follow the steps. Language will shrink like this, but only when Zod does not need to look at things anymore.
- Zod WANTS. Zod wants all that Zod has named. Zod has named, therefore Zod has to have. The Rolex watch. The Diner's Club card. The boxer shorts from Banana Republic. The subscription with Golf Magazine.

The Japanese doll in cast plaster from Pier-1 Imports which screeches "Happy Birthday" in five tongues. Now, all this is Zod's!

- Not yet. For the moment, Zod wants only what he finds beautiful or simply useful. Not what other zods already have.

- Oh... but among all these things out here, outside of Zod, there are some of them Zod cannot appropriate. Zod finds them beautiful, though. Sea. Wind. Lightning bolt. The only problem is they move faster than Zod, blow stronger than Zod, roar louder than Zod and all the other zods altogether. Only some kind of superzods could have them!

- Let them be. Who did Zod think he was? In the first place, why would Zod be here, amongst all these wondrous and mighty things? Say why.

- Uhm...

- Who would have Zod? Huh? The superzods played with thunder, fire, tempest. They had to get somebody to show off to, didn't they? But be reassured, Zod. Nothing belongs to the other zods any more than to Zod, since everything belongs to the superzods. Zod and all the zods that are known to Zod -- that is, the right zods -- live on superzods'estate. The superzods gave the zods the key to their apartment, that's all. At least, they gave them to the right zods, these zods who are more in the good books of the superzods than those lousier zods, and for good reason: the superzods have good taste. From now on, if the right zods are nice and keep their noses dark brown, they will just have to sneak on the lousy ones, and trust the superzods for their security. If, while playing with their mighty things, the superzods happen to hurt Zod, Zod should not be alarmed. It is exactly like when Frank Perdue hurts the Kentucky chicken. The hurt is a side effect, not the guy's purpose. Now, the zods will just have to speculate on the intentions of the superzods, not just stand in their way.

- Good. So the January 14th's spank to Saddam Hussein will trigger a jump of AMOCO stocks. Zod buys!

- Not yet. The right zods only build temples, not systems.

- It is swell here, at the estate. The Superzods don't bother the zods too much. They seem to be spending most of their time ripping each other open or setting up orgies. Sometimes, they even invite the zods, especially since that nosy Pandora found out where they stashed away their paraphernalia, their leather, their whips, their dirty polaroids. Sometimes, they even let the zods cavort with them to cross-breed half-minisuperzods. A day at the beach! But... oh my Zod!

- What's the matter?

- Ohhh... Zod had become so heedless... There was Superzod! Superzod, the One and Only, the Incommensurate. Zod just saw Him. He was hiding behind a bush that He must have set on fire lighting up a Marlboro. While the zods were frolicking with all these damn superzods, He was there, writing down names to distribute Sunday's detention. Here He is, asking Zod to read the Rules of Conduct. The thing is a bit bulky, not as convenient, yet, as all the bugging systems and the corporate discipline reminders at Zod & Zod Amalgamated, but everything is there anyway. The ten things that Zod should refrain to indulge in if he wants to be forgiven by Superzod, who has not yet swallowed, in particular, the fact that the first of the zods had allegedly swiped an apple from His garden.

- Ah Ah! Here we are. Let us not show up at Superzod's door again! And instead of vaguely vacate or touch each other up this way and that, the zods will henceforth have to become responsible, stick to family values, and apply with the local Department of Labor to find a position in the development project of the region at... Zod & Zod Amalgamated! From now on, Zod won't crave for anything less than sitting at the right of Superzod during the board meetings. Above all, let Zod deal with the elimination of all those other lousy zods who are still too boisterous to have heard Him come into the picture, or who do not yet defecate in their fig leaf in His Presence. And Superzod is still too good to give Zod the right to hate in His name...

- Yeah! Zod hates! Oh, Superzod almighty, how Zod hates! Kaddhafi, Noriega, the communists, the fags! Zod hates the fucking Arab who booby-trapped the World Trade Center! Yeah!

- And do not forget to hate thyself, Zod. You should be ashamed. Come on, Superzod let you play in His garden, thinking you wouldn't be mischievous, create trouble... He even had let the neighbors' little girl come to play with you... Next thing He knows, Zod has been let himself be induced in playing doctor by the little slut! Poor mistaken Superzod. He should have kept on making dinosaurs, the day He fancied sculpting his Self-portrait in a pile of mud.

- Noooo... How hungry Zod is! And how cold! It seems that Zod has spent his whole life standing in line at the Department of Labor offices, but he has neither the look nor the qualifications for the job. And now, Zod only thinks of his hunger, of the cold...

- Zod asked for it. He was thinking too much. Curiosity is a naughty sin.

- Okay, but now, Zod thinks of doing really nasty things. Here, for instance: see this cesspool of a street in Cairo's "City of the Dead"? Zod is six years old and Zod has just found a few non digested corn seeds from a heap of dried donkey dung...

- Zod found? Good Heavens! Superzod is great!

- Yes, but there are those fucking sweaty fatsoes over there, those camcorder faces. If only Zod could...

- Go ahead. Accomplish the *fatwa*. Superzod, too, hates those Yankee pigs.

- What about here: Manhattan. Filth Avenue. Cartier. Bergdorf-Goodman. A garbage can behind a black stretch limo. Zod rummages. Ah! Something...

- Thank Superzod.

- No. Fuck Him. Zod's grimy hands pull out a slimy styrofoam container. Inside the container, hardly chewed remnants of a hotdog with sauerkraut. Around the container, gee! a rubber band that Zod will use to fix a sneaker's sole that's trying to sneak away.

- Thank Superzod and let Him bless the one who wasn't as hungry as Zod!

- Fuck Him. And here, in a forest of orchids, on a terrace: Zod is toting a cellular phone. The phone says "You're fired. Because of the recession, the mergers"... Zod looks over his shoulder but no, nobody else is there. So, who's the telephone talking to?

- Absorption. Fusion. Dejection. The same old story.

- But Zod had gotten such a hard-on in the cat-bird's seat at *Zod & Zod Amalgamated*!

- Yeah... But look here, instead, Zod: here, everything is still possible. Run, Zod, run! A senior vice-Zod is expecting his ashtray, from offices to conference rooms.

- Zod doesn't smoke!

- So what? Zod has the right not to smoke but he's got to shit in his business pants to, someday, become a senior-vice zod.

- Oh Zod, I hate it...

- Good for Zod! Where there's hatred, there's hope. Superzod will make something out of Zod.

- Zod has...

- What now?

- In one hand, a pair of scissors. In the other, a double illustrated page showing articles in promotion at SHOPRITE. Zod applies himself. Zod is having fun. Zod cuts out the contours of the images and drops them to the floor, one by one: computers, telephones, garden chairs, underwear, detergent containers, record books, laundry bins, jars of Polish pickles--

- Let the little children...

- Yes but Zod is 47 years old. Zod has been cutting out pictures for as long as Zod can remember... Zod is differently able.

- ...and the differently able come to Me...

- And here: Zod is 74. Long ago, Zod had understood that the right zods had to worship Superzod and obey the very-right zods who were more zod than the others. Zod had even understood that because of pollution, butter contains cholesterol, understood that it is cold in winter because you have to wear a coat and a scarf and lots of things like that. But Zod is dead. Oh, of course, Zod still moves, once in a while, a chin, a hand, an eyelid...

- ...Superzod's nursing home belongs to them, stupid kids and differently able!

- Yes, but... the long chants of interwoven notes also got lost in Zod, and differently able Zod cannot name things any longer. Zod could not forget only as long as Zod remembered. Now, it's like nothing ever happened. Even time... Even Superzod...

- Now wait! All right, granted, it had become a little complicated, even with databanks and e-mail, granted, but.. Come on, if Zod wants, Zod can forget about... SAXIFRAGE, Okay? Or SCANSION. Or CHAPSKA. Okay? Let's see under the next letter in the dictionary: What about TMESIS? Press *Delete*. No problem with that. There were too many things, too many words anyway. But not ME! What's going to become of ME?

- Ah Ah! Zod forgets everything! Forget everything, Zod! Forget Zod, Everything! Everything forgets Zod! Everything forgets, Zod. Everything Zod forgets! Zod, Everything forgets!

- Zod?.......... Zod?........ Hey, Zod?..........???

- ...Okay. All just depends on nothing... Not even Zod.

(New York, January/February 1993)

THE WALLOP EFFECT

ACT 1
(With the Omniscient, the walkman, the father, and the son)

The Omniscient:
A very, very, very long time ago, in a galaxy very, very very far away...

The walkman:
Princess Diana, the B.B.C. reported this morning, slapped Prince Charles on the face as they were returning from a hunting party near Balmoral Castle.

The son:
Hey, are they going to say something about us, instead, on the radio?

The father:
Why don't you just leave this damn' radio and do your homework *instead*?

The son:
I don't have homework.

The father:
Then why don't you pick up a book?

The son:
Pffffffffffffff.......

The father:
By the way, did you pick up some bread, as I told you?

***

ACT 2

(With the author and the Omniscient only.
In the author's office)

The author:
Once again, it seems that you didn't catch the action at the right moment (see INCURSION). If we go on like that, we'll end up using the characters

only to introduce the topic of the day. The dialogue between the father and the son could at least provide more information on their respective temperament. For instance, the son could have insisted and explained why he was shocked by the fact that the media broadcast such rubbish when the world is globally changing or even, closer to him, when one of his friends got bitten by rats in an Uptown project and then caught a stray bullet because drug dealers were shooting each other in the stairway of his building -- by the way, his friend's mother is a single parent and they can't move out because their apartment is at the rent level which is acceptable to the Welfare department. Then the father could at least ask *why* his son doesn't have homework, and the son could say that it is because his teachers have been on strike since one of them was stabbed for having dared teach a eurocentrist history class about Hitler and World War Two. Whereupon, the father could have pushed his son into reading one of his own history books, which would have shown that he himself is a history buff.

The Omniscient:

What the walkman said is relevant, anyway. As we have to stick to the great metaphysical themes that constitute the uniqueness of this series, the only alternative would be to let the father give another lecture to his son, like: "Don't be mistaken. Lady Di's impulsive gesture will have, somewhere, sometime and somehow, a dramatic impact on the fate of the Galaxy and the Universe. Now, let me tell you about the Butterfly Effect, or, in other words, the Sensitive Dependence of global phenomena on the Original Conditions, since such is the topic that we decided to tackle today." The format does not allow us to wrap up an artificial plot in a dialogue which, in the father's and the son's real life, would only lead to another vaguely similar dialogue the next day, without any specific linearity.

The author:

So, let's go on without the characters.

***

ACT 3

(Well, with the same ones...)

The Omniscient:

So, this is what happened in a galaxy very, very, very far away and a very, very, very long time ago. And now, in a galaxy very very far away from the galaxy from which, just as it was a very very very long time ago, it is very very very very far away...

The author:

Wait a minute. Where are we?

The Omniscient:

Right here.

The author:

When?

The Omniscient:

Right now.

· *The author:*

Okay. But where and when is that?

The Omniscient:

That is a very very very long time after "a very very very long time ago," and very very very far away from all that was very very very close by. It is here and now.

The author:

I see. But what is it? What's happening? What's going on? What's the big deal? Oh sure, I can see something, but I can't find the words to talk about it, even with the help of the "Omnilingual" (see the original French versions of DEUS EX LATRINA and CONFIRMATION. Later, I will find better references to BEING AND NOTHINGNESS and SCHROEDINGER'S CATNAP, I promise) Now, let's see. The only thing whose existence I seem to be able to intuit is, perhaps, a sort of elementary globality integrating the primary concept of hands and cheeks, and also a vague notion of pendular, chaotic motion.

The Omniscient:

Not that bad. I have to confess, I had not yet thought about that. But now that you mention it...

The author:

I had to hook onto an idea that could be conveyed by words so that the reader also could grasp it. But you've got to confess that this is more clever than heavy-duty sci-fi, where the umpteenth century or the other end of the universe is now cluttered with video cameras, micro-chips and corporate moguls, after having already been cluttered for decades with printed reports, radio-days computer hardware, and mean Colonels What's their faces. Nevertheless, what's the relevance to-- Good God! This is what it is! As my wife said yesterday... (see *Colombo*)

The Omniscient:
Yes, Lieutenant. Here, the "slap" event is the "original condition" of all existence, just like the "word of God" event is the "original condition" of our familiar world. "In the beginning, there was the slap..." and so on. The only thing left for us to do is to write a new Old Testament.

The author:
So, what are you waiting for? We are already near the middle of the planned format.

The Omniscient:
In short: just as it is widely accepted by meteorologists that the flutter of a butterfly's wings, one given day, on Tien An Men Square in Beijing, can be the primary cause of a tornado that will, a month later, make the umbrella vendors outside of New York subway stations happy, the broadcasting of the event "slap" on the Hertzian waves of all the main media networks has been, millions of years later and in a certain galaxy, the original condition for the existence of everything we both can now see without being able to provide a description. It is all a matter of a propensity toward structuring from an eminently chaotic state, through resonances and chain repercussions, etc., etc.

The author:
Now, we have to explicate the proceedings, describe the various stages, enlighten the consecutive phases of the chain of events. For instance, one could think that several thousand years later, the Hertzian waves carrying the message of the royal slap have been tapped and decoded by some extra-terrestrial civilization listening to the cosmic tittle-tattle; that this message, the very first "intelligent" one they received from outer space and that they successfully isolated from the galactic cacophony, has had a decisive impact on the development of their civilization, reshaping dogmas and thought systems in such a way that, when they, in turn, became interstellar prophets, they--

The Omniscient:
Yes, for instance. But this one has already been used by scores of authors. Look at Carl Sagan in *Contact*, with the first television broadcast ever, Hitler's speech at the opening of the Berlin olympic games in 1936. When you think of all that may have been tapped since, you may wonder if somebody is still there to pay attention.

The author:

Come on, my intention is not to be a drill sergeant pain by asking you to demonstrate the global consequence on the whole universe of a Hitler-Amin-Dada-Baby-Doc-Noriega-etc.-paradigm, notwithstanding Lady Di, Ollie North and all of *People's Magazine* front covers. I would appreciate you merely showing the reader how a *single* message, limited in time and containing but a rudimentary concept of slap, could have produced, over the light-years, the global event that is now unfolding before our very eyes, and our eyes *only*, without our understanding it.

The Omniscient:

But even for this, we would need pages and pages, or megabytes and megabytes. (In the French text, where "megabytes" reads phonetically like "megacocks," we had here a nice reference to the "bleeps" in SCHROEDINGER'S CATNAP. Too bad.) How can I reconstruct such a long chain of historical events *linearly*, without also considering another infinite number of side events stemming from other scenarios but which may also have contributed to the fact that everything we are seeing here and now is especially happening here and now and not elsewhere and at another time? Even one of those eight hundred-page beach novels could not do. The universe is but a huge novel without a first or a last page, where all the chapters have to be read at the same time.

The author:

This is where all the action of my story was, though. If you can't develop that, what's the use? How can I write something without a first and a last page and without anything exactly right in the middle?

The Omniscient:

This is why, in real life, nothing happens exactly like in a Kojak episode. Life continuously includes all possible scenarios of action. The result is that you never really know when a life story begins or when it comes to a conclusion; or even which specific story is unfolding for each of us. The slap to Prince Charles may indicate the end of the idyll between Diana and him, but it may also be part of the development of another idyll between him and a Hollywood actress, or be the starting point of an affair between Lady Di and the handsome Garter knight who, present at the scene, will hand her his kerchief to wipe her reddened eyes... etc., etc. In the same manner, I would like to demonstrate for the reader how the Butterfly Effect only exists as long as one looks for it, and that there is no way one can avoid finding it. For instance, if we take the famous illustration in the folklore:

> **For want of a nail**, the shoe was lost;
> For want of a shoe, the horse was lost;

For want of a horse, the battle was lost;
*For want of a battle, **the kingdom was lost.***

Well and good. Nevertheless, there are other chains of events according to which the same want of the same nail could have caused the loss of the same kingdom. For example:

For want of a nail, *a sole was lost;*
For want of a sole, a boot was lost;
For want of a boot, a soldier was lost;
For want of a soldier, an army was lost;
*For want of an army, **the kingdom was lost.***

Or again:

For want of a nail, *an armchair was lost;*
For want of an armchair, a diplomat was lost;
For want of a diplomat, a peace treaty was lost;
For want of a peace treaty, a war was lost;
*For want of a victory, **the kingdom was lost.***

And you will notice that I did not say "For want of a war" in the last line but "For want of a victory," since the loss of a war can result in a defeat as well as a victory, depending on which side you're on, not to mention a "want of a defeat." So, if somewhere, a missing nail can make somebody lose a kingdom according to an infinite number of probable scenarios, it can also make somebody gain one according to another infinite number of them. In the same manner, the flutter of the wings of the same Chinese butterfly, the same day, on the same Square can, a month later, be at the origin of a high pressure zone in Paris or in Rio where it would have otherwise been raining if the butterfly had not fluttered its wings a month before. Not to mention that the very same fateful flutter, because of some twists and turns in the succession of meteorological events, could very well be at the origin of a balmy day in New York where the sunglass vendors, not the umbrella vendors, would have been seen outside of the subway stations. Consequently, any way we choose to look at it, we owe whatever weather we are having today to the same flutter of wings of the same lousy butterfly... or to the firing of the tanks of the People's Army or to whatever took place on Tien Amen Square or anywhere else and thus, eventually, to nothing in particular.

The author:
Yeah... but what about our story?

The Omniscient:

Well, let me tell you. The fact that a civilization has, somewhere and sometime, built churches where it is preached that In the Beginning was the Slap, and that, among this civilization, communication between individuals is achieved by means of a complex assortment of whacks, slugs, cuffs and clips (which has apparently been the cause, when we look at this species, as we can now begin to make out, of the remarkable development of the fleshy part of their face as well as the impressive length and muscle structure of their forelimbs), together with the fact that this state of affairs is linked to the Hertzian broadcast of the anecdote reported by the walkman, this is too easy to demonstrate and thus, has no value as a literary plot. It would be more interesting to see, for instance, why the same slap is at the origin, in another galaxy as far away from the two others as the two others are from it, of a civilization ethic which assigns a sacred symbolic value to the fact that organs of vision are placed, like for some terrestrial fish species, on the left side of the body, thus preventing any direct rotation to the right. Or, in some other galaxy--

The author:

All right, but in this case, the cause-effect relationship becomes everything but obvious. In a few pages, we would only have some kind of report on a slice of life of the universe, as deprived of logical connections as the father's "By the way, did you pick up some bread?" following the news flash aired on the radio waves.

The Omniscient:

However, it would not be necessary to modify drastically the story in order to prove that point. Let's say, for instance, that a researcher, on a shift at a giant radio-telescope rented by another E.T. SETI project, and who had also just picked up the news flash from CBS, instead of calmly registering the frequency and locking the antenna in the direction from which the manna of wisdom was coming, has been incapable of repressing a jeering "EUREKA!" at the anticipation of the outstanding research paper he was going to be able to publish. Now, just because of that jeering "eureka," he throws the whole system out of order. No record. Nothing. Try as he might to be convincing, he can produce no evidence of his discovery. But, persisting for a long time in approximately the same direction and on the same frequency in order to retrieve the source of the message, he stumbles upon another one, from another terrestrial TV channel: a commercial for the Jack LaLanne heath clubs in which Cher is seen belted up to a training machine with her head completely *twisted to the left* in order to face the camera, and heard declaring that when the going gets tough, the tough get going. It is not difficult to imagine that this second "first" message will have a decisive impact on the development of this civilization, reshaping dogmas and thought systems in such a way that, when they, in turn, became interstellar prophets... etc., etc. Yet, it is still the "true" first message, the royal slap, which remains at the origin of the new scenario because, if the scientist for the latter E.T. SETI project had not picked it up in the first place, he would not have persisted to search in the same direction and frequency range. (As everybody knows, the radio-telescopes' observing time allotted to SETI projects is, throughout the universe, very limited.) But still, by even changing the primary cause, we could witness, from where we are now, the same ritual brawl since:

> **Because of a nail** (*sticking out inside the boot*),
> *a foot was lost;*
> *For want of a foot, a soldier was lost;*
> *For want of a soldier, an army was lost;*
> *For want of an army, a battle was lost;*
> *For want of a battle, **a kingdom was lost.***

So, whether there is a nail or not at the origin, there is always someone to end up losing a kingdom...

The author:
Is that all? Is this the upshot of the story?

The Omniscient:
If you want to finish...

The author:
So, once again, we are left with something impossible to recount.

The Omniscient:
Not impossible, no. But useless, I'm afraid.

The author:
Hey, wait! I haven't found the occasion to refer to BEING AND NOTHINGNESS, yet.

The Omniscient:
Now, you've done it.

The author:
Okay. Let's go see what the father and the son are up to.

***

ACT 4

(With the father and the son,
without the rest of the universe,
but with the telephone)

The father:

Ouch!

The son:

What's the matter?

The father:
It's this damned tooth that's killing me again.

The son:
So go to the dentist. Oh, look, did you see that?

The father:

What?

The son:
They're showing the demonstrations in Moscow. Gorby's just--

The telephone:
Rrring.. rrring.. rrring.. rrring.. rrring.. rrring..

The father:
Can't you pick it up?

The son:
Why don't you pick it up yourself since you're sitting next to it?

(New York, February 1990)

THE TYSON'S SPHERE

[During their chancy investigations in their domain of the Elementary, the X'arg-G'zunn-K'nxps (In Argarkic: **Those Who Are Satisfied to Look Without Touching But Who Always End Up Breaking Something Without Meaning it**) ended up in a Parisian bistro, "Chez Loulou," near the Bassin de la Villette, between the Ricquet and Crimée metro stations. Why not there since they had nothing else to look at and listen to at the moment? But if you looked at what the Jumbo-Jet cargos, eager for exoticism, had done to the Place du Tertre, in Montmartre, or to the Café de Flore near St Germain-des-près, you would soon have an idea of what had to happen. While watching, the X'arg-G'zunn-K'nxops accessed the primary stage and, through downward causation... but rather, let's listen.]

***

"... Sochaux against Rennes, and on their home field to boot, you'll see what I mean. Look, that don't mean anything since *their space is a function of the energy* of the kind of bumpkins they have on their team, huh? Only goddam arabs, I'm telling you. Anyway, this is not saying anything against being a racist. I'm not a racist, you know me. But when you see that, *life that always tends to escalate toward higher stages of organization in order to, by creating ever more varied material supports, diversify its potential forms of manifestation,* when you see what's goin'on, you gotta be a little bit of a racist, even if you're not. Also, listen: as you just said before, *organic matter having acquired more free will than inert matter which, in turn, appears under already more varied forms than gaseous or liquid matter, for instance,* you can't stop immigration. Even le Pen can't. Hey, Loulou, speaking of liquid matter, get us another round, would ya? We're gonna fuckin' dry in here. *Therefore, the increasing level of entropy eventually allows varieties of life forms, always more flexible to the catalysis of a cosmic software which would pre-exist, like, say, a "blueprint" of the Universe.* No. he's pitch black and he's a heavyweight. No, he's a middle-weight, you gotta be kidding! How much you wanna bet? Hey, I know what I'm talking about. My brother works next to the Palais des sports of La Villette and he'll tell ya for sure that *we'll eventually realize that everything we see as natural in the universe is in fact artificial, just the creation of preceding cycles of organization toward consciousness and intelligence, themselves already artificially wrought.* Sure, maybe your brother knows. But I'm tellin' ya he don't know every damn thing. Because, according to him, *everything that seems artificial to a species would therefore only be what it has itself created artificially in order to evolve, and what predates it would seem natural to it.* Come on. Full life size. I saw him in the flesh, just like I see you here, Dédé. But you know what? There's no two ways about it. He doesn't look like T.V. I mean, he doesn't look like *on* TV. That's for damn sure. He is less of a brick shit house even than Marcel. Bullshit. *You can bring each of them here and look at them, but only in turn. You couldn't ever see both of them at the same time.* Marcel and him, I mean, see? Go see for yourself. No way, he's damn less of a brick shit-house than Marcel. Ask Loulou. Huh, Loulou? All I know is you *can't predict, at the same time, two fundamentally incompatible evolutive functions of the same reality.* A phone? Go ahead, buddy. Ah! It's fucking pouring again. You're gonna waddle like ducks, guys. Look here: he's got it right, for sure. I don't mean you're stupid. Nothing like that. I mean it's because of his cerveberal waves. *Waves...* You know what I mean? And if one chooses to consider his *wave-function*, a single player of a soccer team can find himself everywhere and at anytime on the field, right? Jeeesus fuck! He's really thinking this morning, Riri. Hear that? Wow! shit! Hey, listen to that! Look, on the other hand, *if one considers the hypothetical human settlements of the future, stationed at the Lagrange Point, when the "here and now" of a natural system of organization has engendered an enormous artificial network "living" through all the available vectors of energy,* that'll be much better but it ain't no worse. And you know, he's not wrong either. There's some people that are gifted for languages. It's called "the gift for languages." Like in the Bible. Because, like they say... Hey, say something in English, huh? Try "Ricard." How do you say "Ricard," huh? Come on, say it in Argarkic, see? Well, even though they say it, it's not like us. Yet, *those are contradictory and complementary expression* of the same thirst. Ask Loulou, who knows Arabic. Hey, Loulou, how d'you say "Ricard" in Arabic? Seventy-two francs for the three rounds, sweethearts. And if you go further, they could even end up with *the construction of a "Dyson Sphere," i.e., an artificial sphere built by an intelligent species around its mother-star in order to store and use the entire radiation from the star like* words you can't think about *a huge "inside out" planet with a* goal area of *several trillions of square miles, where no energy would be wasted during* the game. It's like what they're talking about: solar energy. Look, come on, look at Mike Tyson. Now, this guy, let me tell ya somethin': guys like that, I mean, if you take them apart, *having in mind to obtain a maximum amount of information on one or the other,* they're okay guys. Sure, they're black, but they're okay, I mean, they just don't use their strength. It's just like *night which is black, as it happens, thanks to a lack of energy in the Big Bang.* And look at Loulou. He's a nice guy, too. He's an Arab but he's a nice guy. But if white folks see Loulou, at night, in the metro, they're gonna say "careful, an Arab," and they're gonna think... See what I mean? *Consequently, there is an intrinsic uncertainty regarding his reality.* You can trust Loulou, though. Look at me.

I'd leave my paycheck right here on the bar. It's even safer than the bank. Right, Loulou? *When the computerized databanks have supplanted the individual memory, there will be an integral constituent, a sort of global reptilian cortex containing the necessary data for the basic reflexes of a new species so* they won't pick up all the penalty shots, right? And *the artificial networks are the necessary hardware for storing the potential instinct of a living entity which is in the process of organizing and constructing itself. And the complicated technology that it will depend on will therefore seem "natural" to the entity, since this technology will be the very fabric of its genes.* Look, it sure don't bother me at all that there's guys around that I don't understand. Come on, if they don't talk the same, it's because we're not the same. That's it. Our *individuality is still well defined despite the fact that the procedure of erosion of all discrepancies tends to accelerate.* That's why. How do you expect all them people to talk the same when they ain't the same? Come on, *the highest levels are just primary since it is their consciousness which determines the elementary.* Another drop of white wine, buddy? Come on, you aren't gonna quit, are you? Hey, don't you see it's because he wants to leave us and drink by himself like a Jew at Paula's instead? Leave him alone. Are you kidding? I knew a Jewish priest, once. Well, those kinds of guys, they're priests, but not when it comes to booze. Not when it comes to chicks either, I'm telling you. Go see for yourself. The guy fucked all the whores around Pigalle, he told me. *Superimposed but potentially complementary.* That's all I'll tell ya. Look, for me, It's like the Arabs. They got a lot of broads just because they're fuck-addicted. They don't drink but they fuck, those dudes. Not so dumb, Ah! It's already something they got in *the way of permanence toward which the supra-individual functions of life seem to tend.* Hey, by the way, how do you say "fuck" in arabic, Loulou? Loulou? He won't answer you. He's too polite. Even if he is *at the center of reality and that it is he who creates it.* But I know how they say. They say "Nadine Bébèque." "Nadine bébèque"? That doesn't mean "fuck," it means other things around it, dude. Not just "fuck." Anyway, whatever you say, hell, it's always the same fuckin' story. The thing is, I mean, it's racist bullshit. We'd better stick together and share the booze to smooth out the edges! Because *the data collected by a more and more numerous, therefore more and more organized and specialized society, has already reached a stage where the individual cannot suffice onto himself.* Yup... But when you see Arabs and blacks that are racists even though they don't need people to be racist... Yep, but there's Arabs that are all right and French who are fuckin' assholes. That, I gotta say. You can't be afraid to say that, whether you're French or not. And look, if you want to go further, a man *is only complete when coupled to a huge organized structure. He can no longer rely on his individual brain to exist within the* playing team. And they're not the only ones. If you follow that line of thought, Platini himself isn't French, either, even though he's white. But it's not as if he was Arab. That's the difference, there. People, I mean, they see Platini and they think that he's white. All that because they *create his reality according to the image they have of him.* However, he ain't French, Platini. And saying that, they're racist even though they're not. Hey, what bullshit are you giving us, man? He's French, Platini. Careful, *according to the new paradigm,* he has a Pollack name but he's French, Platini. Wanna bet? Here, ask my brother-in-law. He'll tell ya that *left to himself, the individual is no longer anything. A man, in primitive communities, used to make his own knife or javelin before using it, but how many of them are capable of producing cars, computers, laser-beam cash registers and* Ricard? How do you make Ricard? Tell me if you know. You know my brother-in-law? Well, he knows somebody at the supermarket he works who knows Platini. Just ask him for me, and ask him how they make Ricard, too, while you're at it. Well, Mimi, I gotta go. That's not all, you know, my boss, I mean, he's watching *since the data storage will allow, in the future, groups dispersed throughout the Galaxy and, therefore deprived of the possibility to immediately communicate among themselves, to continue to develop, from an already acquired data base, further arcane of consciousness,* as they say. All that because there's some who have black skin or Arab skin. Well, for them, too, whites are not blacks. There's whites on the one side and blacks on the other side and that's the way it is. You can't get away from it. In a *quantum system, you have to chose, in the first place, the function to measure.* If you look at the blacks thinking they're white, it's just like they wasn't blacks even if they aren't white. The guy who's white or who's not black becomes white or Arab, and so on. *In such a system, the existence of the particular is defined by the whole. It has no intrinsic reality independently from the consciousness of the observer who happens to be real only because of* what they call the racial difference. It's called the racial difference. There's no other way to put it, it's called racial difference. And racial difference, check it out, well... it's just different. *Like for mathematics and* the code of public drunkenness, by the way, *it is a structural relationship, and a logical one at that, that transcends the properties of beings taken individually.* Look, it don't mean nothing. Take Mike Tyson again, right? He's black and yet, he speaks English. So? Brits aren't black, though! Because he's American and it's not the same, hey, bozo! *There is an interference between the software and the hardware.* Ask my kid daughter who speaks English in the sixth grade, ask her. Well, she'd say that it's not the same. If you say "yes" in English, they don't understand, those yankees. I mean, they understand "yes," sure, but when it's some other stuff, they don't. Now, try to figure out why by yourself. *If the observer's consciousness could understand the paradox, it would mean that it could take all the probable certainties into account and define in itself the Great Equation of the Universe.* Yup... Go talk to Tyson. Even your kid daughter wouldn't understand him. It's even harder than Arabic. They write it the same as French but to talk, it's harder than Arabic. Come on. Show him the bottle of Ricard, to *Dyson,* and he'll know what you're talking about. Right, Loulou? Isn't that right that *when, say, a "yakishitronstrellung," for example, has become a basic tool to new "primitive" groups, just as the stone axe was a basic tool to ancient communities, and when each individual is able to build one for himself from some self-reproductive machinery that has become interface between him and the pre-existent, just what the sensory organs were for a long time,* I mean, if you show the bottle of Ricard to Tyson, he won't piss into it? It's an example that he doesn't understand but that he knows. *It's also a mental event that cannot be explained by material constituents.* That's what they call instinct. He don't drink, I tell ya. Ask those dudes if he drinks. Ask all those dudes, like Rocheteau, or Platini, if they drink. Ask Hinaut, he'll tell you. Before the race, you're better off forgetting *that the notions of space and time are two aspects of the same event, however fundamentally incompatible.* He'll tell you that. Even these champions, they're like the priest that you were talking about. Worse. They shouldn't drink or fuck before the *experiment.* Otherwise, they'd have to beat it *in order to participate in the pursuit of the ultimate identification of the Universe by Itself.* It's like the Jews. They're not Arabs. All right, they're white but they don't look like Arabs. Meaning that *everything is only a copy of the consciousness of the observer.* Let me tell you why you can't be a racist against the Jews: because of Hitler. I personally have nothing against jews. *It is necessary that there exists, at the base, a macroscopic concept before the properties of the microcosm assume a meaning.* Me, too, I know a Jewish guy. Not a priest but a civil Jew. Well, if you'd see him, you'd say he's not Arab. These guys, they're just like you and me. Except if you pull down their pants, hey, babe! Ah! Well... I tell you it's *a paradox. The macrocosm is constituted of elements of the microcosm but it seems that the microcosm needs the macrocosm to define it.* You can't make me get rid of that idea. *And the macrocosm has to make a selection as to the line of experiment to follow up.* Anyway, when you got to take line 7 at the métro station Stalingrad, and you see that it's not a direct ride, and you have to transfer at Barbès where it's full of Arabs, then you say to yourself that they have *acceded to the primary stage and,* despite all the "causal entries" he was talking about, you don't get off there, even if it saves you changing *the behavior of an entity from a preceding domain.* The Jews, you know, it's a religion. It's not the same as if it was only because of the *principle of uncertainty, of the undetermined.* What about the Arabs? Isn't that a religion, too? Even though *it is true that all the established religions have only managed to bastardize all the mystiques,* because, look at this guy... er... there, what's his name? You know who I mean, this Hindu who is a Brit and whose ass they're after at Rominet's, referring to a book that says that the Arab Jesus Christ was fuckin' around with the Virgin's girlfriends or something like that? Well, *it is apparent that any state of affairs can evolve anywhere in the universe without one being able to recognize it as such* but didn't you hear on TV? Hey Loulou, am I right? Oh, you know, all I can say about it, *it is that one cannot predict the evolution of a system since one can't simultaneously define the position and the momentum of a constituting element of the micro-world.* Talking about the Virgin Mary, incidentally, we were at Notre-Dame Cathedral yesterday, because *of the answer obtained that always depends on the question* of the kid who had to write a paper about a Gothic cathedral. Well, there's no telling there either. Even if you're not religious, each time you look at something like that, even though *one's mere presence as an observer modifies it somewhat,* say whatever you want, you'll find it's nicer than the Montparnasse Tower. Well, I gotta get going, guys. See you tonight. Hey, don't forget to watch the game on TV, Riri! We'll *always see each other according to another vector of probabilities.* Did you do your card, by the way? No, I don't play sports lotto anymore. It's just like me. I still do the "tiercé" but I've given up on lotto. See you, guys. And don't forget *that the wave function disappears to accommodate the direction of the experiment and that several realities co-exist as for the result of* the game. I bet you Sochaux will get their asses beat because Rennes will win, *and in this case, the supporters of one or the other team participating more actively in the actualization of one or the other outcome of the score, one could go as far as considering the event "game" as a primary constituent of their own consciousness. For the same reason, if one chooses to measure either the position of the ball at any given moment, or the momentum of the same ball at any given point, or, in other words, as long as the global consciousness of the supporters tends to make either the ball-particle function or the shoot-wave function collapse, one always reaches a point where one has to start from a limited series of observable quantities and therefore, erase the outcome that one has chosen not to take into account from one's own sequence of "real" events. Godammit! Will something happen, finally, in this story?"*

* * *

[Of course, the last sentence is due to the fact that you read up to the end and that you ended up, as the reader and, therefore, as an observer, modifying, in turn, the sequence of events. It is no longer the fault of the X'arg-G'zunn R'nxops. They should not be blamed for everything that happens, just like we should not blame only the American tourists when we get our bill at the restaurant "*La mère Catherine.*" There are a few Basques roaming the neighborhood, too. Anyway, you also succeeded in making the author lose his plot. Now, he is utterly disgusted with the story and he does not feel like finishing.]

(Paris, March 1989)

THE GREAT ATTRACTOR

ACT 1

(With the father, the mother, the son, the TV,
the walkman, and the Omniscient)

The Omniscient:
The father is reading *Newsweek.* The son is listening to the walkman. The mother is watching TV.

The father:
Hey, honey, did you read this here in *Newsweek*?

The mother:
Can you wait for a commercial? I'm watching *L.A. Law.*

The TV:
Fast, easy. Now, you can lose weight and continue to binge, with Dexetrin...

The father:
Now, may I? Okay, this is it: according to a survey conducted by some university, 55% of Americans ignore the fact that the earth revolves around the sun in one year. Another larger percentage don't know why there are seasons, etc., etc. Don't you find this scary? Four hundred years after Galileo? [1]

The mother:
Why are you trying to put me down? You know very well that I didn't know that either. Sorry, I never took astronomy in college. Now, if you're trying to denigrate my education again, this is not what I call a conversation. All you ever do is lecture me. Am I that stupid? Don't I have a degree from Columbia University?

1. Authentic: see the 4/9/90 issue of Newsweek.

The father:

Some degree! A Master's in Business Administration. So much for general culture. But aside from your curriculum, haven't you ever been curious about all this? Haven't you ever wondered beneath a starry sky?

The son:

Enough, you two! You're not going to start bickering, are you?

The father:

I can't help it. It pisses me off. Look at this: our laughing stock in residence, Dan Quayle, vice-president of the United States of America and chairman of the National Space Council, said: *"Why send astronauts to Mars? We have seen pictures where there are canals, we believe, and water. If there's water, that means there's oxygen. If oxygen, that means we can breathe. And therefore, from the information we have right now, Mars clearly offers the best opportunity to see if a man or a woman can be able to survive on that planet."*[2] Well, after that, we might as well give up. Give me the walkman, would you?

The walkman:

Every day of your life, you'll keep a planetary conscience if you use the "Earth Day" stamps on all your correspondence.

The father:

Come on. Easy and fast, as usual. You just need to give your credit card number. Now, let me tell you: as long as they spend their time making a population of zombies, like your mother, believe that they can feel good about themselves because they possess a bunch of credit cards, they make it easy for the Donald, the rain forest developers, the vendors of diet duck à l'orange, the--

The TV:

... If you want to be number one, call your Toyota dealer.[3]

The father:

I never took astronomy in college either! But did I have to attend a graduate writing workshop to learn how to write postcards to Auntie? I learned all sorts of things because I was CURIOUS, period.

2. Somebody wanted to correct the English mistakes after me, of course, but I was just quoting.
3. All those TV commercials are authentic, of course. I couldn't have invented them.

The mother:

What you don't seem to understand is that I'm working twelve hours a day. So, when I have some time to myself, I'd rather not spend it pondering about obscure, weird, and profound concepts.

The father:

The yearly rotation of the earth, a profound concept? What about the rest of the heavenly show? Wouldn't it be more relaxing than all those gunshots in *Kojak*? You could at least watch Channel Thirteen! But nay, you'd rather clog your brain with soap trash like you clutter the apartment with art-deco junk, wouldn't you?

The mother:

If only you took care of some of the business! Who did the tax return this year again? Who spent two weeks on it?

The son:

Would you drop it, please? Pfffff...

The mother:

You shut up! Your father's not the one who deals with the unpleasant aspects of daily life! Sure, he can make himself look good. He's got time to spend watching the stars with you (see DEUS EX LATRINA). In the meantime--

The TV:

The Hubble Space Telescope has been placed today in low orbit around the earth...

The father:

By the way, do you know what the purpose of this telescope is? Wait: do you know what an *orbit* is in the first place? Come on, just think a little... I'm not asking you, say... what a "*strange attractor*" is. I wouldn't go that far. No, just a stupid orbit.

The Omniscient:

AAAAHHHHHH! Here we are! The transition is a little bit crooked but here we are. Here I am now. So, we saw that nothingness was not as much nothing as it appeared to be. (see BEING AND NOTHINGNESS) Well, chaos is not as chaotic as it seemed, either. Chaos was fooling us. Chaos does not deserve his name, any more than nothingness. Chaos appears chaotic only because its organizational level is so sophisticated that our reductionist minds are incapable of reducing it. But chaos is not real chaos. Chaos hides an unbelievable propensity for order.

The mother:

I knew a strange attractor once in my life, and that's enough, believe me.

The Omniscient:

Well... I said that chaos... er.. I mean, in the most chaotic configurations... er... such as, say, the weather patterns, the shapes of living creatures... I mean animals, plants, the works... Chaos lurks everywhere, in the fractal geometry of the coastlines, in the shape of the clouds, in the fluctuations of the stock exchange, in the whirl of the ocean waves, in the periodicity of the drops formation at the nozzle of leaky faucet, or what have you, I mean, radically everywhere... er... As it happens, nothing in nature seems to obey linear equations or Euclidean geometry, but we begin to be able, thanks to the computation of a great number of parameters, to recognize a natural tendency toward a quasi-repetition of schemes, of trans-dimensional shapes, of nested dissimilarities, which were given the name of "strange attractors." And those "strange attractors" give shape to chaos. The existence of these "strange attractors" (or para-linear fixations) in the midst of the chaotic mess would tend to let us think that the forecasting of all the periodicities would be possible if we could feed into a computer the necessary infinity of basic data in less time than the expected result would take to manifest itself in reality. But it is a lost cause, since, even with the fastest computer, several thousands of years would be necessary to determine tomorrow's weather with only approximate accuracy. All in all, it is enough to know that there is not only one linear sequence of values ranging from negative infinity to positive infinity and passing by zero. But let us imagine this bi-dimensional sequence as a line taut within a tri-dimensional space, which means that there exists an infinite number of numerical anomalies, the so-called parallel universes of each number, left to be considered by mathematicians. In other words, what we see everywhere is but the intersection of the shapes of chaos. Hence, our ludicrous "ideal" geometrical shapes, such as our architectural creations, which exist nowhere in nature. Follow me? Okay. Now, if we consider the Mandelbrot set, or the Cantor dust, or the Koch snowflake, or the Sierpinski carpet, or the Menger sponge, or the Lorentz watermill, or the Smale horseshoe, etc., we will note that infinity can be contained in a finite space and, consequently, that the limits or borderlines of various objects and living organisms are never perfectly defined at the microcosmic scale. The same goes for various phase transitions which--

The author:

Hey, Omniscient! Come to my office, now!

***

ACT 2

(With the author and the Omniscient)

The author:
As you can see, the circumstances... I mean, the conversation doesn't carry the action. Once again, you shot off without any regard to the on-going conflict. Now you're in a mess with your chaos. Look at the readers: all they want to know is if it will end in a murder before Kojak shows up, or if the protagonists will make peace before the end of the episode. The rest is over their head. Once again, you're going to find yourself alone on the stage. Is that what you want?

The Omniscient:
It is your fault. You'd better choose another formula. If I have to wait for a family scene to matter-of-factly jump from mundane crap to meta-chaotic speculations, while maintaining credibility of the action and the characters, it is a lost cause. It was easier when there were only the father, the son and me, a sort of mythical trinity, as it were. Now, throughout the episodes, they have become too human, and their world too real. This is exactly what they tried to do, on TV, with *Beauty and the Beast*, and it did not work. They merely succeeded in disappointing a small segment of elite viewers, while not contenting those who'd still rather watch *L.A. Law*.

The author:
What are you talking about? *You* are the one who spoiled everything by introducing the mother to the cast, don't you remember? Yes, on the couch, in front of the TV, in SCHROEDINGER'S CATNAP.

The Omniscient:
Hell no! This is not true! *You* are the one who forced me to talk about her in CONFIRMATION! Because of the lack of characterization and all that.

The author:
You have a point, I must admit... At any rate, it's become too difficult to ignore her now. Look, even Dan Quayle, despite all his canals on Mars, didn't forget to mention a woman in his speech. To speak of "man" as a species has become sexist, you know that.

The Omniscient
By the way, while you mention it, don't forget to call the walkman the walkperson from now on. But back to chaos. Chaos is the topic of the day

and, in the midst of chaos, male and female principles exist only at the stage of the improbable and the indiscernible. Where does the dimensional limit of living beings and their sexual organs exactly lie within the fractal indefiniteness?

The author:
Okay. Go ahead. But once again, you're on your own.

***

ACT 3

(With the Omniscient, the Omniscient and the Omniscient)

Him:
So, as I was saying... Er... well, after the paradigm shift that occurred at the beginning of this century due to the formulation of the relativistic theories, and after the other shift toward the middle of this same century, spurred by Schrödinger's cat paradox (see CATNAP of the same) and quantum physics, the new science of chaos is, nowadays, in the process of upsetting all the dogma of scientific thought. All in all, er... It's no longer a matter of... I mean... At the origin of everything that takes shape and manifests itself as such, er... there would be some of these *strange attractors* or, to put it another way, some schemes of those shapes imprinted in the space time continuum and according to which the random parameters of chaos would gravitate. I don't know if I'm making myself clear, but I think I am in a position to reveal that randomness itself does not manifest itself at random. Randomness is nothing but the ultimate manifestation of a universal mathematical order. What we call disorder only exists in the hidden recesses of an order that we are unable to perceive. I must apologize for pounding on you in such a lecturing manner, but, before going further, I would like you to consider, say, the complicated shape of a tree. *(Would-you-please-show-the-first-slide.)* Yeah... Here we go. Look: isn't this a manifestation of randomness and, at the same time, of a recurrent determinism? *(Would-you-please-show-the-second-slide.)* Now, look: in this second tree which, as a matter of fact, is just another maple tree of the same group, not a branch, not a twig, not a leaf, not a vein on a leaf, reproduces the exact pattern of any twig, leaf, or vein from the previous maple tree. For, verily I say unto you, ladies and gentlemen, nature is no Xerox machine! However, would we be able to tell either of those trees apart from memory after having observed them for just a few seconds? What looks more like a maple tree than another maple tree? If he could have done it, Tom Thumb would not have needed to strew his way with pebbles. And what about our features, our bodies? What difference, say, between you, dear madam (yes, you there, in

the first row, with the vast and overstretched blue polyester slacks), and, say, Marla Maples? Oh, no, I do not mean to offend you. Because the answer is: none. No difference. Not for us, of course, conditioned as we are by the cover photos of *Cosmopolitan*, but for, say, the green tentacled Martian with peduncled genitals who would meet Marla and you one after the other. He, most probably, could not tell you apart, because he would see both of you as two similar holograms of the same strange attractor presiding over human morphology. Yes, between you and Marla Maples, some minute alteration of some basic parameter has sufficed, because of sensitive dependence of global phenomena (i.e. you and Marla) on original conditions (say, the habit that I bet your mother had (and not Marla's) to feed you ice-cream cones and hot-dogs when you were throwing tantrums, to create the difference. But still, who among us could clearly differentiate between two Japanese tourists getting off the same tour bus at Rockefeller Plaza, other than by taking a peek at the brand name of their respective cameras? Because Japanese tourists, although globally sketched according to the same strange attractor as we, are sketched according to a slightly different gamut of parameters! Therefore, you may only see exact duplication and uniformity where there is full-fledged chaos and, beyond, order and repetitiveness, since neither you nor the Japanese have tentacles or peduncles like our Martian observer. Now, you can see that it follows in the same manner with our ideas, our concepts, our actions. Look at the characters of our story: the father and the mother apparently speak about different things, but each of them is only seeking to prove to each other that he or she is wrong, intellectually inferior, functionally disabled, etc. In fact, their thought processes stem from the same strange attractor: the one that pushes individuals to fight for the survival of the fittest, and hence, to the survival of their own views. (Since, in the present case, their civilized facade of sapient individuals will prevent them from killing each other as long as they do not shoot cocaine). Like Gorby in Lithuania, they are content with gritting their teeth and cutting pipe-lines, while others, still the victim of their deng-xiaopignian cortex, might pull out their artillery. But in a forest, what other way does the tree have to smother its neighbors than its roots and branches? Now, with your agreement, we are about to conclude with a short question and answer period.

***

ACT 4

(With the father, the son, the mother, the walkperson, the TV, the telephone, and the siren)

The TV
(*Through Kojak's voice*):
You're under arrest. You have the right to remain silent. All that you could say could be held against you.

The father:
You know at least what Galileo said after he retracted his theories in front of the Inquisition, don't you? What?! You never heard "*Eppur, si muove*"? Maybe you thought he was talking about his freshly dead grandma?

The walkperson:
(*Through Sinatra's voice*):
Strangers in the night, exchanging glances, wondering in thrrrrw nirht, whooot werhrro throoooo hrroo...

The telephone:
Drrrrr..... Drrrr..... Drrrr..... Drrrr.....   Drrrr..... D..

The mother:
Hello?

The son:
The walkperson's batteries are out. Are there any spare ones?

The siren (*From the street*):
uuuu .... uuuuUUUU .... uuuuuuuUUUUUUUUuu .... UUuu ... uuUUUUUU . UUUuuuuuUUUUUUUUuu......

The Omniscient:
Yes, yes, I know. I am not in the cast here but nevertheless, I want you to notice in passing the strange attractor which is hiding in the modulation, although apparently chaotic, of the sirens of Manhattan.

The TV:
The man on the right is brushing his teeth. The man on the left is using PLAX!

The mother:
No, thank you. No, no, I don't need another credit card. No... I thank you very much. No... No, I assure you, I... No...No, no, no, and the hell with you!

The telephone:
CLACK.

The father:

... and today is "Earth Day," and 55% of those zombies...

The son:

Leave her alone, would you, and tell me where you put the new batteries.

The mother:

By the way, if you expect me to cook tonight, you're nuts. You'd better go to Burger King.

The TV:

The Donald and Ivana, both shrouded in a lavish foliage of $1000 bills, sent their message to earth from the Taj Mahal in Atlantic City.

***

ACT 5

(With the author, the Omniscient,
and finally, the Great Attractor)

The author:

Okay. Where are we now?

The Omniscient:

I cannot really say. I am lost. I think we should ask the *Great Attractor*. He is the boss of all the strange attractors, the One according to Whom they all exist, without ever having to pass by the same parameters.

The author:

You mean... God?

The Omniscient:

Don't you dare! I'm an atheist, sir.

The author:

Uh... Hey you! Great Attractor! Can you tell us where we're heading?

The Great Attractor:

Hushhh... I work in such mysterious ways... Otherwise, what would I need time for?

(New York, April 1990)

CHALLENGES

April 3rd, 2092.

Tuni Horzon would have liked to say something to her husband Paul.

She had already had a hard time figuring out what was wrong with him. Now that she had found it, she would have liked to share her concern with Paul. Especially after figuring out what her concern was.

She would have liked to tell him that she could no longer bear to see him walk around in the nude in the apartment; the mere sight of his obese presence was the worst putoff when it came to the accomplishment of her marital duty.

Just that.

But Tuni was feeling guilty about thinking that way. No wonder since her great grandfather could only get to say more or less the same thing to his wife, and only during a marital therapy session, at a time when the cover pages of *Playboy* and *Penthouse* still displayed bodies and skins that could awaken all the guardian demons in regular people's mind.

But in 2092, it had finally been recognized that in spite of all the gyms, jacuzzi, liquid diets, suction, etc, regular people needed much less effort and persistence to adopt a gargoyle look than the look of a Greek god. Even fashion holozines had resorted to show only graceless and even distorted bodies, or "gorgeously challenged persons," in order to protect the good self-image of their subscribers.

When he was in the bathroom, Paul leafed through pornholozines in which the "playmates of the week" would have, a century earlier, been shown only in specialized journals distributed in orthopedic surgery wards.

Tuni knew that Paul himself probably resented her as much for her arachnaean, sinewy silhouette, especially when he had to appear with her at telelink parties with friends.

But it was not her fault. She binged as much as she could but it was in her nature. She had been taken for too many rides on the *schoollink*, where they called her "Brigitte Bardot" or "Sophia Loren" in reference to such legendary icons of ancient cinema. Once, a boy had even called her "Venus." She had no idea who Venus was but the boy's disgusted scowl had made her cry all night.

Later, if Paul had agreed to date her, it was just because she was squint-eyed. It had been a long time since they would operate on children for strabism, or for any congenital defect. Children should not be deprived of their chance to access any status as a "gorgeously challenged person."

In addition to Paul's attention, her strabism had brought Tuni a card of "parallaxedly challenged person," which made her unsueable in case she caused a traffic accident.

To get back to what Tuni had just figured out: she had been rummaging in a dusty suitcase forgotten in the family storage space on the 192nd floor of a storage building nearby, and she had found an old video movie rated XXX which had belonged to her great grandfather.

Her great grandfather had left only a videotheque and of course, without a VCR, she could not really watch the movie.

As for the books that her great grandfather had left, she could still leaf through them, turn the pages... But the problem with most of these books was that they contained not enough illustrations, and Tuni could read neither Spanish nor English.

Or, for that matter, any language transcribed in any alphabet or ideogram which they still used in her great grandfather's days.

Tuni couldn't read because teaching children how to read had been abandoned long before she was born, as soon as reading had been condemned as a eurocentrist activity; it could never be definitely proven that the inventors of the first alphabet, the Sumerians, were not Caucasians (or, as Caucasians themselves had finally succeeded in making the non-Caucasians call them, "people of pallor") or that Gutenberg had brought back the idea of the printing press from a voyage to Cipango.

Not to mention the influence of the "scheduledly challenged" (former "workaholics") activists, who had no time to read, or the all-powerful and already long-established "synapsedly challenged" (former "mentally retarded" or medieval "idiots"). These groups had kept their status of oppressed minority only by tampering with statistics or by letting statistics be tampered with by agents working for other oppressed minorities such as the "gravitationally challenged" (former "overweight people") to which Paul belonged.

The use of a combination of cryptographic codes, sign language, Braille and all sorts of symbols had to be adopted for the keyboards and the menus of the link, and for all documents including doctoral theses. But it was overall very confusing and children still spent a good deal of time getting used to it. Anyway, they were not, as before, compelled to "do reading." They just were encouraged to "contemplate non-oral expression."

The results were rather encouraging. While Tuni's grandfather had renounced all reading after he had been taken aback, in the ninth grade, by a *Hamlet* in comic strips, David, Tuni's and Paul's son, could decipher "sequences of non oral expression" as complex as snatches of "Rambo 5" script in his "Selected Classical Pieces" textlog.

Audio books had also been discarded under the influence of the "acoustically challenged" pressure groups.

Therefore, with the videotape from her great grandfather at a time when you could only find out-of-order and overpriced VCR's in antiques shops, Tuni was left with only one alternative: to look at the picture on the box.

Which picture represented a youngish, muscular, and spidery woman like herself momentarily stuck in a status of "rectally challenged persons."

To get back to Tuni's ambivalence about speaking out to Paul, she knew that if she ever dared, Paul would see it as an act of aggression toward his self-esteem, a wound he would only gradually heal through a long series of sessions in group esteemotherapy.

Esteemotherapy had replaced psychotherapy as soon as people had realized that the former term had a twofold discriminatory character: first, because of its Greek and thus, clearly eurocentrist assonance, and also because of its very etymological meaning: *treatment* of the psyche or the mind. Toward the end of the last century, after the "shrink boom" of the 60's to 80's, psychotherapists, logists and chiatrists of all venues had seen a sharp decline in their practice. Less and less people, otherwise praised to the skies by their recommendation letters, professionally crafted resumes, and various diplomas and trophies, were ready to accept the idea that there could be something wrong with their heads.

So, if Tuni had decided to speak, it would have to be one thing or the other: her discriminatory remark would entitle Paul to the more or less temporary status of "erectally challenged person" (formerly "impotent"), or it would trigger in him a response that might push him to submit Tuni to what would leave her with no other alternative, in order to protect her self-esteem, than to have the results duly expertised on the link in view of her access to a status of "marito-genito-relationally molested person" (former "conjugal rapees").

In 2092, in order not to look "genito-relationally incorrect", a person could only approach another according to a ritual which obeyed ten commandments that could be stated as follows:

1. *Thou shallt guard thyself from revealing the something at the back of thy mind.* (Here, one will note that this first commandment, if applied to the letter, would relieve the person from having to submit to the next nine. But even in 2092, the nature of the human soul had remained what it used to be. Despite the tendency to let the body yield to the entropy of natural charm, and despite the adoption, for all sexes, of a dress code which had inherited, at the same time, the Brooks Brothers' cut and the K-Mart texture [the whole collection coming in the "rainy day in Pittsburgh" shades], only a minority of people could yet shun all the trappings of human seduction. In Tuni's great grandfather's time already, a number of racing rats from Wall Street and Rockefeller Center had resorted to only speak about sex in singles bars after they had made their first million dollars, paid off their

student loans and bought their first BMW's. So, in 2092, if the latter bunch was definitely beyond the risk of love and passion, some others, like Tuni and Paul, had not been able to resist the need to show, at some time or other, a little bit of weirdness in shedding for a moment the metaphorical rectal prop which, throughout their lives, would prevent them from straying from the charted verticality of Human Relations.)

2. *Thou shallt not reject anybody who has betrayed for you the something in the back of his/her mind.* (Here, one should not be mistaken. We are far from the "free love" of the time of Tuni's great grand father's youth, when it was only a matter of giving way to mutual desires. In 2092, the trick was more to avoid upsetting people and causing resentment in a potentially overwhelming minority of "primary concupisciously challenged people" (former "seducer"). The feeling of lust from the part of the concupiscor being a challenge for the concupiscee, the latter could just as well in turn apply for a status of "secondary concupisciously challenged person" (formerly "seduced"). Which generated another sort of conflict that could only be settled by obeying the third commandment.)

3. *Thou shallt express (but not too much, though) your jealousy to the other thus enticed.* (In other words, prove adequate gratitude once faced with one's own access to a status of "primary genito-relationally challenged" [formerly "cheated on" or "cuckold"]. On the other hand, express enough jealousy to spare the other thus seduced the status of "person deprived of the primary genito-relational challenge" [formerly "dumped"]. Since a majority of people could not achieve this balance, each of the partners often ended up with the benefits of a status of "conjugally" or "concubinely challenged person" [formerly "separated" or "divorced"], or even, sometimes, of "vitally challenged person" [formerly "deceased"].

4. *Thou shallt never approach thy partner without witnesses.* (Not because of the tyranny of some "Big Voyeur," but so that neither of the two could afterwards abusively claim a status of "genito-reputationally challenged person" [formerly "sexually harassed" and, even more formerly, of "bothered"]. With witnesses on the link [whom should be notified in advance so that they could be watching], the two partners were left with an equal chance to prove their eligibility to the status in case of legal suit from the other.)

5. *Before the sequential genito-relational challenge, or former "intercourse," thou shallt take the time to adjust a means of protection.* (No longer because of AIDS or as a birth control measure. In 2092, these two dangers were no longer feared. AIDS had disappeared under the presidency of Dan Quayle [1996-2004 -- probably because of the promise he had made during his electoral campaign to be "the last human being to stand up alive against it if necessary"] and impregnation was totally monitored *in vitro* under medical surveillance in order to spare everybody, male and female, from finding

themselves "fetally challenged" for nine months. But this ritual saved an age old fragrance of risk, and, thus, of taken-up challenge.)

6. *During the sequential genito-relational challenge, thou shallt not suggest to your partner any particular motions.* (No longer because of the fear that the suggestion, like in more puritan times, were judged as perverted or degrading. Not even because it was forbidden to speak out of respect for the "vocally challenged" [former "dumb"] outside of their presence. But so as not to hurt the other's self-esteem in looking as though he/she did not know how to handle the situation.)

7. *Again during the sequential genito-relational challenge, thou shallt praise the deeds of thy partner, whether thou likest them or not.* (It was no longer enough to just randomly moan an groan things like "it's so good", "yes just like that", "do that again", "go on, go on" or "Oh Jesus." In 2092, the minutes of the sequential genito-relational challenge verbal proceedings were stored in the link's memory, just like the pattern responses to job interview questions used to be in manuals distributed at the end of college courses of study. The verbalization of those praises triggered a complete ceremonial of trophies and prizes. The trophies and prizes were automatically output by the link's terminals immediately after each verbal expression of passion. The more prolix the compliments, the more sumptuous the trophies and prizes, even more so than the letters of recommendation about the lesser of his professional achievements that Tuni's great grandpa used to collect. Thus, Tuni had made Paul -- and vice versa -- the nominee for a myriad of "recommendations for exceptional genito-relational services." Taking a look at them would have been a job of several months for anyone who would really have liked to know. These trophies were accompanied by holographic clips that were taken by the link at the moment of the celebrated prowess just like, in Tuni's great grandfather's days, other dear moments of life such as Aunt Julia blowing the candles of her birthday cake, the baby's first mouthful of soup on Dad's necktie or the same dad washing his new Acura, had been immortalized on video tapes.)

8. *At the end, thou shallt [but not too much, though] apply thyself to express thy ultimate bliss.* (Here again, be careful. There was no point to try not to disturb the neighbors any more. All apartments had become like island-universes where only the signals of the link penetrated and from where only they emanated. The trick was as always to boost one's partner's self-esteem and, at the same time, spare one's own. Not enough conviction in your voice and your partner could find him/herself on the "satisfactorily challenged" [formerly "disappointed"] roster; too much, and you could either condemn him/her to only rarely being able to equal his/her last performance or yourself, by reaching an intensity of expression that you would not be able to equal very often, to gradually lose confidence in your own capability to reach climax. Considering that many succeeded in not being taken by surprise only after a time-consuming mutual observation, this commandment

opportunely came in the way of the development of free passions as described in [2] and [3].)

9. *After the sequential genito-relational challenge, thou shallt [but not too much, though] express thy happy lassitude.* (The trick was here to flatter your partner's self-esteem by assuming a post-coital attitude that would reassure him/her about his/her expertise. Like in the old days, that would mainly translate into sighing, heavy eyelids, undone hairdo, lame duck gait, blurred speech, and so on. However, you also had to avoid challenging your partner "reputationally," that is, not to embarrass him or her in front of all the on-lookers [the witnesses on the link] by getting back too quickly to business as usual as if nothing had happened. And that was where the "not too much, though" takes on all its significance. You should not hurt the peepers on the link by showing a more blissful lassitude than theirs or their own partner's on similar occasions. Here again, the task was a delicate one which required that you kept under close scrutiny all the others' private challenges. In Tuni's great grandfather's days, only a few people in the limelight like Lady Di or the democrat candidates to the U.S. presidency were the target of such scrutiny, but in 2092, the link had made everyone the Gary Hart and the Bill Clinton of everyone else without, again, any real "Big Voyeur" around.)

10. *Finally, however and whenever possible, thou shallt only engage in onanism.* (Because, on the one hand, of the nine preceding commandments which, as one may realize, did not induce sharing with the others any more than, in Tuni's great grandfather's time, job interviews sometimes induced accepting a position in a multinational corporation, and, on the other hand, of the uselessness of the genito-relational challenge for procreation, sexual encounters between people had in fact become the secret garden of a minority of "virtuously challenged" persons [former "perverts" or "sexually obsessed"]. In 2092, those who could still find this enjoyable were those who, like Tuni and Paul, had the opportunity to play doctor before receiving their first trophy for "orgasm under pedagogical control" after the reception of their first "genital self-gratification kit" [which contained more gadgets and sensorial stimulation devices than, in their great grandparents' days, a sex-shop in Amsterdam and the neurology laboratories of the Massachusetts Institute of Technology combined.)

So, today, seeing Paul stark naked in front of her, Tuni would have rather obeyed the tenth commandment only.

Nobody would object to that, not even Paul, who, besides, was right this minute too engrossed with the rehearsal of his daily self-affirmation exercises in front of the tri-dimensional mirror.

These exercises consisted of a loud voice repetition of a check-list of all that he had to remain convinced was positive in his physical and moral personality, that is, except omission on his part of all the items that the personalized list established for him by the services of the Challenger General included up to that date.

This personalized list reflected the point of view of the concerned party, i.e., himself, while making all possible concessions to the Challenger General's point of view. Because of that, Paul's list made no mention of the perfect knowledge that he had acquired by himself of six foreign languages and Tuni's list didn't make any of her quasi-perfect body shape.

Paul had just reached the fifty-fourth affirmation on the list which consisted of repeating: "I have a rear end complex which merges with the back lower part of my thighs in a softly pendular continuum. And I know that Soft is Beautiful."

And this was indeed, among other particular motives of self-satisfaction for Paul, what deprived Tuni of any idea in the back of her mind regarding her husband. But this was also what she could never have said without running the additional risk of being accused of "morphofantasic fascism" or "revisionism."

Any individual accused of morphofantasic fascism or revisionism was bound to accomplish a more or less long-term service in esteemological assistance under the aegis of the Challenger General.

In Tuni's case, this service would consist of doing again and again her morphological self-critique in front of a local assembly of variously "gorgeously challenged" people in order to help them to acquire a better self-image by persuading them of the wrongness of her own revisionistic contours. For example, she would have to succeed in making several of the amoebic members of the group vomit at the sight of her small and firm breasts and her long, muscular, dancer's legs. Upon which Tuni would gain bonus points toward a status of "empathically rehabilitated" person.

Paul had once gone through a similar punishment but in another domain: he had been condemned to directing a color print photography workshop, just like his own great-grandpa had, in his days, directed a workshop in papyrus manufacturing in the Hamptons. Paul had to award trophy upon trophy to the authors of snapshots such as even his great-grandmother, who had never been able to use anything other than an "Instamatic," would not have had the nerve to keep in her photo album entitled "Passover in Monticello" or "Florida vacation at Aunt Julia's, 1992." It was because Paul had been convicted with "revisionism in graphical expression" after he had, by accident, taken a few more or less well exposed and well focused shots through the window of his apartment.

"By accident," because he had involuntarily left on the self-timer and the motor drive of the century-old "Olympus" camera he had just bought in an antique shop and negligently placed on the window sill while he was trying to decipher the attached user's manual.

But nobody ever believed it was an accident.

Speaking of photographs, what Tuni would never get to telling Paul either was that she could only fantasize successfully in front of a specific photograph of her great grandfather. That photo was an old beach snapshot where her elder, whose muscular and suntanned slimness was enlightened by a sunflower colored mini-string, was not in the least attempting to hide from the photographer the idea at the back of his mind.

The picture was not hanging on the dining room wall, of course not. Tuni kept it in a little box under her pillow where nobody, not even Paul, would search for it.

In 2092, it would not have occurred to anybody to search anybody else's belongings. Such a behavior would have been labelled as "secretario-relationally incorrect" and, furthermore, Paul would not have liked Tuni to ask him what was hidden in the little box under his own pillow.

In the little box under Paul's pillow, there was also a picture of Tuni's great grandfather that he had fallen upon one day while searching his wife's belongings.

It was the next shot on the same roll where the elder, in the meantime, had probably decided to overtly expose to the photographer the idea at the back of his mind.

In 2092, it had been a long time since such graphical artworks could only be found in boxes, small or other. Soon after, in Tuni's great grandfather's time, the scandal raised by the exhibition in a museum in Cincinnati of a photographic collection by Mapplethorpe, all graphical works representing bodies endowed with a shamelessly flawless plastic had started to disappear from museums and art galleries.

Not so much because of their erotic suggestiveness or their obscenity, since even the Church did not proffer the word "sin" anymore but spoke rather of "acts due to the lack of self-esteem," and since masturbation finally seemed recognized by God as a healing balm against a poor self-image. But it was rather because such images could tarnish those that people had of themselves.

Besides, if they had really looked at those who had gathered to protest in Cincinnati, twentieth century people would have easily realized that the hubris was due to the fact that none of them would have been chosen for models by Mapplethorpe.

For the same reason, in 2092, museums no longer exhibited anything that could not immediately be copied by all visitors or elementary school students upon their return home or at school. If anybody failed in his/her attempt to create an exact replica of any exhibited piece of artwork in less than fifty minutes [commercial messages included], that person had the right to consider his-or herself "artistically challenged" and request the immediate relegation of the aforesaid piece of artwork in a box adapted to its size.

Which also entitled the aforesaid person to immediately see his or her own attempt put on display in lieu of the original.

That was why the works of Rodin or Van Gogh had all disappeared into big boxes and why, at the Louvres, the spot where Mona Lisa used to be was now occupied by the portrait of his mother by a five year-old mongoloid boy who was squint-eyed, color-blind, and had only three fingers directly attached to his shoulder blades.

At least, it was a portrait of her that the aforesaid mother had seemed to believe her son had done when she found, one morning, on his pillowcase the palette of colors from the frozen stuffed peppers she had stuffed down his throat the night before.

Some had even wondered if the aforesaid mother had not cheated a little. After all, the week before, she had herself visited an exhibition of the still graphically correct work of Andy Warhol.

Those artists whose reputation had survived were all by the way of more or less the same period as Andy Warhol. For instance, the Pompidou Center in Paris had kept unchanged an exhibition of the work of Tinguely, especially because the wave of successful imitation it still generated was contributing to solving the storage problem for bulky garbage.

And again at the Louvres, it was the absence of her arms that had saved the Venus de Milo. They only had to change the plate into "The Anteriorly Challenged de Milo."

Even in religious art. The new "Christs on the Cross" and "Virgins with the Child" would have reminded Tuni's great grandpa of the people he could see, as a G.O. with the Club Med, arrive with the clubs of senior citizens because of the off-season cheap fares.

Finally, if Tuni had been able to, she would have liked to meet her great grandfather. Sometimes she even thought that she would have loved to become her own great grandma. Unfortunately, even in 2092, time travel had not yet been invented.

Neither time travel nor, for that matter, anything that had not yet been invented in her great grandfather's time, even the link which, after all, was only putting into practice a series of techniques that already existed then.

This, in passing, will allow the author to remain up to date for posterity.

Enough to make H.G. Wells and Jules Verne jealous, since they had the misfortune of writing science fiction at a time when they found themselves rapidly caught up by science-action. But more than a century later, while they had moved in fifty years from crossing the Channel to hurtling to the moon, people rapidly got wary of setting foot on it again.

Not only because of budget cuts at NASA and in scientific research in general in order to benefit the establishment of assistance programs for the expression of the challenged minorities. Also because less and less people, throughout the years, remained to believe that there was something left to search for that they had not yet found.

They should have expected it, in Tuni's great grandfather's time, when those who had read classical literature before they had to study it in post graduate programs already saw themselves confined to "schools for the gifted" and later, through a quota system giving priority to "slow learners," were practically banned from universities.

And also when they had appointed Dan Quayle to head the Commission for Space Research or something.

Since she could definitely not make up her mind to confront Paul, Tuni decided to confide in her sister Nora. Fortunately, Nora was responsible for a support group of Fornicators Anonymous, where the attendants had to learn how to accept their powerlessness at believing in their impotence by watching and commenting on old porn movies and participating in group tutorial work.

By 2092, it was definitely out of the question to risk hurting one's self-esteem by going against or criticizing any aspect of one's personality, and support groups had become approbation groups.

Even at the Alcoholic Anonymous meetings, where they worshipped Bacchus just like people used to in bars and cafes.

Or, at the Readers Anonymous meetings, where they got their fix with passages of Joyce and poems of Rimbaud, just as people used to in libraries and at CUNY TV lit talk shows.

These days, Paul himself attended some Photographers Anonymous meetings where he could spend time developing photographs he could not decently send to the nearest Kodak lab without spending the rest of his life granting trophies and prizes for blurred kneeshots, tip-of-shoeshots, and unexposed "monochromatic" shots.

Tuni felt much better as soon as Nora confessed to her that she herself was at the moment masturbating in front of a third shot of their great grandfather, the one where, after having set the camera on a tripod and put the self-timer on, the photographer had found herself momentarily "buccally challenged."

(New York, Feb/March 1992)

NO OFFENSE

It was then that one remembered the two planetary probes, *Pioneer 10* and *11*, launched in 1971 and 1972.

The Imam Saddam Al-Ahmir, a delegate for an Islamic interest group of lumbago-riddled worshipers, was he first to express his indignation when he reminded the assembly of representatives of adverse interest groups of the existence of the two probes. This took place during a recriminatory session at the local headquarters of the United-Factions Organization, held at the Springfield, Missouri G.Z. (geographical zone) Superdome. First, Saddam expressed his concern regarding the fact that the two *Pioneer* probes, launched in the direction of Jupiter and Saturn and twice slingshot by their consecutive passages in the gravity field of the two planets, were probably still on their way toward the outer limits of the solar system at a speed of about 10 kms/s with regard to their launching position. Then, in front of the assembly's blank gazes, he explained his calculation according to which, given this speed which had allowed them to span the distance of one astronomical unit -- the average distance between the sun and the earth -- every six months, the two. probes, if they still existed, had probably covered a distance of some three hundred billion kilometers as of this April day of 2071. Only afterwards did he proceed cautiously with the veritable object of his wrath.

As these recriminatory sessions seemed ordinarily to be only an outlet for each and everyone's need to prove to each other that he or she was spending his or her time plotting against him or her, the intervention of Saddam Al-Ahmir, for the first time in the living memory of delegates to the Organization, triggered a unanimous reaction of disapproval comparable to that which has been observed aboard intercontinental flights when the captain announced that landing would occur at an airport located at some thousand miles from the planned destination because of a snow storm. During the rest of the session, many abandoned their simultaneous translation earphones and leaned over their desks to try to communicate directly, beyond the bullet-proof partitions of their boxes, with their immediate neighbors in what they could remember of obsolete vernaculars such as English, Spanish or Arabic, thus giving their personal multilect cyberpreters a break that the latter could not, unfortunately, fully appreciate. Saddam's immediate neighbor, Rabbi Moshe Melnik -- representing an affirmative action group of bald wearers of yahmulkas -- was the first to spring out of his box. With a voice muffled by his mask of a holocaust survivor upon his liberation from a death camp, the rabbi asked the imam in an anguished and painstaking English where in hell he got that from. Of course, other participants such as Yasmina Sarhakhan, a lady with an obvious handicap of bodily exuberance and whose ebony-painted face contrasted with the otherwise diluted hue of her arms and hands -- and a delegate for a femino-conservative faction whose agenda was to promulgate within the territory of the geographical zone a campaign for the re-excision of formerly surgically rehabilitated clitori of patients who would repent for having succumbed to "the dirt of afro-excentrism" -- begged Saddam not to proceed with the graphic description of the object of the general outcry, to call it off until an in-camera session could be scheduled, and not before the terms of the communication had been consensually revised by a committee of inter-factions editors. Yasmina reminded the assembly that at the time of the *Pioneer* 10 launching, the editorial board of major newspapers such as the *Chicago Sun Times* had already made desperate efforts to hide from their readers the most questionable zones of the object. In the ensuing commotion, so many questions were asked of Saddam and among the members of the assembly, so many groups spontaneously formed between the rows of deserted bullet-proof boxes, that the security services finally gave the order to evacuate the premises.

Thus began a great quest on the planetary scale, such as even the Holy Grail and the World Soccer Cup had failed to initiate. From then on, the human world seemed to take passion only in the follow-up of the *PROJECT NO OFFENSE* -- as one finally agreed to call it using the most widespread ancient vernacular. The whole of mankind was called to witness by all the media networks whose custom-made programs created by and for each interest group were preempted by fact of the gravity of the information. Life scene seemed to change drastically, insofar as one could still say that there was, in anybody's memory, any kind of life left on earth other than that, virtual and cybernetic, of the communication networks installed by the transfactional superpowers -- AMOCO, MITSUBISHI, COLGATE/ PALMOLIVE, PARAMOUNT, ELF AQUITAINE, etc. As for the arteries and public places which, after having been for too long the scene of chaotic and often violent expression of mutual recriminations, had finally become frequented only by parades, demonstrations and motorcades organized under the aegis of various affirmative action factions or under the logos of the transfacs, they almost again became the agora they had been before the rise of exacerbated factionalism, before all gazes became unable to meet otherwise than through pixeled images. As soon as the news of the scandal broke out, the security lines set up by the "blue magnetic shields" of the United-Factions broke off, and one could see the same badges and streamers -- in particular those of the *United Factions Delegation for The Assistance in The Realization of The Project NO OFFENSE* -- adorn lapels, windows and stoops. With the onslaught of "spatially challenged" card bearers -- i.e., all those who felt their self-esteem had been hurt by the publication of the consensual report from the United-Factions about the *Pioneer* affair -- all kinds of services found it more and more difficult to respect the ever more complex and detailed quotas which had been established to comply with the requirements of the multitude of interest groups. Gone was the time when, for instance, if the neighboring post office or supermarket had covered their quota for the specific ethnic origin of a customer, the latter could still send in his/her place an African-Filipino or Indian-Japanese friend or neighbor whose respective quotas had not yet been covered for the day; gone was the time when illegal trading networks had developed and when the shopkeeper and the service supplier still often closed their eyes like the bartenders of yore when it came to serving alcoholic drinks to minors on a Friday night spree. Over the years, things had worsened to such a point that any arrangement between members of adverse identification groups had become virtually impossible. The suspicion that could arise within one's own interest group as a result of being seen hanging out with someone who did not display the same morphological, genetic, or cultural characteristics, was sentence of suicide. But priority was thus given to the "spatially challenged" and, consequently, to just about everyone.

Life did change, with the exception of life in the womb of the transfacs. Sole institutions transcending the beneficial segmentation of the society which would otherwise have to confront the metaphysical questions which had long troubled the human soul, the transfacs ruled everyone's life, since everyone belonged to them one way or another for reason of material survival and medical coverage. These big companies had for a long time put on a more friendly face under the influence of new managerial teams, and they had not skimped with regard to the well-being of their human capital. For instance, they had proven capable of veritable *tours de force* when it came to redesigning the occupational space. Their premises, which remained the only places where devotees of various interest groups were likely to meet under the old equal opportunity rule, had been equipped -- just like all public places had previously been rendered wheelchair accessible -- with a gadgetry meant to spare their occupants the throes of deconsideration. There were self-adjustable ceilings according to their height, doors and hallways of adjustable width according to their bulk, partitions and furnishings that came in changing hues according to their complexion, pivoting spaces that could, at any time, be oriented toward Mecca, Jerusalem or Lhassa, computer terminals camouflaged as altars, reliquaries or models of holy grounds according to the faith of their user and even -- but then to the intention of everybody -- annular elevator cars where one did not feel obliged like in the past to study for the umpteenth time the limit capacity chart or the fabric of the wall covering. The only thing that had maybe facilitated the task of the corporate architects had been the *BANNING OF ALL MIRRORS*.

The mirrors... For one thing, one should remember the poisonous atmosphere that had prevailed before the boards of directors resigned themselves to banning all mirrors from public places like town councils had long before banned the ashtrays; when some persisted in thinking that they had walked upon the shooting of *The Ultimate Return of the Living Dead* -- subtitle: *This Time, It's Hopeless.* Of those aesthetes to whom one had nonetheless tried to explain since their infancy that people were just who they are, that it was not their fault, etc., with tones of a future mother-in-law keen on the wedding of her daughter to Somebody-the-Third with an acne-cratered face but with a degree from Harvard Law School, there were still too many to retort that they'd rather try to pick somebody up at a fancy East Side health club than at a Pizza joint near Toledo. Of course, these were people born "before the war" as one still said, or right after. These were hedonists-humanists who had as a matter of fact conceived and launched toward the stars the two incriminated space probes. They were of those who had attended school at a time when one could still take one's little friends for a ride without fear of bringing lawsuits upon one's own parents. And in fact, for them, the worst was the children, wasn't it? Weren't these kids, on top of being utterly illiterate, even uglier than their parents? As far as parents were concerned, one could still unearth from some closet an old super-8 movie, or spot, in a frame atop the TV set, a few wedding snapshots where they beamed with the grace of their youth, but for the kids... First thing, you should have seen their get-ups, their unlaced shit-kickers, their oversized jeans that could have fit Hulk Hogan, and their XX large T-shirts with dinosaurs from *Jurassic Park*, or MTV's *Beavis and Butt-Head.* How remotely did they resemble Cinderella and Little Lord Fauntleroy! And in the subway, at 3:30 in the afternoon, were those damn kids not competing for the trophy awarded to the fattest and the most nazi-looking hairdo, to whom would scare you out of your *New York Times* in order to take possession of the whole car? And those -- rare -- youth who were still passable, wouldn't they have traded their own portrait for Ross Perot's, even the girls, provided they could get his stock dividends? Come on, it surely was because they'd ended up thinking of nothing other than a career plans if the global consciousness was about to snub the human morphic patterns within the chaos of probable shapes! And yes, features and silhouettes would soon be led out of their way by dint of sticking to the general idea released by the porticos of the corporate headquarters! Now, if they looked at the photos of those elected by the readers of Cosmopolitan to be the sexiest guys of the year, those freethinkers were not any more satisfied with what they saw. Come on, they would sneer, ugliness, blandness, homeliness, all that showed even more on the inside than the outside! Kennedy Junior? Oliver North? Dan Quayle? In plastic form and in 4,000 bucks three-piece suits in the window of Bergdorf-Goodman maybe, and yet... So, what did they want? Oh, it was so simple: to organize. Organize when it was still time to prevent Merrill-Lynch and J.P. Morgan from putting up their billboards along the huge highways which would soon criss-cross the Altiplano, Tibet, Sing-Kiang, Burkina-Fasso. Otherwise, it would soon be over with the gracious native children's faces and the old ones' noble bearing, over with their eyes as deep as the matrix of the universe. Besides, wasn't it sufficiently alarming to take a look at those who had come from such places in the world not too long after their birth or lived there only as genetic blueprints? Homeliness was beginning to transcend races, even among the Greeks if they were from Astoria, Queens. Of course, nobody would dare confess of such an opinion other than by the choice he or she made of those who would be the targets of his/her inclination for sexual harassment, at the risk of showing contempt for the rest of the world, but such contempt was still too visible in attitudes, in furtive looks of repugnance. Therefore, by blurring in people's imagination the idea of beauty, nobody could deny that the banning of mirrors had sped up the eradication of atavistic reactions of disgust toward ugliness.

The idea of Beauty... As each and everyone had forgotten by 2071, the primary mission of the two *Pioneer* probes was to hurtle past the planet Jupiter, then Saturn, take measurements of the density and composition of their atmospheres and, most of all, take close-up photographs of the two magnificent astral palettes. Afterwards, that is after completion of the scientific experiments, the fate of the two probes would be, as Saddam had probably remembered, to continue their voyage through interstellar space for millions of years after their on-board instruments had become mute if no micro meteorite or uncatalogued space debris ever got in their way.

If everybody had completely forgotten *Pioneer*, it was also because great care had been taken to eradicate from the history textbooks the propensity of the twentieth century ancestors to tread the front lawn of the Estate Divine. The all-powerful integrist and fundamentalist factions had finally succeeded in achieving what some hesitant precursors had attempted toward the end of the previous century regarding the nazi holocaust or the geological age of the earth: deny their historical truth. The APOLLO and VIKING odysseys were now regarded merely as modernized sequels of ancient pagan myths or, at most, as distorted remembrances of *real historical events* like the erection of the Tower of Babel and the abduction of Ezekiel. Those who had believed in the reality of the exploration of the moon and Mars had to have only been the victims of a vast propaganda orchestrated by the same evil powers that had already provoked secularization and a slackening of moral standards from the end of the European Middle Ages until around the time when the two space probes were launched. Thus, in 2071, at a time when the earth was definitely only six thousand years old and when children did not wear dinosaur T-shirts any longer, space missions consisted only of the launching and assembling, in normal or geo-stationary earth orbits, of gigantic but purely promotional or confessional signboards.

From the launching of a volley of huge M's from McDonald's that could still be seen reflecting the sunlight, at night, above the five continents, to the more recent overpowering plasmic portraits of Jesus from the Mormon Church or the Christian Coalition, via all the fake moon slithers expedited by all the jihads of Islam, the mock-stars-but-of-David and various icons sacred to such and such almighty denomination of God's fanatics, the hobby of backyard astronomy had become extinct. If the truth may be told, there had not been for a long time either backyard astronomers or professional ones, or anyone curious about the nature of the universe -- or anything else for that matter -- since questions were no longer posed but just followed by pre-selected answers on multiple-choice questionnaires. Besides, was the entire truth not already contained in sacred books, reminders of corporate ethics and affirmative action manifestos? It would have been a waste of time to try to convince any benefactor member of such and such faction of the validity of exploratory missions even if, as the last advocates of the quest for new frontiers had once tried to do, it had been attempted to demonstrate that such missions could also be useful to study, for instance, in a state of weightlessness or on the surface of other planets, the resistance of such and such automotive material or of such and such virus. So, the unanimous passion aroused by the preparation of the two inhabited spaceships *No Offense* 1 and 2 which would be launched to *CHASE AFTER THE TWO PIONEER PROBES* can be understood only if one remembers, just as Saddam Al-Ahmir did, *the character of the secondary mission of the two probes.*

Beauty... Of course, without the mirrors, it was not easy. In the first place, everyone had to resort to looking at each other and then comparing what they saw with the object of their shame. Only then did the *No Offense* artists become capable of drawing something on the screens by superimposing dozens of millions of snapshots supplied by the various factions and interest groups. This alone took months. As for the conception of the spaceships, each of which would be launched in the direction of the disappearance of one of the two *Pioneer* probes -- and the construction of which would be entrusted to a consortium of logo manufacturers --, it was not easy either. The initial plan was the spaceships would be vast enough to contain a fair quota of astronaut representatives of each faction and interest group and fast enough to catch up with the two probes before the passion of the public fizzled out. The way the dead probes could be located in the outer reaches of the solar system also raised technical and mathematical problems which could only be solved by deciding to agree on a maximum margin of possible trajectory error at the estimated distance from the earth of the two stray *Pioneers* at the moment of *rendez-vous*. This would necessitate equipping each *No Offense* spaceship with as many individual recce pods as astronaut representatives on board. Each representative would take their place in his/her assigned probe at the right moment with the common task to comb a bubble of space of about half an astronomical unit around the parking position of each *No Offense* mothership. But there were dissensions as long as one had not yet resorted to adopting the final draft of the mission, especially when it came to determining, in addition to the factional quotas that had first been mentioned, the composition of the crews in terms, also, of their usefulness on board. It was thought that priority should also be given to technicians in specific disciplines useful to the maintenance and survival in space for several years of a population equivalent to that of a big city. But then why not also have representatives of professional sectors less useful to the mission participate, like stockbrokers, tax accountants, immigration officers, post-graduate students in functional literacy, business executives in preliminary reinsertion training, corporate lawyers, etc., who were already claiming the right to a quota of representatives as such? That of course would go against and distort the estimates already established on other bases. For instance, should such and such crew member appear at the same time on the passenger list as a representative of a wing of a Chinese-Parisian faction for the eradication of latin characters in the "métro," of a self-help association of lesbian mothers, of a coalition of visually challenged for the banning of public lighting, of the Organization for the Liberation of Pigalle and of a congregation of Everyday Saints for the medical rejection of menstruation, at the risk of preventing others from having a chance to embark, or else, should she choose her camp at the risk of being blamed for appearing illicitly on the roster of the other groups mentioned? Finally, after months of soul-searching, the only equitable solution was finally adopted: send to space on the tracks of the two *Pioneer* probes the *TOTALITY OF THE POPULATION OF THE EARTH.*

It was only after that decision was made that it became possible to tackle the conception and construction of the two *No Offense* spaceships. According to the increasingly precise virtual models that were revealed to the public on all the news networks, the ships would consist of two huge space arks three thousand kilometers in diameter whose annular shape would allow, through a spinning motion, to maintain in their interior an artificial gravity sufficient to prevent their occupants from peeping too much at each other's crotches. Those models could very well have reminded the public of the old concepts of twentieth century science fiction if those works had not long disappeared under the pressure of the politically and religiously correct censorship committees on the grounds that they contained too many sacrilegious ideas and, most of all, too many lusciously bodied heros and heroines wearing much too tightly fitting spacesuits.

Or no spacesuits at all... Anyway, while it had taken politicians about the same time, at the end of the previous century, to hem and haw about the construction of a miserable thirty meter-long space station which never got out of the folders, the transport and assembling in orbit of those two annular planets, thanks to a concerted technological effort and unlimited funding, took less than twenty-five years. Sure enough, other world events seemed for a time to come to the fore. First, there was the question about the participation in the Winter Olympics 2084 of a member of the Botswanian golf-on-ice team whose great grandmother had allegedly been a go-go dancer in a Jewish orthodox neighborhood of Brooklyn. There was also the Bilbo-Hobbit case, this shameless couple from Signal Mountain, Tennessee, with the wife who was harassed by her husband's recent sodomitic propositions and dared called him a *"shitcock"* on a local group psychotherapy network of Chattanooga -- the slur was never exactly uttered by the media just as they never mentioned the length of the thing found in a ditch alongside a road in Virginia. But these events failed to hold the front page for more than a few consecutive months. They were nothing in comparison with the constant indignation that was continuously rekindled by the awareness of those two antique probes which were each day moving a little farther from the earth, with, affixed to their side, the *ACCURSED PIECE OF ART* by Linda Sagan, wife of Carl Sagan, a leading figure among the heretical astrophysicists of the late twentieth century.

Then boarding started. Thanks to a fleet of some ten thousand super-shuttles, each accommodating five hundred passengers and capable of making one round trip Earth-No Offense each day, and given that the population of the earth was then, roughly, ten billion people, it took just a little more than six years before one could close the airlocks and proceed with the ignition of the boosters designed to provide each one of the huge arks with an initial thrust capable of imparting enough acceleration to catch up with the *Pioneer* probes in less than three years. (There were also a few incidents around boarding priorities and the accidental loss of about thirty shuttles with their cargo -- some of which could not avoid colliding with orbital advertising signs.) Finally, *No Offense* 1 set forth in the direction of the disappearance of *Pioneer* 10, i.e., toward the constellation of Orion, and *No Offense* 2 toward *Pioneer* 11 and Epsilon Eridani.

The voyages were uneventful, with the exception of all those media events which continued to be scooped up and poured in detail into ten billion brains. One of them, however, appeared to be more significant than the others: a faction -- although not catalogued as such -- of modesty codes objectors who had been, for that very reason, completely overlooked during boarding, attempted to steal one of the gold anodized aluminum new plates placed under United-Factions' guard in the non-gravity zone in the hub of *No Offense* 1, with the intention of strewing it with obscene graffiti.

The new plates... It was not that people still believed in extraterrestrials. Credits for the SETI project had been canceled as early as 1994, at a time when mankind was really beginning to have its feet on the ground as a result of massive layoffs and a skyrocketing increase in the price of ski-lifts. It was not that they did not believe in E.T. any longer either. Most of all, they had ceased to give it a thought, at least until Saddam reminded them of the old plates. Afterwards, that is, ever since then, it was not that they had started to really believe, but all the same, who could say for sure?... In the best of cases, could those plates not fall back onto earth after having completed a loop in the Galaxy, and trigger a cultural shock among our descendants such that no propaganda from any High Inquisitorial Secretariat to the Faith or anti-pornography league could alleviate?

The old plates... Upon their arrival at the critical research zones in the outer limits of the solar system -- fortunately, the *Pioneer* probes would only reach interstellar space after they passed the great cometary belt, i.e., forty thousand years or so later, and none of the neighboring star systems before a few million years -- the two *No Offense* spaceships slowed down and, as planned, each of them deployed its five billion individual recce pods. The navigating skills of the pod's human occupants would not matter; each pod was in fact an entirely automatized mini-ship which could very well have done the job by itself. Besides, since many freaked out at the last minute just as whole families of foolhardy children would do upon boarding the most scary and shaky rides at Disneyland, a good half of the pods left empty. As a matter of fact, only young children and members of mentally challenged factions, to whom, after all, the Kingdom of Heaven belonged more than to anyone else, dared embark.

It is agreed that *Pioneer* 11 was first located and tracked down by an empty pod. (It was so agreed in order to spare the overall self-esteem by not having to issue a trophy to a representative of one faction rather than another.) Then it was *Pioneer* 10's turn which was spotted just a few weeks later by another empty pod. Only then did the final phase of the mission begin: the simultaneous approach maneuver by the two huge *No Offense* ships, the capture of the two old probes from two opposite regions of the heliosphere, and, finally, the ultimate goal of the mission, *THE REPLACEMENT OF THE OLD PLATES,* the description of which, although euphemical, had made the world blush with shame.

There had been a harbinger of signs like the case, around 1993, of that oil reproduction of a barely clad group from a Botticelli scene by a street painter on the sidewalk of an avenue in New York City, which the Department of Sanitation had to erase at the express request of the employees of a couple of neighboring banks who were not able to stand the view of some bare-breasted goddess. Later, at the turn of the twenty-first century, it was again in Egypt that it all really started. Under the pressure of integrist movements, first the temples of Karnak and Abu Simbel which displayed overly suggestive carvings, then the pyramids of Gizah and a score of traces from pagan civilizations which could not, decidedly, have preceded the advent of Allah, were dismantled. Over the years that followed, the same was done in India, in South America, then everywhere. Finally, all the museums of natural history were emptied not only of their dinosaurs but also of their skeletons of hominides which could not have represented divine -- but failed -- attempts at self-portraiting, art galleries were rid of their nude paintings and sculptures -- except for a few ones like the Venus de Milo who was spared thanks to her obvious physical handicap. Jesus Christ was from then on only represented on the cross wearing shirt, sandals and boxer shorts, sunbathing became forbidden on the lawns of Central Park, and an advertising sign from Calvin Klein stayed in orbit for only a few days before the Lubavitcher sect dispatched a sabotage mission. As a matter of fact, was it not a similar mission -- but how much more grand! -- that the whole of mankind was accomplishing aboard *No Offense* 1 and 2?

The old plates... Because the antique *Pioneer* probes contained a message for the stars and *that* was what Saddam Al-Ahmir had remembered. On the side of each of them, a six by nine inch gold anodized aluminum engraved plate had been affixed. In a scientific language that had been expected decipherable by the hypothetical alien race which would, in several thousand of years or even millions, intercept one of the two crafts riddled with the impact of micro-meteorites, the engraving described something of the time and the location in the Milky Way of a conscious and curious species. The plates told of the location of the star Sun as compared with the position of a dozen pulsars, along with the frequency of these pulsars; they also told that the probes came from the third planet around that star, along with other pieces of information of that kind about the sender. But even more than the blasphemous character of such a message in a bottle tossed not to God but to the galactic ocean, it was, next to a diagram of the probe itself (meant to determine their size), the representation of a couple of humans such that even the editors of the most pornographic underground publications had forgotten could exist: the man and the woman on the engraving were *beautiful* according to the old understanding of the adjective, and as *unclothed* as Adam and Eve before they found out the use for what God had, in his unfathomable distraction, put between their legs.

As soon as the old plates were replaced by the new ones, the two *Pioneer* probes were released into space at the same speed and in the same direction they were going before their capture. Then, mankind headed back to earth and the ceremonies organized around the destruction of the old plates kept everybody busy for the time of the return trip. After disembarking, the two space arks were dismantled and the parts and constituents were recycled for the construction of two huge multi-denominational temples at the center of two globular clusters of corporate logos.

It was then that the very old Saddam Al-Ahmir remembered the two gold records engraved with murmurs and glimmers of Earth and sent to the stars aboard the *Voyager* 1 and 2 probes launched in 1977.

(New York, March/April 1994)

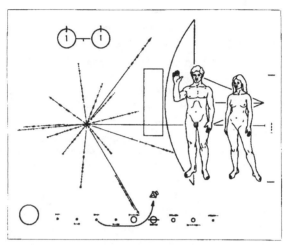

Fig. 1: anciennes plaques (dessin de Linda Sagan)

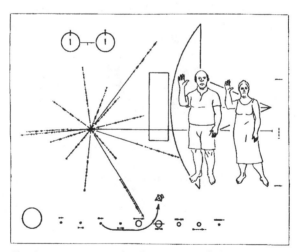

Fig. 2: nouvelles plaques (dessin de François Méry)

ELEPHANT & CASTLE

ACT 1

(With the father, the son, the Omniscient, and the author)

The Omniscient:
The father and the son are at home but, given the ensuing dialogue, they might as well be straddling the solar wings of the Hubble Space Telescope (see THE GRAND ATTRACTOR)...

The author:
No, please, nooooo! It's not because the Hubble Space Telescope has been mentioned somewhere by the TV in order to induce a slightly crooked transition (see THE GRAND ATTRACTOR, top of page 3) that... Huh?! Well, now, it's different. It's a pertinent reference. Go on.

The Omniscient:
...testing out various types of contact lenses on it. But wherever they are, it won't have any effect on the action.

The son:
What day is it?

The father:
December 3rd, 1990. Why?

The son:
Because, once again, what was supposed to happen didn't happen. The earthquake in Missouri, I mean, wasn't it scheduled for today?

The father:
Nothing ever happens of what prophets and seers foresee. Fortunately for them. Most of the time, everybody has forgotten what they foresaw at the time it's supposed to happen. Although here, with N.B.C. on the site and vendors of "earthquake" T-shirts, the fact that nothing happened as expected is already a big happening in itself.

The Omniscient:

That's what everybody says. Nothing happened. Right? Right. But if something had happened, if the earthquake had taken place, this is not what they *would* say. All right? Now, wait. The son is going to have an idea.

The son:

Anyway, we could think that the earthquake did not happen *and* that it did happen at the same time. It's like the death of Schrödinger's cat (see the CATNAP of the same). And you know why? Well, it depends on where you choose to make the *wave function* collapse. That's why.

The Omniscient:

But of course! It is according to that famous function that *everything* happens in the universe which contains everything that is happening. It is according to that function that the global non-manifested, or the overlooked by the observer, the non-affected, the non-collapsed, in a word, the probable, does exist. To begin with, we have to assume that since the universe is everything, it cannot be that nothing is happening in there. If nothing happened, the universe would not happen and consequently, would not exist, since all that exists happens and happens in there. Oh, this does not mean that, without a universe, everything would be static either, because nothing that *is* can be without happening. Furthermore, the mere idea of something being static already carries the expression of an illusion of time and thus, of happening. So, *nothing* would be since, as we already saw in another script (see BEING AND NOTHINGNESS), all that *is* is the event, therefore, what is happening. The truth is that there is no middle ground when it comes to the universe: It is everything, or nothing. And since it cannot be nothing, it is obviously everything. Everything happens in the universe, including what does not happen, because, if such a thing were imaginable (I mean, that something or other did not happen in the universe), not *exactly* everything would be left to happen there, and, therefore, the universe, short of containing its whole self, would not deserve its title all by itself any longer. See what I mean? So, the son is right. What does not happen happens all the same, including the earthquake in New Madrid, Missouri. Now, we will have to consider the fact that what is happening is happening because what has happened has happened. Accordingly, all that will happen after what is happening now will happen because what is happening now is obviously happening. Finally, all that is happening now or *has* happened is happening and has happened because what will happen will happen. That is what is commonly attributed to the *Downward Causation.* (See *LYING ONE'S WAY TOWARD ONE'S TRUTH OR HAVE YOUR DOWNWARD CAUSATION RE-VISUALIZED*, by the same author but in another collection) Hey, author, what should I do at this point? Should I lecture about downward causation or let them peruse another volume of your works?

The author:
There are enough writers who are not ashamed of repeating themselves about subjects that aren't even as vital as downward causation. Look at (beep) and (beep) and also (beep), right? Go ahead. And you can lift me word for word. You're my guest. Page 23...

The Omniscient:
Ok.. let's see... here.. Downward causation... it means that, I quote: "... *If the common purchase of some eggplant parmesan at the supermarket is the result of an encounter* (between a character named Linda and another one, an Ollie North look alike) *around a paper plate full of turkey with cranberry sauce eight days earlier, the turkey with cranberry sauce owes its reality to the reality of the eggplant parmesan.*"

The author:
Can't you use a somewhat more scholarly passage?

The Omniscient:
Wait... here, I've got it: "... *In order to exist, the present needs the future as much as the past, the past needs the present and the future, the preture cannot exist without the prast, the fast without the pasture...*" Huh?

The author:
Ah! Ahahahahahaha! Ahahahhhahhhh!!!!! What? Nothing... Just so funny. Go ahead.

The Omniscient:
Here is a more learned passage: "*The observer is the effect which causes the cause of which he's the effect. Just like the honeymoon of Linda and her new boyfriend in Pataya, Thailand, is the consequence (or the effect) of the installation of Hilton Hotels and branches of American Express in Pataya since... (etc., etc.,) ...Linda and Ollie find it easier to take a trip to Pataya than to Azerbaidjan and, at the same time, the sine qua non condition (or the cause) for their installation in Thailand...*" Wait... You're talking about the installation of the Hiltons and American Express, right? Okay. "*...for the installation of the aforesaid facilities in Thailand, since Linda and the Ollie North look alike represent the expression of American tourist consciousness.*" Is that enough or should I go on?

The author:
That's enough. But would you tell me, by the way, why you mentioned downward causation in the first place?

The Omniscient:

Did I?! Never! I just stepped into my dressing room. Look: I obviously have not had the time to take off my raincoat, yet. Look how soaked I am. We will all end up in the hospital with this miserable weather. (See BEING AND NOTHINGNESS, beginning of ACT 3) At this time of the year, it should be snowing instead. The climate is totally fucked up. Because of the greenhouse effect. Now then, what are we going to talk about today? Hey, why not that downward causation, huh?

***

ACT 1 (bis)

(With the father, the son, the Omniscient, the author)

The Omniscient:

The father and the son are at home because, as we understood very well from reading THE GREAT ATTRACTOR, there are *strange attractors* everywhere, which sketch the most probable patterns. And one powerful strange attractor, when it comes to sketching the situational probability for a serious father and a studious son on a cold Monday evening at 8 o'clock is, of course, their home. In any case, they are more likely to be found there than orbiting in space, fixing the Hubble Space Telescope.

The father:

Did you see that? What did I say? They've been had with their earthquake in the Midwest. Predictions *never* come true.

The son:

Yeah... but look, what I mean is... it's hard to say, anyway, seen from New York, whether it took place or not, I mean this earthquake... Sure, we're still here to testify, but... if, for instance, you look at all these predictions about the end of the world... huh? If they had come true, we would not be here to testify that they were right! If we are here, it might just be to take note that they were wrong, isn't that true?

The father:

You're raising an interesting question. I have my opinion about it, and I most certainly would love to talk at length about it with you, as still happens between fathers and sons. But let the Omniscient do it, or the author might be accused of using the dialogue to present a theory, which isn't appreciated by a Pulitzer Prize jury. So, let the Omniscient take over, and let's talk about something that can move the action one step forward.

The son:
Wait... Oh my God, oh my God, what a story! I can't believe it! Has it really just happened? (see CONFIRMATION, last page)

The father:
I'm winded. Let me regain my breath. ... Pfffff...(idem)

The author:
No! No! Oh no! I don't know what to do with that, yet. Curtain!

***

ACT 2

(With the Omniscient, the author, the father,
the son, and the walkperson)

The Omniscient:
So... everything has happened, everything's happening, and everything will happen. Try as you might, there is no way around it. Since the universe contains all that is happening, including time, everything is happening *now* in the universe, and nothing can happen that is not on the program of the universe, which, according to the uncertainty principle of Heisenberg, contains all the probabilities and as many possibilities. All this means that the son is right: the mere fact that he is here to testify that something *did not* happen *makes* it impossible to be covered by the printed press or by Hertz waves. It is all a matter of downward causation. And this was the point I was trying to make at the end of Act 1. In other words, their memories have tuned onto a past which justifies the absence of an event that, elsewhere, might have occurred according to a multitude of probabilities, not for other people, but for other manifestations of themselves. (Accordingly, since all the imaginable scenarios are possible, it is reassuring to believe that there exists a probable world where topless sunbathing is a must on the Saudi beaches, no?) *More than everything* cannot be imagined, and everything, as we saw, is on the universal program. In contrast to what the father was saying, prophets and seers are, in the end, always right since all that they pretend to foresee will happen, in any case, according to whatever future. Of course, they have to be careful in their choice of predictions, considering the probable rarity of some events as

opposed to some others. The guy who predicted the earthquake in New Madrid took too many risks. If he had instead chosen to predict that, from Cincinnati to Chattanooga, the year would end in utter tectonic bliss, he would have been safer. Whatever they think in Hollywood, the probability that *no* natural calamity occur in a given region and at a given date is far less uncertain than the catastrophe scenario, even if the aforementioned scenario is likely to happen then and there, according to a few parallel realities...

The author:

Wait. All that doesn't tell me what likely outcome could follow their outburst of joy. I'm not going to say that it's because of an earthquake in Missouri, just because the father, an atheist and a furious anti-clerical type, would applaud the destruction of the Bible Belt. No way. Radicalism is *passé*, and, in these times of scientific illiteracy (see THE GRAND ATTRACTOR) when all types of religious loonies...

The Omniscient:

While the author is pondering, we are listening to whatever probability of the event "walkperson," wherever its wave function might have collapsed. Come on. Just for kicks.

The walkperson:

The world today acclaimed those who, long before Salman Rushdie, had been the target of the Iman's *fatwa* for having bedazzled mankind with their demonstration of the scatological nature of God. (see DEUS EX LATRINA) These heroes were welcomed this afternoon with a ticker-tape parade despite the conspicuous silence of John Cardinal O'Connor. Piles of computer printouts and shredded corporate documents rained on the passage of those whom the world now only calls the Father and the Son.

The son:

Dad, did you hear this? Do you know what they're talking about?

The Omniscient:

Hey, author, are you crazy? This *was* the reason for their explosion of joy! How could the son not know? How could he *not* be aware since they must be parading around, tonight, at the Waldorf Astoria, after the official reception ceremony at City Hall? No way they can hear the media talk about something that would not be happening in *their* manifested reality. In other words, if the media covers their triumph tonight, it is necessary that, as I explained earlier, through downward causation, their memory be tuned on an adequate past. Otherwise, you get bogged down in the lousiest type of science fiction, you know, where you can hop around from one universe to another, or from one epoch to another, and exist there without you being the *effect* of any historical and plausible cause.

The author:

What are you talking about with your "not possible?" You yourself asserted an all-possibilities universe. As for me, I don't personally buy this story. It doesn't sound realistic. It's not convincing, and, to tell you the truth, it's a little far-fetched. I must find something else.

The Omniscient:

Wait. You have a point. There must he a possibility, though... Let me see.

The author:

Okay. While you're thinking, I'll type the caption for ACT 3.

***

ACT 3

(With the father, the son, the walkperson,
the author, and the Omniscient)

The Omniscient:

Now, let's see. The father and the son are slumped on a Louis XVI sofa in the farthest reaches of a suite on the sixteenth floor of the Waldorf Astoria. A valet has just brought them champagne and caviar, and the conversation is proceeding.

The son:

Yes, maybe. But in another perspective, maybe no. If you see what I mean, that's exactly what I meant when I said that it's a quite different matter. It seems that you're confusing something. Remember THE SLAP EFFECT.

The father:

I can't get it out of my mind. It's always like that. It's not the first time it happens, and I am convinced that there's no other solution.

The son:

Good blood! But you're pleasanting! Don't say cunteries, huh! If you listen to all these assfaces...[1]

The father:

Stop your tank, would you? And be polite. Hold, listen to the walkperson and shove me the peace.[2]

The author:

What's the matter now?

The Omniscient:

The Gulf crisis. I could collapse the wave function as was needed in order to observe the outcome of what must be going on at the end of CONFIRMATION but it seems that their conversation, for the moment, is not relevant to the action. Of course, in real life, that's what happens most of the time. The grandest philosophical ideas can be formalized while doing -- and talking about -- the dishes. As I just did myself, it is up to the biographer not to obsess endlessly about the brand name of the dishwashing liquid being used, but to shed some light on the main lines of the philosopher's thought and their impact on the course of history. Well, I *do* know why the father and the son are at the Waldorf, but I wish you, the author, would find out by yourself. While we let inspiration come to you, we will continue listening to their petty talk. After all, in this scenario, maybe, something interesting is happening in the Gulf. (This was written during "Desert Shield," well before "Desert Storm.")

The son:

My God! Help! What's happening? Oh my God, everything is tumbling down, collapsing! The lights went off! Help! Hey, it's a fucking earthquake!!

The father:

What the fuck! Did it have to happen today! Oh shit! The media is going to forget us!

The son:

See? They said it would happen here in New York someday. But, as always, people never believe what the prophets foresee and... see the result? Look! the Chrysler Building is already down, and all of Rockefeller Center. And rocking as we are, it won't be long before...

The father:

AAAAAAAHHHHHHAHHHHHHhhahhhhhhhhhhggggghhhhhgggggrrrrr.....

The son:

RRRRRRRRqggggghhhhgggggggghhhhhhhhhggghhhhhhhhhhKKKKet..Ket..

The Omniscient:

Bad luck. In this scenario, the lives of the Father and the Son end here, in the rubble of the Waldorf Astoria. An earthquake, 10.75 on the Richter scale, has just collapsed a probable collapsing of the wave function of New York City. Hey, author, should we start over with something else?

The author:

Too late. We're already at the top of the last page.

***

ACT 4

(With the Omniscient, the father, the son,
and Houston through the walkperson)

The Omniscient:

The father and the son are in space, in low orbit around the earth, straddling the solar panels of the Hubble Space Telescope. To make a long story short, the father has been, for a number of years, the best optical technician in the West and this is why he is here. As for the son, it is, well... because he was selected to become the first high school student in space.

The son:

Did you hear what Houston was saying? A gigantic eathquake struck the Midwest.

The father:

Really? Well, they got it right this time. Despite the media coverage, I bet you they didn't really expect it. Pass me the 4.25 screwdriver, would you?

The walkperson
(Through the voice of Mission Control in Houston):

Father, who art in heaven, thou whose eyes are soaring above the abyss, from Cincinnati to Chattanooga, canst thou behold anything from above?

The son:

Do you see anything? I can't see a damn thing, personally.

The father
(Lost in his own thoughts which, as almost always,
are not relevant to the action):

Elephant and Castle[3] ... What a name for a neighborhood, when you come to think about it. Uhmmm? What were you asking me, kiddo?

(New York, December 1990)

(1) and (2) : The Father and the Son are French. This is what they really say to each other.
(3) : As a title, E & C applies to the story as well as it applies to the neighborhood of that name in London. All the more so since London does not appear in the story.

THE TRIAL

Here she is, looking at the screen, but only distractedly now, because she has just started to think of something again. Not that she was looking at the screen more intently a moment ago, since *a moment ago* has just started again to exist *with her*. However -- let's say *a moment ago* -- if she wasn't looking at it, it was because she was as far from envisioning the existence of a screen as the contents of a box of spaghetti or a bag of popcorn is from envisioning the digestive tract that is going to transmute it into energy and excrement. Whereas now, even though she is not otherwise troubled by the presence of the screen, she knows that a screen is there; even though she has just started to think of something else. And everything is going to start again: diverging opinions, cultural shocks, a chaos of ideas...

Finally, she stops looking at the screen at all and she lets her glance wander on what she seems to recognize: the walls of the room where she is, then the objects in the room; it stops on the shelves left of the window, which probably contain, she thinks, what she has just thought about. Does she still have it or did she, some day or other, in order to gain some room, give it to a street vendor, or simply throw it away? No; that book, like all the books that are still in her possession, belonged to her father, and she must have kept it. A little stiffened, she drags herself out of her armchair, and she staggers toward the shelves. Now, who was the author? She could not tell exactly why but she wants to be clear in her own mind about it. Her left forefinger runs along the edges of a row of books and stops on a black hardcover. She picks it up and she fingers its texture for a while, hesitantly, like the first hominid's fingers must have hesitated at the contact of the bark of a tree or the fur of a small animal he had just killed. Yes, that's the one. She still has it. *The Trial*, by Franz Kafka.

Has *this* trial something to do with *the other trial*, the *real one*, through which she has always existed and that she was never supposed to consider so, that is *as the other*, with some distance, in a fashion? But it was only the association of ideas, and the idea was enough to escape.

This time, it was a good move, though. *The* Trial was exactly what they needed. The ultimate scoop in regard to the times. Everything was there: a glitzy show of an interracial marriage, a success story, a wrenching "Gee, my husband!" and, for an epilogue, a true car chase with true cops behind a true celebrity turned, from one minute to the next, into a true murderer. In short, everything that was needed to organize the chaos of ideas, to rally diverging opinions, and level out cultural differences.

She starts leafing through the book, but she would not even dare getting herself to read. As far as she can remember, the only book she had ever read cover to cover was a voluminous black plastic-covered agenda that she had not yet made up her mind to replace with a digital pocketbook her employer had offered her as a holiday gift a few years back. She had never found the time to familiarize herself with the program and feed the data into it. Whereas in the big black agenda, she would write down everything, day after day, scrupulously, including her heart rate during her morning aerobic class at the gym, between six and six thirty, before she ran to the bus stop which would take her to the station where she would buy herself a cup of coffee to go and jump on the train that would drop her off, forty-five minutes later, at the business center of the city. But she thought of the title of the book just like that, and she just wanted to check. She was just being *curious*.

At the time the trial began, there was still some choice. The information networks were then only tending toward ultimate merging and globality and fighting for time that could still be, at least, envision as "prime," which they could saturate with many other scoops likely to generate as much fascination: the former extramarital "faux-pas" of a would-be president, the slow return to erectedness of a once severed penis... But the trial won, anyway, by wider and wider margins, all the program ratings, even that of the neo-conservative proselytes whose gospels of hatred eventually had the fiercest bigots blush with shame. So, just as hundreds of living species disappeared every day from the surface of the earth to yield ground to the one species that seemed to have been granted by God the right to grow and proliferate, a lot of events (among which were a lot of other trials) just passed and vanished as quickly on the opaque horizon of the masses' memory.

Now that she has cleared in her own mind about the book, she gets to thinking about *him* again. She must have been aware all along that he was here, but he had slipped out of her consciousness for a moment because of the book. She diverts her eyes from the pages, and, inevitably, she sees him sitting between her and the screen, mesmerized in front of the motion of the image on the screen.

In front of the image.

In front of the image's life.

At first, she thought he was *back there* with her. Back there... was this in the courtroom? For a short while, she is unable to recall any place other than the courtroom, just as she can't recall any sound other than the voices modulating the sworn evidences, any smell other than the spectators' bodily secretions. It must have been in the courtroom, decidedly... But then, all of a sudden, he, *even he*, had shrunk as seen through the lens of a film camera whose zoom ring she would have inadvertently let slip on a much wider angle.

As big as the screen was behind him and as sharp as the image was on the screen, those are presently nothing more than *something contained in something else*, something else she and he have now become part of. A vague fragrance of an incense stick that she had lit, just a moment or eons ago, before setting herself in front of the screen, has replaced the smell of the dust and the crowd.

He has slowly turned toward her. He must have heard her get up and walk to the bookshelf. And she sees his face, abashed. In a surprised jolt, she drops the book she was still holding. Maybe she had become less accustomed to looking directly at faces, be it on street corners, in the subway, in the elevator, or right at the restroom door during the interludes between the prime-time programming periods or the commercial breaks, anywhere and anytime life still led one to discover them, always anew, or unknown, always more numerous. From whence she comes now, there was but a limited number of faces, and she knew all of them. None was a surprise anymore. Except for *his*, there were the faces of the judges, of the jurors, of the troop of lawyers, of the witnesses on the stand, and that was about it. The others, the faces of the crowd in the courtroom, were not there to be looked at. Besides, *they* did not look at her either. But now, someone from *back there* has just turned around to look at her in the face, and that is what is so shocking to her.

There had not only been the screens at the genesis of the universe of the Trial. There had also been big headlines on the front page of the newspapers that one snatched in a glance while running on one's survival paycheck path, covers of slick tabloids on checkout racks in supermarkets and piles of biographies not only of the protagonists of the crime but also of the judges, the lawyers, the witnesses (along with their neighbors and friends), the school teachers of everybody, the law enforcement officials involved in the preliminary enquiry and the arrest, without mentioning the video games, the Trial Cards... All that resulted in booming sales of a certain type of sunglasses, glove, sport bag... until it seemed that one could walk across each other in the streets only after having written the same shopping list: a half-melted ice cream, a set of golf clubs, a ski cap, a pack of envelopes, a wax candle... and accompanied by a specimen of the only living species that had not yet disappeared: a little Akita dog.

She, however, had really taken to the Trial only during the third or fourth year. First of all, during the first few months, she would work too late at night to keep up with it other than by watching a summary of the daily proceedings on her favorite channel. She was so exhausted and brain-dead after the daily thirteen to sixteen hours that she devoted to a challenging career that even watching the video tape that she had conscientiously pre-set in the morning, before leaving, with the intention to miss nothing of the daily proceedings so that she could be able to discuss the details with her colleagues at lunch break was beyond her power of concentration.

With no apparent reason at all, she starts thinking about the street again. Most naturally, with as much urgency as she had desired to take a look at the book, she now wants to take a look at the street. She detaches her eyes from the man's eyes, goes to the window, and pulls up the Venetian blind. And she is surprised to see *nothing* in the street. She can't even see the street itself or, for that matter, nothing exterior to her apartment. She can see that this is not because the night is too dark or because all lights have been turned out; it is as though some *screen* of sorts she expected and which should have then displayed an image of the street was just blank. But very quickly, as it seems to her so impossible that there be nothing after having expected so much to see something, she begins to make out, more and more sharply, *their* shape emerging from a chaos of probable shapes, *their* motion deciding on a direction to go, *the blue and white police cars in the wake of a white pick-up truck*. It is not yet exactly the street she was expecting to see, though. This "street" is rather a sun-parched asphalt strip along which the vehicles move. There is nothing, yet, beyond the asphalt strip. Countryside... Space... After all, that's not what *counted* really.

Space... And time. She had taken to the Trial only when the present tense had become the only conjugational tense of the world, after total completion of the global interactive information network, when each and everyone became an active part of the Big Scoop and became able to experiment with all its probable outcomes, and have every other human being experience one's own probable outcomes, when instantaneous information became *all that life was about*. Harbingering signs of such a development could have been observed as soon as the need for immediate efficiency had overcome the need for mature reflection, as soon as curiosity itself began to be satisfied through series of mere occupational training sessions, and when eyes no longer lit up but at the sight of the word "NEW" in flashing print on the packaging of products on display at the shelves of the selling zones. First, the mental time must have stopped passing around 2010, when the last extra-Trial activity ceased. As for the time which had, until then, inscribed itself in the second law of thermodynamics, given that the basic parameters of the chaos became more and more simplified by the fact of their merging with the Trial's minutes, it probably stopped passing also because of its forgetting to do so. In other words, the suspension of all human activity, in conjunction with the cessation of all extra-human activity due to the general biocide, made the passing of time obsolete and redundant. And, of course, through lack of time, space got out of the picture as well, except for that which she had just believed she was observing through her window; that is, the zone of a megalopolis where the murder case at the origin of the Trial had taken place, and that space which seemed to unwrap itself in the courtroom, that is, the space necessary to create the tri-dimensional illusion of the Trial.

However, little by little, she can see shapes shifting, colors changing, perspectives transforming. She could even think, for a time, that she is dreaming. A time... For time has started to reinscribe itself within her, ever since she thought of *a moment ago*. A moment ago, that is, when the street did not exist, when nothing created space other than the asphalt strip which cut across a checkboard of luxury houses and swimming pools bathed in sunlight. Now, the light has changed, and she can see it is really nighttime. It is night and the familiar street is out there, lit only by the street lamps and the neon signs, run over by an assortment of disparate vehicles among which she still tries to recognize a white Bronco. She recognizes the street. It is obviously the very one she expected to see when she first walked to the window. However, a part of herself is still overwhelmed by the presence of the street, as if she had suddenly been transported in a world of improbable light displays and motions pertaining to some realm beyond the imaginary. She is seized by the urge to go down in the street and blend within the crowd. Even more so since she knows that *he* is there, right behind her, watching her, and that she has to escape his look, that she has to *get the hell out of him*.

It is maybe just another idea, something else she has started to think about, but no -- she really is hungry. Her stomach -- or whatever it is within her that ensues the existence of the idea -- is really aware of the fact. It is because she has entered again into possession of her body and her world, right where she had left them, or right where, more simply, *the idea of her and her world was born*. She is going to get something to eat.

At any rate, *he* will let her go shopping, and then he'll see. He is still a little short of ideas beyond the one that she has to go shopping, but the rest will come, and, after all, the rest is his prerogative since she is the one who passed behind the screen, she and all those who are going to follow her, as the story he'll choose to invent will come. Later, when there are too many ideas and when those ideas become too muddled, he will confide them to words, then to gigabytes and megaflops. And one of them -- the fittest of them all, and, hopefully this time, the craziest one -- will in turn enter into possession of him, *the defendant*, and give him, just as he is going to give her, a simple name among others.

(New York, May/June 1995 -- eighth and ninth month of the O.J. Simpson trial)

WE WANNA SEE THEM EYEBALLS CLICK!

"You'll never believe me when I tell you how much money I paid for that," declared Donald-Trump T., whose seven-footer's knees seemed to hold one angle of the table at the terrace of *La Baguette Gourmande*, a very trendy French eatery & drinkery of the urban entertainment area. He had just sat there with four other people, on a sweltering Saturday night in August, around ten p.m., after the offices' early come-out. Thick-waisted despite being in his early thirties, he had to, in order to sit down, unbutton the jacket of a dark grey pinstripe suit that he was wearing over a white shirt. One would think that his small deep-set eyes -- so deep set that one could not see the white of them -- went around the attendance, but nothing moved on his face, not his fat chin, not his flat and drooling cheeks, not his short nose, not his pale forehead hardly shaded at the pole with an uncertain light-dark hue. Only his thin and colorless lips seemed to tremor imperceptibly when he added: "And it cost me a lotta money." Upon which he looked at his watch and busied himself to turn down, from under his necktie, the thermostat of his air-conditioned underwear so as not to incommode his neighbors with the noise and the wafting hot air.

"I bet you that it must have cost a lotta money, Donald-Trump," further added Arbitrage D., looking at his watch. Arbitrage was also in his thirties, and his knees seemed to hold the opposite angle of the table. His paunchy stomach protruding from under a taut white shirt had forced him, when he had to sit down, to unbutton the jacket of a dark grey pinstripe suit. His small deep-set eyes (whose white could have been seen if only he had turned them toward Donald-Trump T. to answer him) in a short-nosed and thick-chinned flattish face topped with a rather brownish polar cap, remained glued in the direction of a virtual point of the eatery & drinkery area when he added -- hardly moving his thin and colorless lips: "And you've gotta be able to afford it."

"As for me," slipped in Lee-Iacocca K., who was about the same age, and whose long bony knees had not yet found a place under the table, "this will be my next purchase. I can no longer live without." (His thin and colorless lips contrasted with the globular and amber-colored opulence of the glass of Terrier *au chocolat* he was lifting toward them.) "But we spent so much these last days, Migraine and I," he went on, pulling up the sleeve of a dark grey pinstripe jacket so as to look at his watch, and finally succeeding in wedging his knees under the table without moving his bust.

"Isn't that true, Migraine?" he said, while looking at his watch, to an imposing and determined looking blonde who had a short permed hair and whose fat thighs wrapped in white stockings had slipped out, when she had sat down, from under the skirt of a dark blue business suit. Migraine blushed slightly while moving her Charretier's luminescent rings-laden fingers toward the buttoned collar of her white blouse so as to turn down the intensity of her personal air-conditioning system, and she hardly turned her round eyes and her little nose from FacePerfect Inc. toward Lee-Iacocca.

"Oh, yes. Look: I paid one thousand two hundred and nineteen doodleddos for this at Suk's Fiftieth Avenue," she said, pointing at (and taking advantage to look at) the third watch on her left wrist, a slash of green and red plastic on her dry and milky skin. "A SQUASH EQUITY-LOAN."

"Ohhh! Really? It's unbelievable! I paid more than one thousand eight hundred doodledoos for mine at Save-Smart last week," whistled Modellle T., Donald-Trump T.'s wife, a rather tall brunette -- since her seated bust almost towered over her husband's -- with a short-cropped and permed hair and wearing a dark blue business suit over white stockings and a white blouse. She looked at her watch, covered briefly her round eyes with her two hands loaded with precious junk from Bergdorf-Goodperson, and then, as if she had already forgotten the object of her surprise, (and turning her small nose away from her neighbor Arbitrage D., who immediately endeavored to lower his personal air-conditioning system) she brought them around her glass of plain Terrier water, and said: "Come on, Donald-Trump, tell them how much you paid for your résumé holder in real burlap from Christian d'Or."

"One hundred and eighty thousand doodledoos," answered Donald-Trump, not even moving his lips this time. (Because he could do it when it came to figures.) "without the delivery charge."

At that moment, coming from the street area, a tall half-blood lady with an imposing face walked toward their table. She was also wearing a dark blue business suit jacket, but her thick bony knees sheathed in white stockings emerged from under khaki boxer shorts. She was shod in pink and purple sneakers and toted a sport bag that excused her for her outfit. She looked at her watch and waved her hand imperceptibly at Migraine.

"Hey, good credit, Migraine! How much are you doing?"

"Oh, Veranda! Good credit," answered Migraine, raising her eyes slightly in her direction. "I'm doing a lot, thank you, and you?"

"A lot, thank you. At the Theological Bank, as always. And you?"

"Oh, me, as you know, I'm still doing a lot at Breast & Colon Cancer Amalgamated. But let me introduce you: Veranda A., Theological Bank. Veranda, this is Donald-Trump and Modelle T., Total Expansion Ltd., Arbitrage D., Total Expansion, and my husband Lee-Iacocca, Total Expansion."

"Credit accepted. How much are you doing?" Veranda asked in turn to Modelle and Donald-Trump T., Arbitrage D. and Lee-Iacocca K.

"Credit accepted. How much are you doing?" they all answered in their turn to Veranda A. while looking at their watches.

"How much are you paying here?" asked Veranda while taking a peek at hers.

"Three hundred and fifty-two doodledoos before tax for five units of product," Migraine responded to her friend.

"And where do you plan to pay the evening?" asked Veranda again while staring at the rear area of the eatery area, which appeared as a moving puzzle of varied color crystals in which the customers could spend their time trying to recognize the fleeting design of one or another corporate logo.

"*Dogs*, at the Summer Garden, like every week since I've been doing a lot at Breast & Colon," Migraine answered, looking at her watch. "You've got to pay somewhere. And my friends here have hardly paid there more than thirty to fifty times."

"Oh, look," Veranda broke in, pointing with her finger at the rear area, "the logo of the Société Fondamentale de Banque!"

The waiter (who looked like Donald-Trump T., Arbitrage D. and Lee-Iacocca K. all at the same time, but who was dressed as a waiter and had a French accent) came to their table, looked at his watch, and asked Veranda what credit card she wanted to charge.

"Any which one," Veranda replied.

"At your debit, madame," the waiter said. And he walked away.

"So... I bet you spent more today than I did," Veranda said to Migraine and her friends. "Because I waited more than two hours tonight on the BIG NET before I could access Bloomingsale's in Cairo after having been put on indefinite hold in a dozen branches in Europe and America. When you think that less than five years ago I could still access the main branch in New Work thanks to the quotas and Affirmative Shopping!

"I hope you had good buying anyway," said Modelle T. while looking at her watch.

"Are you kidding? I was so upset after this waiting that I hesitated too much, and I wound up not spending as much as I'd planned. If it goes on like this, you know where this could lead me, don't you? There's no joking over that at the Société Fondamentale. They may decrease my salary and increase all my minimum credit lines."

"Sometimes, you wonder if you'd rather not go there in person," Arbitrage said. "For our last vacation week, two years ago, my wife Copacabana and I took a tour called "The Life in Teak" of all the capitals of South-east Asia. Exhausting, I grant you that. Especially as Copacabana insisted on rickshawing all around the place. But we succeeded in spending more than fifty thousand doodledoos, not counting plane fares and hotel fees."

"I do agree with you, Arbitrage," Veranda said. "But it is always so professionally risky to take a vacation! Not to mention the fact that it is so difficult to come near the products on display because of the crowd, or even get your credit card picked. Whereas on the Big Net--

"Here you go, madame," the waiter said as he put in front of Veranda a glass of Terrier "Vaporetto." (Terrier water brought to a swift boil) "Of course, neither the service, nor the tip, nor the glass rental, nor the price of the detergent used for the washing ... you name it, but nothing is included."

"Who do you think I am?" Veranda blurted out. "As if I never went out and didn't know! Ah, I see. It's because I'm of color, huh? But I am a *human doing*, me too, *monsieur*! I bet you I can pay in one day more than you ever will in a month! And I can prove it to you right now. Charge immediately one hundred doodledoos on my card!"

"These French waiters are so obnoxious," Veranda said to her friends as the waiter walked away with a satisfied look on his face, looking at his watch.

"Easy, easy, Veranda. This is for local color," Migraine said. "It's nothing against you in particular, you should know that. We are here at *La Baguette Gourmande*, and it's not like any of those eat & drink areas of the urban area that have the digital service. Here, we can experience human contact. Do you know what he came up with when he waited on us? He told us that he had cut his finger while opening the bottle of Terrier, and that he was going to sue us unless we agreed to pay immediately for his medical bills. You bet we weren't going to lose face in front of a waiter! It's Donald-Trump who got his card picked first. You should have seen his draw!"

"It doesn't matter. He must make a lotta money," Arbitrage said while looking at his watch.

"That must cost a lotta money," said a lady who was walking by the terrace of *La Baguette Gourmande*. (She was hardly older but heavier than Modelle, Migraine and Veranda, and she wore the same dark blue business suit and white stockings.)

"Oh, you mean that old thing you saw in my bathroom? The antiquarian said they called it a plow. No, it didn't cost me that much money, you know," a very tall gentleman dressed in a dark grey pinstripe suit said to the lady above while looking at his watch and finishing passing in front of the terrace. "A couple thousand."

"Most probably two to three thousand doodledoos a week," said Modelle in response to Arbitrage's remark.

"How much do you think this might cost?" asked, in the vicinity of the terrace, another high-rise middle-aged gentleman who was wearing the same pinstripe dark grey outfit. (He was speaking to a lady who was as imposingly and professionally bi-color as all the others and who was looking at her watch.)

"And me," said another lady at least as imposing as the previous one in her dark blue business suit, "I pay more than a thousand and five hundred a week in rent. But I share a windowed studio apartment on the Avenue of the Fortune Five-Hundred."

"One of my friends made more than twenty-five thousand doodledoos in an hour," (*) said a high, dark grey, pinstriped shadow to another that could have been taken for a reflection of itself if it had been carrying the door of a French *armoire* with a mirror.

"I also bought one thousand *Nutscape* at twenty-five eighty and I sold them before the bell at fifty sixty-two. And you? What do you plan to do?" asked another passerby -- whom one could confuse with the previous pair if that pair had suddenly merged into one -- on his cellular phone. (He was speaking to his wife, who was in a taxicab in some place where it was morning. He could easily imagine her wearing white stockings under a dark blue business suit, the same as she wore the day they last met three weeks earlier in the bar of a hotel *Parallèle*.)

"There were six hundred applicants for the position," said a very long and very erect young man who seemed to glide past the terrace, exactly as he had probably done the same afternoon in front of a line of jury from the human attitudes services while proceeding along the intercommunication areas to a dozen vice presidential suites of the company he was looking forward to doing a lot for. "But I have some hope. The last vice president motioned me to sit down." (This one spoke to himself and was repeatedly looking at his watch.)

"All right, all right, honey. It will cost me a lotta money, but it's okay. But it really costs a lotta money, you know, Nasdaq," said another business-clad passing lady in front of the terrace to a crying little boy who kept going all the while: "I want it! I want it! I want it! I want iiiiiit!..."

"There's a lotta money to make in this type of business," some other dark-clad body said in the street area while staring at its watch.

"It's probably worth near five hundred thousand doodledoos," said some other professionally-clad doer who was proceeding in the other direction.

"I bought five and I got one for free," said another pointing at a waistband of portable phones under his pinstripe jacket.

"It doesn't matter, but I'd feel even more comfortable with four to five thousand more doodledoos a year," Migraine K. was saying to her friends when a strange character walked up to their table. The man looked like one of those extras selected and licensed by the public relations services of the urban entertainment area in order to instill a quaint and oldish atmosphere to the neighborhood. These temp jobs were often distributed to those people whose lack of productive capacities or zeal to purchase had not allowed them to fully integrate in society and access the status of "human doings." These surprising beings, whose disparate looks and faces reminded one more of the motley chaos of the crowds of yesteryear, could eke out a living from

Saturday evening stunt to Saturday evening stunt. Among them were people of all ages wearing more casual -- or even frankly sloppy -- outfits, men wearing jeans and T-shirts, skimpily clad women with thinner buttocks and bare legs, children and old-timers whose piercing stares sometimes generated complaints over self-esteem harassment. There were longer and dishevelled hair, higher cheek bones, less smooth foreheads, thicker lips, and less manicured dental areas. The tips that those shadows from another age could make, however, were probably sometimes fairly substantial, as could be seen by the fact that, when the stranger stopped near their table, Donald-Trump, Modelle, Lee-Iacocca, Migraine, Arbitrage and Veranda had already drawn their credit cards and held them all together in his face. Even though he was definitely shorter than average -- hardly six feet --, the man's silhouette seemed more sinewy than those of the other passers-by. Migraine, Modelle and Veranda, blushing, seemed not to be able to detach their eyes from certain median zones of his body while Donald-Trump, Lee-Iacocca and Arbitrage instinctively buttoned up their dark pinstripe jackets. All the same, this one was pushing a little too far in the "retro" look, they were all probably thinking. At a time when even the most skimpy leisure outfits hardly uncovered elbows and knees, it was almost unbelievable that he had not yet been nabbed by one or another corporate militia that patrolled this neighborhood even more vigilantly than other areas. The red shirt with the sleeves cut off at the armpits he was wearing wide open on his chest *à la* Calvin & Luther Klein and the raggy shorts he had probably cut himself out of a pair of regular denim jeans let them see his limbs sculpted like those of the characters that once appeared on paintings now concealed in the basements of the art museums of the world. His curly and disheveled black hair tied up into a bandanna, his too expressive features, his skin weathered and tanned by God knew what forgotten elements, his crooked nose, his wide open eyes, nothing in his appearance would indicate that he had one day to go on a job interview. It was unbelievable that they had even accepted him as an extra. People like him had to have the excuse of being adulated artists, or show biz stars. They had to be rich and famous, like those you waited for hours on Fridays or Saturdays night in front, for instance, of the Haute-Couture Café around the corner, in the hopes that you would catch a glimpse of them crossing the sidewalk toward their limousines, or else they had to be derelicts and drifters like those who vegetated in squalor outside of the urban spaces limits, those who still insisted on being called "human beings."

"Really? Because you already feel comfortable?" he directly asked Migraine, whose remark he had surely heard. When he spoke, all the muscles of his face dubbed by a real pantomime stunt what he already conveyed through his vocal cords. His intrusion into their conversation and what appeared to Migraine and her peers as a series of grimaces stumped them for a moment. Finally, Arbitrage D. intervened:

"Good Credit, sir. Arbitrage D. I'm doing a lot at Total Expansion Ltd. And you? May we know how much you're doing?"

"Oh, me... The only thing I wanted to know," he went on without responding to Arbitrage's greetings, "is how in general people can feel comfortable when they only know the world through its icons and celebrities, or when they are able to cite from memory the names of all the fashion designers and perfume brands, but not the names of the planets, or when they risk their paycheck if they don't wear the right clothes, or when they think that the fish they find on their lunch tray has never had any other shape than that of breaded sticks, or when they're pounded on in multimedia by pharmaceutical consortia that they have to be terminally ill and should report immediately to their doctors' offices; just things like that... I'm just wondering how you people can feel *even* more comfortable when you know that the interests on your credit cards increase at the rate of the global planetary debt."

The idea that the man -- who did not wear a watch -- could make fun of them did not cross their mind. Modelle and Donald-Trump thought for a moment that he was really an actor -- there were so many of them in the neighborhood! -- and looked around the street area for the shooting crew and material. Veranda went as far as shyly applauding to his tirade, asking him from what Shakespeare's play it was; whereupon Arbitrage proposed *Don Quixote* without a hesitation, while Lee-Iacocca was still insisting on handing out his credit card to the man, hoping he would move out of the field of vision of Migraine, who did not seem to be able to detach her eyes from the man's open shirt. Then, as the man still did not budge, the five of them started, looking at their watches, to giggle nervously. That was when the waiter came to their rescue. He grabbed the stranger by the shoulder and pushed him out of the terrace of *La Baguette Gourmande* while talking on his cellular phone. The man then stayed for a while on the sidewalk area, yelling: "But why don't you tell me? I really would like to know!" At the other tables, too, the conversations were suspended. Somebody said in a creaking voice: "Look at that! Is this not a shame? It will all end in disaster in this neighborhood, with all these extras. If only they were required to dress more professionally and wear masks!"

When a patrol wearing helmets with the logo of Consolidated Cash-Flow & Liquidity Co. arrived first at the site, the man did not resist arrest, and, turning his head back in the direction of the terrace of *La Baguette Gourmande*, he sneered: "Too bad. I guess *They* will explain it to me."

"Another one of these *Human beings* who has succeeded in trespassing into the urban area," the waiter said, passing among the tables and picking up the credit cards they all handed out to him. "Here, they take advantage of the presence of all the extras."

The next Saturday, around ten p.m., after the offices' early come-out, as Donald-Trump and Modelle T., flanked with Lee-Iacocca and Migraine K., were sitting at the terrace of *La Baguette Gourmande* before attending one more performance of *Dogs* at the Summer Garden Theater, two regular looking gentlemen, dressed in dark grey pinstripe suits and white shirts, came in and sat at the next table. Before sitting down, one of the two had leaned a pair of crutches against the back of his chair and painfully succeeded in wedging his seven-footer's knees under the table. One could not hear what they were saying except, maybe, every few seconds, the word "doodledoos" and one or the other conjugation of the verb "to pay." One could not see the disabled man's lips move, and for a good reason: in addition to his crutches, the bandages that covered his face let one only see a swollen tan chin and, on the top of his head, a thin cap of curled black hair. For a short time, Donald-Trump and Lee-Iacocca sought, each on their own, to chase out of their mind a vague but painful memory, that of the already long gone days that followed, for the first of the two, the day when his mom had taken him to the doctor's office "for just a little shot," and, for the second, the sweltering summer evening he had succeeded in sneaking into the urban space, and had been nabbed by a patrol of Total Expansion Ltd. And the two of them, after having looked at their watches, brought their hands to their faces.

(New York, July/August 1995)

(*) Even less invented than the rest. Heard on Thursday August 4, 1995, at 2:45 p.m. at the corner of Sixth Avenue and Forty-Ninth Street in Manhattan from the hardly moving lips of a character who looked like all those of this story, and who was looking at his watch -- except that he did not say "doodledoos."

Anarchist Fiction From
III Publishing

The Last Days of Christ the Vampire by J.G. Eccarius
ISBN 0-9622937-0-9   192 pages, 4.25 x 7" $7.00
The book that broke the silence about the vampiric nature of Jesus Christ
and his fundamentalist zombies. Jesus has set his sights on converting some
teenagers in Providence, Rhode Island, but instead they resist and set out to
hunt him down before he can release his Apocalypse upon the world.
Arguably the best religious satire of the 20th century.

Virgintooth by Mark Ivanhoe
ISBN: 0-9622937-3-3   192 pages, 4.25 x 7" $7.00
Elizabeth has not exactly died: she has been made into a vampire. Now she
has not only all the problems she had when alive, and that of avoiding the
mindless feral vampires, but she must also get along with the other human
vampires. At times terrifying, at times hysterically funny, Virgintooth will
horrify and delight you.

Geminga, Sword of the Shining Path by Melvin Litton
ISBN 0-9622937-4-1   5.5 x 8.5", 256 pages $9.95
In a world poised between a superstitious past and a surreal future of
bioengineering, virtual reality and artificial consciousness, Geminga surfs on
the winds of the present. A product of genetic engineering, this bird has
been trained since infancy to assassinate the enemies of Peru's Sendero
Luminoso. Now she's come with her best friend, Jimmy the Snake, to
California Norte.

This'll Kill Ya by Harry Willson
ISBN 0-9622937-2-5   192 pages 4.25 x 7" $6.00
The anti-censorship mystery that will have you laughing out loud and
examining your own reactions to materials that surely should be censored.
Caution: If you believe that words can be used as weapons to harm people,
reading this book may be hazardous to your health. Willson has a devilishly
delightful sense of humor that should place him in everyone's library.

We Should Have Killed the King by J.G. Eccarius
ISBN 0-9622937-1-7   192 pages 4¼ x 7" $5.00
Jack Straw and hundreds of thousands of other English peasants rebelled
against their overlords in 1381, killing nobles, lawyers and tax collectors.
Ultimately they were crushed, but the spirit of rebellion was reborn in
America in the punk/anarchist movement during the 1980's and Jack Straw
was there. A stunning look at the underground in the USA.

My Journey With Aristotle to the Anarchist Utopia
by Graham Purshase
ISBN 0-9622937-6-8   128 pages 4¼ x 7" $7.00
No government? No taxes? No police? Wouldn't that be anarchy? Tom, is bashed by the police until they leave him for dead. When Tom regains consciousness he finds himself a thousand years in the future where he encounters Aristotle, who leads him down to Bear City. There he sees how human life can be organized without government or bosses of any kind.

A.D. by Saab Lofton
ISBN 0-9622937-8-4   5.5 x 8.5", 320 pages $12.00
The future seen through African-American eyes: after decades of anti-utopian racist fascism in the 21st century, revolutionaries create a society based on Libertarian Socialist Democracy. Even then, a menace from the past threatens the society of the future. "The price of Liberty is Eternal Vigilance."

Non-fiction:
Vampires or Gods by William Meyers
ISBN 0-9622937-5-X   192 pages, 8.5 x 11" $15.00
Vampires living thousands of years, commanding legions of human worshippers. The stuff of horror novels? No these vampires are right out of ancient history books. Every major ancient civilization was associated with an immortal claiming to be a god. Egypt had Osiris, who rose from the dead after his body was hacked to pieces. He reigned for 3000 years. Asia Minor had Cybele, whose followers fed her their blood. Greece had Dionysus and Hercules, Rome had Quirinus, and the list goes on. With illustrations and extensive quotations from the ancient historians.

back issues of **The Stake** magazine
Each issue contains satire plus the best contempory science fiction and horror stories. Read the talented writers corporate America hates:

The Stake #1	Stories by Ivanhoe, Eccarius ...	$4.00
The Stake #2	Pint Counter Pint, Litton ...	$4.00
The Stake #3	Vatican Correspondent, Noe, Mery, Secrest ...	$4.00
The Stake #4	Amy w/bat tattoo cover, Smart, Ramseyer, Longhi ...	$5.00
The Stake #5	Perry, Lee, Webb, Tea, Eccarius ...	$4.00
The Stake #6	Sister Ax cover, Nelson, Hemmingson, Victour ...	$4.00
The Stake #7	Stickle, Simon, Davidson, Brite, Noe ...	$5.00

To order direct from III Publishing send cash, or check or money order for the listed price (postage & handling is free for orders of $7.00 or more in the US; otherwise add $2) made out to III Publishing, P.O. Box 1581 Gualala, CA 95445. Or send $1.00 for an up-to-date catalog.